I0723279

Shattered

from

Within

A collection of short stories and novellas

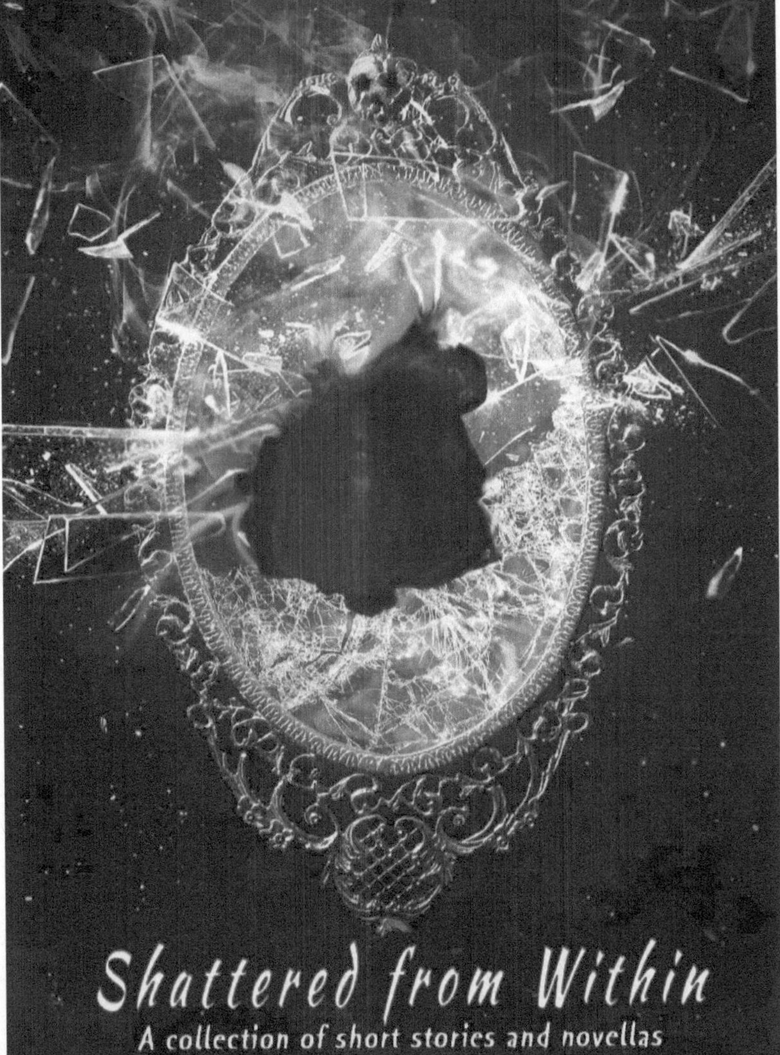

Shattered from Within
A collection of short stories and novellas
by Kathy-Lynn Cross
Bonus story; Lonely Hearts by Amber Hassler

Inscytheful Publishing

Shattered from Within:
A collection of short stories and novellas
by Kathy-Lynn Cross
Bonus story: Lonely Hearts by Author Amber Hassler
First print edition: Copyright ©2024 Inscytheful Publishing &
Both Authors, Kathy-Lynn Cross, and Amber Hassler
All rights reserved.

ISBN# 978-1-7337890-7-3
Cover Design by: Inscytheful Publishing
Typography by: Inscytheful Publishing
Editing by: Amber Hassler

(*) Trigger warnings: All works are fiction but some touch on real-life problems such as mental health issues, drug and alcohol abuse, implied physical abuse, and traumatic situations.

Table of Contents

Dedication

I would like to say a special, "THANK YOU," to the following:
To my husband for listening to my writing woes.
To my kids for their support.
To my family and friends for standing by me.
To you, dear Reader, thank you for allowing my characters a chance
to share their stories with you.

Stay Scythetacular x.x

Here's a taste of what to find.

When Emily was Here – Locked away in her bleak forgotten world, Emily wanted what every caged bird does, freedom. Surrounded by patients who have succumbed to their way of life in the asylum, Emily works to convince them to leave the confines of their hell. But as certain events shake her resolve and pieces from her past threaten to realign her fractured soul she begins to wonder if the doctor is right. "She can never escape the evil within, but only learn to live with it."

Maryanna's Mirror – Before you play her game, ask yourself, "Am I ready to die?" Maryanna is a product of privilege and wealth in sixteenth-century southern, England. After her father's untimely demise, she is invited to her uncle's home with a promise
to host her twentieth birthday party. When the day arrives, Maryanna is given a cryptic family history lesson that drags her into certain events unlocking an evil both her father and uncle have tried to conceal for the last twenty years.

Tainted Currents – A change of scenery is exactly what Ceanna's friends believe she needs to mend her broken spirit. A hiking trip to Skelton Lake may help to relieve her pain. But whispers of vengeance lie beneath the currents awaiting such a heart to release their rage from the river's depths.

Clipped Wings – For over four hundred ninety-nine years, Raziel has protected her cemetery and the souls placed in her care. Once an angel in charge of maintaining justice was now bound to pay penitence as a Judge for damned souls.
Devilkin Breckford finds himself in a difficult situation, he's dead and about to be judged. Unfortunately, for Raziel, this demon poses a perplexing problem, she is unable to judge him and may end up having a new cemetery sidekick.
Did exercising free will doom their future or alter their destiny?
Misplaced – Pranic Cyphers are wandering soulless creatures cursed to exist as spiritual parasites. Curiosity gets the best of one and

it wonders if imitating a human is possible—for a spell. After a botched-up aura transfer, leaving both host and cypher on the brink of death, it is determined to claim the broken body and life of Ava. Once certain characteristics are discovered, pretending to be Ava might be more than this Pranic Cypher can handle. What happens when a predator becomes prey?

Lonely Hearts by Amber Hassler – Loner, Mila Webber is persuaded to attend a class trip to Stayville Asylum. While exploring, repressed memories from a year ago emerge, and Mila has to decipher if it's a hallucination or if what she is seeing is real. Can Mila set herself free from the mental chains holding her mind hostage, or will she become another twisted family secret?

when Emily was Here
"She can
never
escape the
evil within,
but only
learn to
live with
it."
By Kathy-Lynn Cross

Copyright

When Emily was Here

When Emily Was Here

A bite from the worn mattress jolted me awake. Taking a deep breath, as if I'd been aroused from death, caused a dry tickle in my throat. A coughing fit soon erupted, dampening my eyes.

Lanterns from the grounds below shone through a caged glass window, casting a web-like shadow across the poxed ceiling. My vision adjusted to the dim light. I pretended to skip on spider legs from line to line toward the only reminder of my unattainable dream. Freedom.

Arms heavy, I pushed off the bed to stand, then reached the paint-flaked window frame. My fingertips ran across the light-grey wood to the edge. A bolt of lightning emphasized several tiny notches decorating the entire circumference. Gauging the stretch of silence, my misgivings released in a huff when I brushed across a smooth spot.

Body quivering, I thought, *'Just one more.'*

Using a sharp pinky nail, I feverishly moved the finger, making a little gash to match the others. The motion caused the fingernail to split and break under the pressure. A wood splinter pierced under the nailbed. Instinctively, my jaw locked from acknowledging the pain. Unmoving, blood dripped into the new indentation. It seemed fitting since it would be the last.

Riding an exhale was a silent giggle. I spoke loud enough for confirmation. "Yes, very fitting for today. This makes four thousand seven hundred and forty-nine." Quickly, I did an about-face to check the metal door behind me. The view window remained closed.

Relief was a balm to the emotional panic from believing a guard might be watching. Noticing the silhouette cowering in the shadows,

I smiled and motioned it to come closer. It held up its dark hands to display one finger on the right hand and three on the left.

"Yes, today does mark thirteen years, doesn't it?"

Another flash from outside scared Mistie into the darkness. I resumed the task at hand. A smear of blood marked where I absentmindedly steadied myself to acknowledge her. Blood trailed from the window's frame to the floor, causing me to inspect my shirt.

'Damn, if the guard notices, she might alert the doctor.'

The room illuminated at the same time an idea struck. Removing my shirt, I mindlessly cleaned the blood trail from the wall using the sleeve. I turned it inside out, then slipped it on. Fingers fumbled behind matted hair for the tag to rip it from the seam. Not sure what to do with the evidence, I slipped it under the mattress.

To address the puncture, I decided to stop the bleeding by sucking on it. Liquid salt and iron coated my tongue, replacing the stale, warm Dr. Pepper and dirty penny film. This new flavor was a refreshing change that caused me to pull harder.

I ran my tongue over the torn skin to find the splinter. To extract the foreign object, I pinched the area with my teeth. Once obtained, I sprayed it onto the concrete floor under the bed in a pool of crimson-diluted saliva.

Strobe brightness brought attention to the caged glass in front of me. An ashen female face glowered. The female wore a broad sneer, wide enough to expose canines and bloodstained teeth. The presence made me apprehensive about moving the plan forward. Kaye might try to convince me to bring her along again.

Her eyes narrowed as the darkness from both pupils inked out, coloring each orb in a hollow blackness. Tightness grew in my chest. A panic attack threatened to consume me as I gulped air, turning me into a drowning fish. She was vexed.

Instantaneously, a metal latch from the window unlocked, and I took a jarred step back, anxious the sound might rouse my roommate. Several rapid snaps from the last two made me wince when the glass splintered and cracked from the force. A cold breeze slipped through the partially open window, causing my fingers to cramp.

Moisture poured into the room with a promise of rain. This made the little hairs on my neck stand at attention. So many emotions, anxiety, joy, alarm, and jubilation, made me unsure whether I wanted to clap with glee or vomit.

Kaye looked down at the one-inch opening. The wood protested and then fractured under the pressure she was applying. Breath held, I waited for the familiar heavy footfalls from the morning guard.

Instead, my roommate rolled over and broke the room's silence. "Geez, all the noise you're making is going to get us into trouble."

I crouched so she could hear me. "Hey, if you helped me, we both could escape. Do you want to stay here trapped with only Kaye and Mistie to talk to?"

The human-sized lump squirmed until the opening produced an angry caterpillar with the blank glare of a sixteen-year-old girl. Hair tangled in a wicked case of bedhead, which was common since Arora slept like a cat.

She yawned and used a knuckle to scrub the crusties from her eyes. "Honestly, there's nothing out there for me."

Disgusted, I turned my attention to the door. "You should stop taking those drugs. Eventually, you'll lose yourself to them. Ever watch a zombie movie?"

Arora answered me through another yawn, "Yeah, maybe I'll turn into one right before I cut my boyfriend's heart out."

I coughed, knowing full well that she was a compulsive liar. "You are a few sleeping tablets away from being one."

A gust of wind made its way down my shirt. Nature's timing was better than a slap. From under the door, a thin line glowed, which meant two things, it was five a.m. and Ester was coming.

My escape plan would have to wait. Jumping away from Arora's bedside, I never felt my feet leave the ground, but the landing caused my calves to cramp. Ignoring the pain, I spun around on a heel and smacked the window shut before diving onto my bed. Readjusting the blanket, Kaye stared at me in disbelief. Her mouth opened to protest, but I quickly signaled to be quiet. Disappointment drained her skin paler than normal.

At the last minute, I checked the room for anything out of place before I pulled the cover over my head. Across the room, Arora cast a judgmental snort.

"Stop it," I hissed from under the blanket.

"You'll never get out."

The statement made the band around my heart squeeze. "If you could've helped, we'd have gotten out in time."

She sighed. "This way is easier. You'll see."

Frustrated, hot tears trickled down and threatened to drip from my chin and nose. I pushed into my pillow and screamed. This wasn't easier, and I didn't belong here. Deep down, I knew if I didn't get out, I would die in here.

Click-click-slam.

I made a fold big enough to see the door. Ester peered through the honeycombed screen. "Emily, get up. Wesley will be here in five minutes."

I lay there trying to control my breathing.

"Be a good girl. Don't make me call for assistance."

'Oh crap,' that meant needles. Flipping the blanket to the floor, I sucked in the lint-filled air then croaked out, "I'm up. Now go bug somebody else."

Keys jingled when one slipped into the lock. I shook my head while chewing on my lower lip, cursing this existence. Ester extracted the key. It was a sick game she enjoyed torturing the inmates on a daily. We had passed the morning test when her laugh echoed down the hall toward the next victim. Once the footfalls grew faint, I could breathe again.

Ester's menacing cackle used to invade my nightmares for the first year. Now, it festered under my skin like a crippling disease.

One I didn't imagine a drug could cure or control.

I envisioned Ester choking on her tongue from laughing too hard. This helped me relax, but then I noticed sweat dripping down my hairline. I wiped my tears using a shirt sleeve. If the doctor knew about these ill thoughts, she might up the dosage, but if I kept these sugar-coated wishes to myself, all would be none the wiser. Besides, the daydreams helped better than any drug could.

Arora propped herself on an elbow. "See, I told you, sleeping is the best escape."

I kicked my legs over the side of the bed. "I'll sleep when they close the lid on my coffin."

Religiously, I began the morning routine. I pushed the smelly blanket to the other side of the bed and untangled myself to stand. Once I stripped the mattress and folded the bedding, Arora moaned.

"You know, Ester will be here to let Wesley in. Better get up. I'm not going to do your chores for you." It was the only free warning she would get from me.

In the corner, the blanket mound on Arora's bed squirmed. Then, two hands gripped the pillow she used to pull it under the covers. A muffled yawn filled the silence. Finishing in a flippant, casual reply, "They don't care about me."

"Yeah, because you're a compliant captive," I said while placing the pillow and folded pillowcase on my neat stack of monthly laundry.

"You may not understand my reasons," she sighed. "But being ignored makes me unseen. I like flying under their radar."

"I don't want to be ignored. I want them to listen. My brain is fine and isn't as twisted as any normal human walking the streets." The springs creaked from my weight when I sat down.

A bitter chuckle came from Arora. When she calmed down, her

head popped out. "Sleeping is the best escape. It's like diving into a movie or reading a book and getting lost in it. I'm someone special in my world."

The morning rays fought through the rain-filled clouds. The overcast light touched her unspent tears. Arora was crabby, uncooperative, and a sloth, but when she opened up and spoke about herself in this way, it created an imploding star of emptiness.

Not wanting to acknowledge her mental state, I scrutinized the room, landing on the partially unlocked windowsill. Then I whispered, "I dream too."

Arora blinked away the moisture before it spilled over, and her expression shifted to shock. "You do?"

A key slipped into the lock. The familiar sound renewed my attention from the window to the door. Waiting, I clasped both hands and placed them in my lap. I stiffened my posture while sitting on the mattress's edge.

Quickly, I murmured, "Yes, I dream of running. Oh, there are so many ways to run away from here."

Arora butt-scooted to the edge. She sat across in a crossed-legged yoga position, giving me a warm smile. I started to comment, but when the lock clicked, she shrugged and swung her attention to the door.

My head mimicked her reaction. The rusty metal door swung wider into the room; its creaking protest was a daily reminder of our reality. My existence resembled a caged bird with restrictions on how long I could sing.

Squeaky wheels meant my nurse was coming. Wesley rounded the corner, looking concerned. His sandy-blond bangs parted briefly on each step, revealing his eyes. Today, the sun's dim light changed his hazel gaze to a stormy gray.

My hands prickled to touch him. There was a familiarity between us, a distant relative or perhaps a childhood friend. I could never put my finger on it.

He was composed and understanding most of the time. Wesley's gentle demeanor would slip when I pushed Ester too far, and things between us would get heated and then physical. The guard would demand he intervene, medically.

Ester never made it easy for us to talk in private. In the past, she had mentioned once or twice that it wasn't proper protocol for us to be alone. It wasn't like that between us. If I had a friend on the outside, they would be like Wesley.

Solemn, he said, "Good morning, my favorite patient."

Coy, I tilted my head. "I bet you say that to all of your patients."

Taking my morning vitals was the one ritual I didn't protest about, much. The cart stopped. He sidestepped around it, picking up the pressure cuff. Placing the device next to me, Wesley slipped the stethoscope from around his neck. He winced before putting the ear tips in both ears. The nurse once admitted to me the pressure was annoying.

Ester lingered by the open door, checking her watch while twirling a key ring with my cell number on it. The glint coming off the silver number seven mesmerized me as it chased the key. It was her way of taunting me into making our morning more interesting.

Wesley placed the stethoscope's diaphragm above my left breast and told me to take a deep breath. When he moved behind me, I held my hair up, but only high enough so he wouldn't see the missing tag. One last exhale, and he dropped the drum. It made a muffled thunk against his chest. He penciled in my info before securing the pressure cuff around my arm. Light air puffs filled in for small talk as he worked.

Movement from behind the nurse distracted me. Arora was making silent gagging gestures and air kisses. Baffled by her behavior, I inconspicuously altered my view from her to Ester leaning against the doorjamb several times. *'Was she looney?'* She'd for sure get smacked if the guard noticed Arora's childish actions.

There was a pinch from the pressure cuff, and then Wesley released the air. The *pshhh* died, and he turned to remove it. I tugged on his lab coat, not wanting him to see Arora making out with her hand.

My throat muscle tightened when his smirk began to defrost the emotional ice wall I encased myself with. Wesley pivoted as though he forgot to check my pupils. Clearly, he didn't want Ester to know I had physically gotten his attention. We were so close that I could detect the lingering effects of a breath mint. He used them to mask his vanilla coffee breath.

Since I missed the opportunity to talk, he gave me another chance, snatching a silver and black ophthalmoscope. Shining the tool into a pupil, he whispered, "Emily, how are you?"

If anyone in this godforsaken place expressed genuine concern, I was grateful he did. Since Ester could see me, I tilted my head. Catching on the slight movement, his frame shifted to block Ester. I answered, with an inaudible, "Fine."

Squinting, he asked, "Did you want something?"

Nervous, I kept looking over his shoulder.

"She's on the warpath. I'm not sure if we'll be able to talk today." Moving to the other eye temporarily blinded me until the one he checked adapted, and I could see his name tag. He grumbled, "I'll see what I can do. If I can come later, I will."

Arora fanned herself and pretended to faint. Ester turned in her direction, eyes narrowing. She bolted to a compliant sitting position. A sigh slipped out from concern.

Wesley misunderstood and hastily added, "Is it important?"

I gave him a slight nod.

He packed the cart when Arora gushed, "Me next."

Ester glared.

Wesley covered his reddening cheeks. Then he mumbled, "And things were going so well."

My stomach twisted from his comment, and a wave of nausea crashed against my rib cage. Not wanting to see what the guard would do to Arora, the scene became blurry. Wesley was right; 'things were going well.'

Even though my roommate wanted to sleep more than live, Arora didn't deserve this treatment. Guilt clawed within me as I remembered our earlier conversation. Heck, we both didn't deserve this bleak life.

Bile burned a trail up my esophagus. Unshed tears growing cold, I forced my eyelids shut. The last thing I heard was the repetitious hand-smacking of Ester's baton. Then Arora grumbled a few obscenities before her screams matched my own.

I stirred my blob of cold oatmeal. It was beginning to retain the consistency of Playdough. Pushing the thin plastic spoon into the middle of my creation, I tried to test the laws of physics by flipping the bowl upside down. The cereal and spoon remained stationary.

"Look, magic." I tried to break the depressing stillness in the room.

After several attempts to eat, nothing worked. Dejected, I placed the bowl on the ground and moved to sit on the bed's edge. It took some time since I was in pain. Arora's pleas had gotten to me, and without thinking, lunged at Ester's swinging arm. I caught the first of many strikes to the ribs.

Arora lay in her usual position under the blanket. This time, she tightly pulled the cover around her fetal-posed figure. Gradually, the sobs that had filled our space quelled to hiccups and painful coos a few moments ago.

Wesley was forced to assist the nasty woman. Once restrained, we were given a different medication through a syringe. Seriously, Ester needed the couch time and solitaire more than we did. Anyone with eyes could tell she enjoyed beating everyone in her care. However, my assumptions of her actions could be misconstrued because Dr. Reins claimed I tend to exaggerate certain situations.

Mentally, I buried the memory. The secret place where my soul resided was a bit crowded. I envisioned myself standing in the middle of a private cemetery with unmarked moments writhing under layers of negative emotions. At least they were in a place no one, not even the doctor, could gain access to. As long as my soul kept a safeguard over the primary grave, normalcy was one session away.

A sniffle brought me back to the problem at hand. Arora's impression of a pill bug was getting better. I couldn't tell where her head was, though. Taking into account her condition, a thought occurred to me. *'If only I could cheer her up.'* Remembering the breakfast tray and the clear two-ounce cup of pills, I snapped my fingers. Not even thinking twice about how it appeared, I shook it like coaxing a pet to come. When she didn't move, I held it out and shook it again louder.

It baffled me why guilt had me defending my actions. She knew better than to provoke the passive-aggressive hippo. From afar, they seem non-threatening but approach one, and you'll find yourself stuck to the bottom of their foot like ABC gum—already been chewed goo.

My roommate moved with grace, and it dumbfounded me how fluently she slithered under the cover. At the foot of her bed, she emerged from the makeshift cocoon. Arora's hair resembled a mound of fresh cotton candy. Her eyes were swollen from crying, and her features were marred in pain. Turning away from shame, I held the treat cup out to her.

Arora cautiously straightened and wiped her nose with her sleeve. Springs twanged and popped as she winced from adjusting her weight to cross her legs. An arm extended, exposing scratched knuckles.

Using my long hair as a black curtain, I peered through the split. Purple and rouge patches darkened parts of her left cheek and continued along the jaw, fading by her puffy lips. The lower lip had a dried gash from where Ester punched her with the key ring.

Arching an eyebrow, she probed, "Are you sure?"

"You need them more than I." Using a finger to dig through the cup. "Besides, Wesley might have snuck in a pain tablet."

"Nurse's pet, that's what you are," she said tartly.

I rattled it again. "Do you want it or not? Going once, going twice, going–"

"Okay, yeah, I want it." Licking her lips, she stopped when her tongue touched the small wound. "Sorry, I didn't think asking to be checked would trip the behemoth into a hail and brimstone frenzy."

"Ester has always been unpredictable. She even gives Wesley trouble."

Mistrust heightened, she queried, "Really? It didn't seem like he was holding back this time." She rubbed both forearms. There were finger-sized bruises from where Wesley held her down.

"She's a basic power-wielding tattletale. If he doesn't comply, he could lose his job."

Exasperated, she pulled the threadbare blanket around her like a tee-pee. "He doesn't like me, Emily. I should've stayed asleep." Cautiously, she stood to fix her bed. Preparing for another period of hibernation.

Her comment made my heart drop into a pool of emptiness. A shadow darted out from behind Arora's headboard. Mistie's hand pointed at the handle. I motioned for Arora to get under the blanket.

From the window, Kaye watched Arora squirm in pain as she stood in a patch of light examining her work. Right then, Kaye's hazy reflection distorted into a toxic hatred as she assessed our roommate. Tilting in my direction, she pointed to the door. Someone was definitely coming.

Defeated, I removed myself from the mattress. A shared silence grew between the two of them. Then the angry girl gave me a wicked smirk before the both of them shifted their view to the windowsill, where a drop of blood remained. I wasn't interested in the notches anymore but in the sun's position. It was hard to tell the time because of the cloud cover. Ester was probably ready to take me to the showers.

Teetering on my tippy-toes, I overcorrected and hugged myself. Hissing in pain, I plunged into a dark place. Picturing the guard bloody, beaten, and not breathing. This caused my lips to curve from the 'what if' daydream. Behind me, Kaye and Arora laughed. My newfound good nature took me one step closer to our little hell.

Arora crawled into bed. Kaye stepped away from the window,

and Mistie dove under one of the beds, leaving me alone in the center of the room.

Ester appeared in the opened doorway, twirling the key. "Time to scrub off the crud."

Gradually, my lips parted enough to show a hint of teeth. "Yes, I'm ready."

Showering alone sucked. The room had an oppressive presence that always hovered. The lukewarm spray was a blessing. Most days, you were a popsicle by the time you reached for the soap. Ester must have bumped the shower time as an apology since I wasn't her direct target.

Humidity added to the air's heaviness, making it hard to breathe. Conducting a self-examination, I probed each rib, pressing certain spots until I found an area that almost made me pee. Frowning, the conclusion was bruised ribs, but none felt broken.

Arora was pretending to snore when Ester ushered me from the cell. Mistie was afraid of the guard and the doctor, so she moved to a safe spot. As the door closed, Kaye's face twisted from betrayal for not inquiring about her shower time.

Savoring the moment, I played with the little pillow pouch of the generic shampoo and conditioner. The packaging reminded me of the ketchup packets from fast food restaurants. I used my teeth to rip it open. Squeezing the contents onto my palm, I scrubbed the white slime through my hair.

Humming a few bars, I recognized the song and froze. Eminem's lyrics faded as Rihanna's voice echoed the chorus, and when it reached the part about being crazy…

Ire boiled under my skin, making the drops of water sting like hail. "Et Tu, Emily? Of all the songs you could be thinking about," I scolded myself.

The guard cleared her throat to remind me she was still there.

A thunderous boom ricocheted through the shower room. If my skeleton could have jumped out of my skin and run, my husk would be a puddle on the floor by now. An invisible force popped my ears, and both hands instinctively whipped up to cover them. The caged fluorescent lights above me flickered and buzzed like a nest of angry hornets.

In a controlled panic, the guard asked, "Emily, are you okay?" Her words were muffled and strained, assuming she'd fallen trying to get to me.

"Yeah," my reply was shillyshally, over the water's sputtering streams.

Another cannon boom echoed, but this time, the building seemed to tremble in fear. An electrical spike, similar to a photo flash, in the glass tubes plunged the room into a blinding black.

Unmoving, I listened for Ester, wondering if she was going to suddenly appear and drag me into the hall naked and dripping wet. Picturing it, I slapped a hand over my mouth to make it harder for her to find me in the dark. Using the water spray to mask my movements, I waited to see what she would do. To my amazement, Ester did the unthinkable.

"Emily, stay where you are, I'll be right back." Her booted footfalls echoed until I heard the exit door's hydraulic pressure protest from the abrupt motion. Then, the *ka-shhh* of air as it closed, followed by the handle's click, confirmed she had left.

I was alone.

A constant ticking warned that the backup lights were attempting to draw enough battery power to come on. When the yellow emergency lights grew brighter, a realization hit me: I was blissfully by myself–no guard, no nurse, no Dr. Reins, and no clingy-needy friends.

Naked and about five feet from my towel, I estimated how long it would take me to find my clothes and hide. Absentmindedly, my hand found the wall lever for the shower. Fingers shaky, I turned off the water. Spurring forward, I recalled a laundry cart in the Strip and

Search room on the other side of the wall.

"Could this be the opportunity I had dreamt of?"

Ester's decision to check on the unforeseen problem was that she had no idea her bad day was about to get worse. Nervous, I whispered, "Thank you, Zeus, for the lightning bolt."

The lights above flickered in sporadic pulses, a little reminder that time wasn't on my side to spring this plan into action. In between the flashes, I placed a foot on the slippery soap-scum tile. When I took my second step, guilt pinged within my skull. It resonated like the peal of a grave bell. This disturbed my calm little cemetery–I kept within myself–from one of the plots. Faith awakened furiously by pulling on those heartstrings.

I ignored the distraction. Optimism was a dangerous illusion of an ambiguous promise. In contrast, pessimism was the cushion that broke your fall when fate decided to let go. Thinking this way helped me plan for the 'what ifs' when others who believed in fate's control dotted their 'i's' with little hearts.

On a bolted plastic chair, folded neatly, was a powder-blue bath towel. Reaching for it caused me to whimper as several ribs warned me I was moving too fast. Frustration burned the discomforts away after I wrapped the cloth around me.

Worried, I bit my lower lip. The painful spot throbbed from the pressure. Laughing nervously, I said, "That's all I need is a cold sore." My tongue pushed on the annoyance, and I tasted blood.

White-knuckling the towel, I followed the wall using my left hand. Each row of lights lost its fight for power, and I found myself in darkness again; this time, even the emergency lights flickered before fading out. Fumbling for where the wall ended, my foot struck something hard. Freaking out by the sudden stop, I overcorrected, and my ankle gave way. I went down without a lumberjack hollering timber. Disgusted, I thought, *So much for protecting my ribs.*

Coughing, I inhaled a sharp gulp of air. The world became two-dimensional. Objects were crudely outlined in black permanent marker, and everything was colored in a cascade of greys.

I readjusted the towel before scooting toward what stopped my momentum. Curiosity needled my resolve, and using a free hand, I cautiously patted the floor until…four fingertips grazed stubble.

Recoiling, I strained to see the figure better. Mustering some courage to lean in, the lights hissed to life. Wesley gazed at the ceiling. His perfect expression, empty of emotion, frozen dilated pupils emphasized parted blue lips. Modesty be damned. I screamed, and then lobster-crawled to put space between us.

The male nurse wasn't wearing his typical uniform. He was dressed in a Fallout Boy tour shirt. There were several dark red stains on the front. Mind numb, vision swimming, I noticed his torn black jeans and a pair of muddy black-silver Nikes. He was dead.

Hands over my mouth, one of the band's songs began to play in my head. Free falling into memory, I said, "You loved Fallout Boy." My fingers were slick, and the smell of rusty pennies made me pull both hands from my mouth. Blood dripped from them. Horror smashed into me as I grasped that the blood was not mine. Unable to contain it, I screamed again.

Crying, I yelled, "Get up. Wesley, stop playing."

He didn't move.

"Get up," I shrilled in demand.

Escape plan and dignity forgotten, I lunged forward, clutched his shirt, and straddled him. Fiercely shaking my male nurse until his head wobbled, Wesley's expression stayed fixed. Dropping him, I started CPR.

Hot tears burned trails over my skin. "Who did this to you? Who did this to you?" I asked between puffs of air.

My heart must have taken leave because the erratic pulse running through my veins ceased, realizing my attempt to revive him wasn't working. Curling over Wesley until my forehead rested on his, one phrase echoed. *'Kaye did this to you.'*

Sobbing, I cupped his face. "I love you. Why would she do this?"

My world inverted as I tried to see through sticky tears and past heaving breasts. One of my hands was wrapped around the hilt of a knife protruding from the middle of his rib cage. Sobbing uncontrollably, a disembodied voice pled, "I didn't do this. This isn't me. I love him. This isn't me."

The shower room door swung open before Ester stepped through the threshold. The familiar *shhh* the door made seemed appropriate, telling Ester to keep what she was about to witness, our dirty secret. Through stringy hair, I could see her brown eyes widening, taking in the horrific scene.

Just as I turned away, hopelessness glued my eyelids shut. I didn't want to see Ester's ugly sneer before the baton made contact or noticed Wesley's lifeless form beneath me. *'How was I going to explain this?'*

Boot scuffs made me stiffen. Praying, I prepared for the first swing of her baton to crack my skull hard enough to send me to wherever Wesley was. Then a hand clapped my shoulder as she leaned in to whisper, "What are you doing?"

Reality flashed before me. I was hunched and straddling...no one. Freezing and shaking uncontrollably—wet onyx hair draped over my head from leaning forward. Wanting to dump my guts out, I started to dry-heave.

Patting my back, while using a mocking motherly tone, she said, "Did the storm scare you? Or are you afraid of the dark?" Sanity drained from this reality as she continued, "It's all right now. The generators are working. Come on, let's get you dressed."

Traumatized, I said through quivering lips, "There was a dead body here. I saw it."

Caught off by my blunt confession, Ester's hand quit moving. "What?"

I didn't want to say his name as a taboo sense of dread skidded over my skin. Inspecting my hands, they were clean. Reluctant, I craned around her slightly to scan the room for Wesley's dead body.

Disbelief punched me in the gut. Thoughts scattered when reason slipped from random unanswered questions, and sporadic statements swam in my mind. *What happened?* I didn't know the nurse personally. *Love, I didn't love him.* Wesley had to be alive. *Could what I witnessed be a premonition?* Nothing was making sense. A rumble of thunder added to the guard's demeanor as I watched her confusion shift to understanding.

Ester looped one arm under mine to help me off the floor. "Wesley might be right. You are a little off today." Supporting my weight, she steadied me before I took the first step. "I'll inform the doctor."

Apathetically, I stared at a crumpled powder-blue towel where Wesley's lifeless body had been. Not wanting to make Ester upset, I tried to keep pace as we passed a few metal cabinets before reaching the charcoal-painted lockers.

I finally stopped taking my morning cocktail Dr. Reins prescribed. It took a couple of months to dwindle down the dosage. *Maybe this was a side effect?* I tried to go cold turkey before and ended up in the hospital wing for a few weeks. Arora didn't want me to get in trouble this time, so she hid them in a hole that she made in the mattress. This way, I had them if the side effects worsened. Ester propped me against the lockers. "Your clean clothes are inside." She wiggled five digits in the air and grumbled, "Five minutes. Get dressed, and I'll be back."

Nodding, she gave me some privacy. It didn't matter since I had already walked here nude. Facing the ceiling, I inhaled sharply to swallow the pain. Counting to ten, then exhaled to clear my mind.

I saw his lifeless body.

Tasted my fear.

I smelled his blood.

Heard my screams.

Death's presence had claimed him in this room.

Memory replayed the negative image of Wesley's glazed-over expression. His lips parted from death's final kiss. The two smears of blood left marks on either side from where I held his cheeks. Remembering how my fingers were slick from the knife's blood-soaked handle sent chills.

A single drop of clarity disrupted my pool of madness, and the earlier statement resurfaced.

Why did I believe Kaye killed him?

Curled up, muscles sore and stiff, I placed a pillow against my middle and stretched. I moaned. The combination of internal pain, physical chill, and broken mental balance kept me from sleeping.

Several creaks from the protesting metal made me aware of my roommate. The harsh whisper of hands sliding across a sheet meant Arora was on a mission. It had to be paramount if she was putting that much effort into whatever she was doing.

My body shut down. I didn't care enough to roll over or ask why. Depression's only positive side effect was fatigue. Maybe this was why Arora slept so much.

A long gurgle came from my stomach, but I wasn't hungry. *'Can you consume your emotions,'* I wondered. Consuming multiple servings of pity pie, with two or three scoops of 'I-don't-care' and topped with a mound of whipped despair. Saliva pooled inside my cheek, and I swallowed to keep from choking.

The smoky shadow of a head poked out from behind the headboard. Hoarse, I croaked, "Hi Mistie."

Pale light shone through the wired double-pained glass, creating a silhouette of me on the wall. Mistie thinned and moved in a distorted blur to lie on the shadowed blanket. She wanted me to confide in her, and my heart broke.

Tears dripped over the nasal bone as I lay on my side. I placed both hands between my cheek and the mattress. They were getting soaked from the waterworks. Snot thinning, I sniffed and used my sheet to dab away the tears. Heaving a groan, I watched Mistie's outline rock slightly; she was trying to be patient.

Taking a moment to collect my thoughts, I whispered, "I'm never getting out of here." The words sounded final, which made me cry harder.

"What?" Arora's voice held a hint of astonishment.

With a one-shoulder shrug, I repeated the realization through hiccups and sniffs.

Mistie's head bobbed as airy fingers tried to push a strand of hair behind my ear.

"Don't listen to her," Arora shrieked.

Shocked, I flipped over to gawk at my roommate. In a flash, there was an accusing finger pointed at me, and outrage colored her pasty complexion. Scared by Arora's outburst, Mistie bolted to the other side of the room and disappeared under the adjacent bed.

"So, you're giving up," my roommate accused.

Tears welled, but I didn't dare blink.

"All you keep talking about is getting us out of here." Flaying me with her words became overly dramatic before both hands landed on her hips. "Out there–out there–really? Why do you want out so badly? What's wrong with staying here?"

Mouth agape, I rocked my head. Words failed me as I sputtered like a drowning frog. Her behavior floored me. She was passionate about one subject: sleeping. Different positions, and which was the most relaxing. What pills did she prefer over others? How she would brighten when reminiscing about her bedroom. Arora often shared about the decorations, furniture, and the collection of plush fish toys she slept with. Finding Nemo might have played a part in the obsession. I watched her gray-socked feet slowly amble toward the window.

I sniffed.

Then she did the same.

Standing, I joined her to stare out the glass. Kaye glowered at us like she was expecting us to say something. The silence began to poison the air, spurring Kaye to pace like a caged cat riled from being darted. A glint of a predatory nature was present in her smile.

Concerned, I stole a glance at Arora. Sparkles trickled down her chin. In front of us, Kaye's reflection kept pacing, her way of waiting to see what I would do. Since we were having a group intervention, I decided to go next.

Quietly, I said, "There was an incident in the showers today."

Kaye didn't stop pacing but hesitated.

Arora looked out the window. Her reflection was speckled with raindrops, which I found fitting. A few trailed down the glass, emphasizing her sorrow.

Nervous, I reached for my hair and began to comb it with my fingers. Taking a shallow breath, I explained every detail about the storm, the power outages, and how Ester left me alone in the dark, thus exposing an opportunity to escape.

Kaye quit pacing and scowled.

Guilt zinged down my spine as I averted my position from Kaye and focused on Arora. "I wanted to see how far I could get."

"You were going to leave without us?" Arora's eyes held betrayal.

Blocking her view so she couldn't see the tells of the lie. "I would have come back for you if I did."

Bam!

We both jumped as we watched the glass splinter in a web-like fashion from two fist-sized indentations in the window. The whites of Kaye's eyes were hollow and empty. Her fury radiated from behind the glass.

Arora nodded at Kaye. "Yes, I know she's lying." She spun on a heel. "What I want to know is, why are you lying to us now? I thought we were in this together."

Rubbing my knuckles, I could taste regret's rancid bite. *'How could I have left them behind?'* We were a team—they had my back—and I had theirs. No matter how annoying, they understood me better than anyone else.

In a gesture of forgiveness, I pleaded, "It was stupid to try and leave without the both of you." It was mainly for Arora, but I knew deep down Kaye would force me to bring her along. So, begrudgingly, I acknowledged her too. "I mean, both of you."

Kaye was livid, but at least her eyes were normal again. My roommate gave me a tremulous smile. It made her seem fragile; if I acted differently, she might have shattered. Reassuringly, I tried to return the gesture. I didn't think this discussion was over, especially since I had a few questions for both of them.

Observing Kaye, her dark eyes delving into my soul, her lips progressively curling, I knew this was far, far from over.

Exhausted, I fell onto the mattress. There was a plastic rattle above my head. I cracked an eye to see a clear plastic pill cup. Arora shook it again, and I opened the second one.

I lifted my head suspiciously and murmured, "What's this?" Then I held out my hand as she placed it in the middle of my palm.

"Remember, I've been saving them for you." She spun on a heel and, within two steps, jumped onto her bed. The frame protested from her effort, and she giggled while crawling to the far corner.

I regarded the small pink suppressants. Counting, I was impressed with the amount. "Wow, there's a week's worth in here. How did I manage to do that?" I shook the container.

My bewilderment faded to concern. Trying to piece together the last few days made my head hurt. Each moment was smeared in clouds of fog like time didn't exist. I whispered, "Impossible."

A phlegmy rattle came from Arora. "Duh, you gave them to me after you pretended to swallow them. You're lucky Ester doesn't swipe the upper part of your mouth. By the way, Dr. Reins must have upped your dosage because I noticed the milligrams and code on the tablets. They are different than before."

Digging out one of the capsules, I eyed it. "I don't recall her telling me she changed it." Frowning from this new information, I wondered what she knew. "Do you remember yesterday?"

She laughed. "Of course I do. That's a song."

"Come on; I'm serious."

Her giggling slowed. "I am, too. It's a song." Arora sounded incredulous. "Um–hello–the Beetles." Then she started humming the tune.

I threw my pillow at her. "Come on. Arora, I need you to think. What did you do yesterday?"

She scrunched her nose in thought. "I slept."

Infuriated, I shot up. "That's a cop-out. What did you have for breakfast?"

With her back against the wall, she side-slid down and pulled the blanket over her head. "Why does it matter? Every day is a paid vacation from reality." Her finger pointed at the window.

Scared, the emotion triggered the shakes. "You don't know, do you?"

"Listen, why poke around the past when the present is right in front of you? Enjoy the now." The cover muffled her reply.

On edge, I uttered, "What?"

Flipping the bedding away, she motioned at the cup of prescriptions. "Take one of those: sleep, forget, recharge, and repeat. It's easy. And bonus, you don't have to deal with the three of them." Waving at the door, she continued, "They'll leave you alone if you play their game." Punctuating her advice with a yawn, I realized why I had tried to leave without them.

Then, the memory of Wesley's dead expression flashed into my mind. *Was this vision something from my past?* I tested the hunch. "Arora, what about my past that I'm not supposed to remember?"

She rolled toward the wall. "Like, how should I know?"

"But you do, don't you?"

Her answer was barely audible. "Maybe?"

With a slight ping of hope, I asked, "Can you help me?"

With her voice quivering, she answered, "Trust me; you don't want to dig up the past." Sitting up, she scooted into the shadow so Kaye couldn't see her. She gave me an earnest expression, "You aren't going to like what you'll find."

"If you help me, I'm sure it'll be okay," I said with confidence.

Becoming somewhat dejected, she hissed, "I'm not your strength. That's Kaye's department."

A screech from the door startled me. Head raised, Ester held the door open for someone. Awashed in uncertainty, a voice in my head asked, *'How would he look? He wasn't dead if his cart was rounding the…'*

A man with raven hair and squinty obsidian eyes glided over the threshold. Panicked, I pushed away, clamping my hands over my mouth. With my head, I motioned 'no.'

Ester sighed. "Emily, this is your new nurse. He's going to–"

"Where is Wesley?" I couldn't hide my anxiety.

The stranger addressed Ester, "Is she the–"

"The crazy one, yes." The guard cut him off.

He cleared his throat. "I was going to say special."

Special, he wasn't allowed to think of me that way. Only Wesley thought I was special. I didn't know this guy well enough for him to assume he knew me.

The new male nurse approached me with a cup overflowing with pills. "This will help you forget why Wesley is gone."

Frightened, I yelled, "What are you talking about?"

He shrugged. "You'll have to ask Kaye if you want to know more."

Instantly, she appeared behind him. Seizing his neck with one hand and in the other was a raised knife over his chest.

Mouthing the words, "I'll protect you." She plunged the knife into his chest and then twisted; he grunted from the pain. Body slack, Kaye released the guy, and he crumbled to the floor. I couldn't take my eyes off him, and his head lolled in my direction.

Wesley replaced his image. I shrieked. "Why? Why? How could you? I loved him. I could never."

Kaye slid her open hand down the blade. With the wish of death sparkling in her irises, I watched in revulsion as the blood ran down her arm. "But, I could."

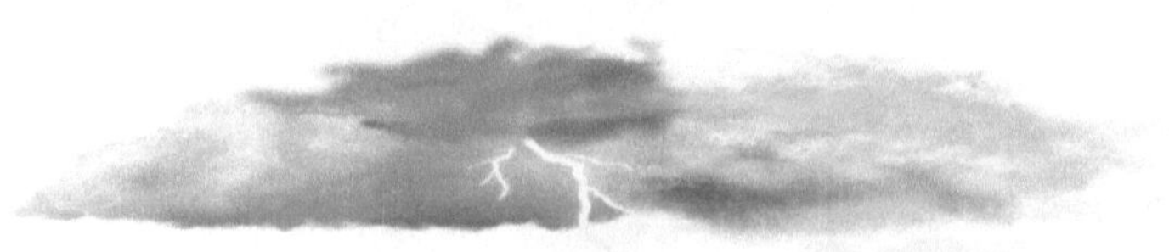

Someone shook me and yelled. Then, a harsh sting exploded against my cheek. I gasped as tears marred my vision, and I tried to settle down long enough to realign my reality.

Ester was over me, and Wesley had a hold of my ankles. The guard's mass pushed me into the springs. My nurse released both ankles and removed a vial and sterile syringe from a locked drawer on his cart. Removing the packaging, he plunged the needle into the clear bottle. When he withdrew it, I heard the tapping on the plastic to release the trapped air. Then he picked up a tourniquet and alcohol swab. He nudged Ester to the side so he could reach my arm.

Madly, I skimmed the room for Arora. She was hiding under a pillow. Resentment rising, I thought, *I defended you, and you're not going to return the favor?'*

Using my best in-house voice, I calmly spoke to Wesley. "I'm fine. I'm fine. I don't need it."

Troubled with whom to believe, he hesitated. I could tell he was battling to accept my previous actions or my words. Lowering the shot, he cocked his head at Ester. "What do you think? I don't want to use it if she is rational."

She grabbed my chin. Invading my personal space, I could see my reflection in her pupils. The twin images of me appeared frantic and petrified. Breathing was difficult as fear made the lump in my throat expand.

Dropping my chin but not letting go of my shoulder, she said, "Dr. Reins said if she has a fit, sedate her. It's your call if you want to go against orders." Ester squinted at me. "Her appointment with the doctor is in thirty minutes."

He kept working, placing everything on the green medical tray. Solemnly, he requested, "Ester, can I have a word with her?"

She straightened and then released me. I rubbed blood into the area she held. Gauging her co-worker's demeanor, the guard touched her baton and drummed four fingers. "Sure, I'll be right by the door."

Walking around him, Wesley placed a hand on her arm. "Can I have ten minutes with her alone?"

I was in disbelief. Wesley was asking her to break the rules. *'Was he crazy?'*

Cheek's red, Ester blew out hard. "You know I can't leave you alone with her."

"I would like to try. I believe I can reach her." The pinch in between his brows relaxed. "Ester, ten minutes, please. You can time me."

She turned on a heel. "If she goes out of her freakin'-ass mind and kills you, your blood won't be on my hands." Glancing at her watch, she turned to us. "Ten minutes, starting now." Taking the silver seven from her pocket, she fingered the ring, twirled the key, and then grabbed the handle to close the door. I didn't hear the lock, which was her way of saying she was right outside.

Wesley released a profound sigh. "Well, that wasn't as hard as I thought."

I massaged the arm he was going to stick. Skeptical, I kept my jaw locked, figuring it was better to remain silent until he revealed his reason for being alone with us. Bringing my knees toward my chest, I wrapped my arms around both legs and peered at him from over my kneecaps.

Arora was still hugging the pillow but tighter than before. Her body shook as though she was crying. Grimacing, I turned my attention to the male in the room.

Lost in thought, Wesley stood in front of me with an expression that made my heart pause as I pictured him dead. His presence in the room made it hard for me to breathe and it peaked my anxiety meter to new heights. I wasn't sure if this talk would benefit the situation, but I gnawed on the inside of my cheek and waited for the executioner's axe to drop.

"May I sit?" He motioned to the foot of the bed.

I nodded.

Arora whimpered into the cushion. *'What was her problem?'* He wasn't sitting on her bed. She wasn't the focus of his attention. When the inner reproofs stopped, another round of inquiries circled. *'What if he wants to ask me a question? What if I answer it wrong? Would he end up using the needle on me anyway?'*

Wesley cleared his throat. "I can see the questions behind your eyes. Emily, breathe. I need you to keep calm, or there won't be anything I can do to help if you lose control." He crossed his legs. "Understand?"

I agreed with a head bob.

Pleased, he said, "Good." Then, his lips pressed into a thin line. Taking a moment to continue, he said, "Emily, I'm going to be direct because I think this is the only way to get through. I need you to listen. Some things will sound unbelievable, but you need to pay attention. We don't have a lot of time."

Giving him a half-shoulder shrug, he continued, "Do you remember the night we met?"

Wide-eyed, I answered, "No."

"During our senior year, we moved in different circles. I knew about you, but you stayed pretty much to yourself. A friend was having a party, and I asked her to invite you as a favor."

Unsure, but a name resurfaced, "Wendi?"

Sparking the correct answer from me spurred him into the rest of his explanation. "We left the party, and I overheard you giving Wendi the excuse to go home to feed your fish." He grinned at his memory. "I introduced myself as we headed to our cars. I found how secretive you were peculiar, so I challenged your reason for leaving.

"You gave me the cutest smirk and thanked me for walking out with you. Before getting into your car, you asked if I'd like to get a coffee. You were giving me a chance. I didn't even hesitate and agreed."

Suspicious, I pushed for more information. "What are you getting at?"

Wringing his hands, he continued, "Our trust grew, and over time, we became friends. Four months later, we were dating. At the end of our senior year…" His voice trailed off.

Petrified but intrigued, I sat straighter. "What happened at the end of senior year?"

"I asked you to marry me."

Gaping, I perused our surroundings. "How did I end up here?"

"This is where it gets hard to explain."

"I'm finding most of this unbelievable, but continue." Nervous, I munched on a hangnail.

"It was the end of summer, and we were on our last date before heading to college. Our date didn't end well." He became pale.

"What, did we fight," I asked sarcastically.

"Yes, we did. Now, thinking about it, it was silly at the time. Still, you got out of the car and stormed off. I couldn't leave you and followed to apologize."

Raising a hand to his chest, he paused to catch his breath. "Your complaints turned to pleas for help. They echoed through the darkness, and I began to search for you in a panic." Tears formed along the rims of his eyes.

Breathless, I asked, "Wesley, what happened?"

"A group of cloaked men was in the woods performing some ritual. I think they might've been deranged or drunk; I'm not sure, but they were evil." He started to sob. "They raped you and then beat me senseless so I couldn't save you."

I choked on my saliva. "They what?" My temperature rose, and I began to pat my body to quell the heat. "What?" I screeched.

Wesley moved forward and clasped my hands in his. "Look at me, Emily," he said sternly. "It gets worse."

"Worse, how can it get worse?" I tried to pull away from him. "Oh my, are we dead? We're dead, aren't we?"

Leaning in, he sighed. "No, we're not dead."

I relaxed and bowed my head with a relieved sigh.

His words became distant. "No, we're not dead, just me."

Jerking away, I shrieked.

The asylum alarms blared throughout the hall. Ester came crashing into the room. Wesley tried to shelter me from the guard.

Arora yelled at Ester to leave me alone.

Before she got to me, Wesley yanked me closer. "Those sadistic bastards gave you a choice. If you killed me, they promised to set you free. I begged you to do it. I loved you. It was the only way to save you. Even though you kept wailing and repeating, 'You couldn't.' But after the man with raven hair attacked you with a knife, something happened."

Breathing shallowly, I didn't want to know, but the words were slipping from my mouth before I could stop them, "What? What happened?" Horrific images flipped uncontrollably through my head, and I knew before he even confessed.

"You killed me, Emily Kaye."

The crack of Ester's baton was a blissful godsend.

Epilogue

The alarm's screeching grew louder, branching the nightmare into reality. My lids were heavy, and I realized they were crusty, probably from crying in my sleep again. Debating whether or not it was worth hitting the snooze, I decided to roll out of bed and smack the button to make the annoyance stop.

Dealing with a headache there wasn't enough room for my brain to think. Sluggish, I made my way into the bathroom. Adjacent to the sinks was the walk-in closet. Picking out my clothes for the day, I hung them up next to the shower so the wrinkles would steam out, then reached in to turn on the water.

Waiting for the water to warm up, I headed to the dresser, opened the top drawer, and picked out stockings with matching undergarments. Glancing at a picture of a blond man holding up a girl's hand with short pink hair and showing off a ring. I reached over and laid the picture face down. For some reason, I couldn't look at it today. On the frame, someone penned Wes & Kaye with an infinity sign.

Lightning flashed through the bedroom windows; its leftover presence was hard enough to shake the second floor. I raised the blinds to look outside. The rain was turning to hail. I had to hurry to make my first appointment.

Before entering the bathroom, I retrieved my cell phone from its charger and checked for messages. Then, I placed the phone and undergarments on the counter. I ached all over when my heart fractured into six different emotions. Turning on the faucet, I froze.

Steam clouded the mirror but failed to conceal the six sets of eyes staring at me through the reflective surface. I froze in disbelief as Ester tapped her baton. Arora yawned from inside the bathtub. Kaye's angst raised the room's temperature. Mistie zipped past and into the shower stall. The presence of an eighteen-year-old Emily was the most dominant. She began to cry when Wesley's misty form emerged from the closet, and the rest of us gasped in unison.

Brain-fried, I clutched my chest. *'Why were the seven of us in this room?'*

Ozzy's "Crazy Train" interrupted the silence between us. In a panic, I reached for several prescriptions. The volume rose from the unanswered call. Cursing, I snatched the cell, and proclaimed, "All of you can't come to work today."

'How much longer must I endure this torment? Relive this pain? Wasn't thirteen years long enough?'

Maddened for not discovering a way to cure myself, I swiped the bar and answered, "Hello. This is Dr. Emily K. Reins. What's on your mind?"

Maryanna's Mirror
By Kathy-Lynn Cross
Before you play her game, ask yourself,
"Am I ready to die?"

Copyright

Maryanna's Mirror

Maryanna's Mirror

A set of keys jingled as the guard stepped around me while studying his collection for the specific one. Another male stood out of my peripheral vision; his lack of personal hygiene was accompanied by the stale stench of used chew and laced weed, triggering a gag reflex. A few sweat-soaked strands draped over my face when I coughed, so I used the guise to glance behind. Ben was stickered on a brass name badge, the letters slightly crooked. His eyes were bloodshot and glazed, a sure sign he'd be crashing soon.

I perceived the hum and quick sessions of hiss-pops from the fluorescence light fixtures in the hallway as a warning. Chewing on my lower lip, I played connect-the-rusty dots on the poorly painted blue door.

When the guard acknowledged his co-worker, the glint from his name tag caught my attention. After a brief exchange of words, Cecil inserted the key, and the metal latch unlocked in protest. With force, he shifted his stance to wrench it open. Stale air blew past us as though a collection of broken spirits escaped. It prompted me to balance on the balls of my feet. I struggled to remain in control and force myself to adjust to the multiple degrees of darkness. Eventually, certain objects began to form. A chair in the middle of the room was a similar scene from a generic spy movie. And as expected, it faced an ominous, one-way window.

I wrapped both arms tighter to conceal the only possession that linked me to this era, unsure of what would happen if it were discovered.

Fear was normally our drug of choice—in the right circumstances—but this rotted residue was from thousands of uncured and broken souls. The stench rooted me to the floor. Readjusting the gray hospital smock, I fidgeted with the object in the sleeve.

Fingers pressed into my back to shove me over the threshold. The action caused me to bite my lip. Instinctively, I sucked on the puncture while stumbling forward. There were several clicks from the hanging bulb until its illumination worked as an invitation to sit. Even though the chair was bolted to the floor, it was the only sign of refuge.

High above, a male's voice with an electrical crackle tested the volume. "One, two, three. Can you hear me?"

I winced at the one-way glass and noticed the seat. *'This could be problematic,'* I thought.

As if on cue, a heated whisper penetrated my skull. *"Keep your head down."* A shift in the air from an additional presence encircled me. The oppressive bout of frustration turned to a more complacent understanding. *"Keep your eyes roaming or fix on a point in the room. Preferably the floor. Try not to make eye contact with them through the glass, and we'll be fine."* Testy, the voice confirmed, *"We've been in worse situations. Keep them talking. I'll figure something out."*

With a fleeting exhale, I nodded like a defiant child and then clasped both hands until the nails bit into the skin. Pacing around the chair, a Southern accent, much softer than before, said, "Please take a seat, Maryanna."

Muscles tightened while I fought the knee-jerk reaction to respond. As a distraction, I spotted a crack running along the cement floor. The point of origin was possibly from the bolt securing the chair leg by my right heel. The cracked webbing pattern seemed fitting since I was trapped like a bug.

Electrical pops from the ceiling speakers caused me to jump. "Maryanna, did you hear me? Please sit down."

I complied.

"Ready? First session, November 3, 2020." The female's voice drifted overhead, indicating she was preoccupied. Probably filling out forms, I assumed. "Subject number 840236-Cambridge, M. Age approximately twenty."

Internally, I scoffed. Oh, if they only knew the historical events I've witnessed.

"Birthdate unknown. Sex," There was a pause as I felt their eyes on me. I remained silent. Those C-cups pretty much indicated what I was. "Female," Echoed through the room. "Turn the volume down, Franklin."

"Yes, Ma'am."

"Caucasian. Black hair. Blue-gray eyes. Weight?" Papers rustled as the woman's voice became distant as she shifted her attention to ask an associate the question directly. "Her weight and height; did you get it?"

A terse conversation from the back of the room continued. Infuriated, the person answered, "No, not yet."

My lips peeled back to expose teeth when I recalled fighting three men and the gratification when I latched on one of the guard's forearms. Then, the pleasure was ripped away when a faint throb reminded me of the outcome.

"I'll need her weight to prescribe the right dosage." She cleared her throat. "In case she needs medical help."

"Yes, Ma'am," Franklin responded robotically.

The doctor timidly coughed away from the mic before asking, "Maryanna, do you know where you are?"

I shook my head from side to side.

"This is Finite. An institution for humanity reprogramming and medical rehabilitation. My name is Dr. Sheila Worthington."

An asylum; how fitting. Flipping through memories, I couldn't recall the last time I was admitted against my will or for self-preservation. Our situation struck my funny bone, and I filled the space with laughter. The pressure would have killed me a second time if I held it in.

"Curious. Why do you find this humorous? You do recall why you are here?"

Greed and jealousy were two main reasons I found myself in this predicament. Like a curse, and on cue, memories replayed two searing eyes, a room engulfed in flames, and continuous screaming—maybe some pleading, mostly from me. I found it surprising how death's melody can be beautiful depending on the person.

The repetitive pen clicking brought me back from my Shakespearean tragedy. I feigned innocence, using a scared child's demeanor. "No. No, I'm not sure why I'm here. Please let me go home."

"We found you at a murder scene. You were non-responsive and covered in blood. At the hospital, you were sedated to check for any defensive wounds. They documented several long gashes along your chest and a few shallow punctures across your abdomen, but no wounds on your hands. You were treated but healed remarkably fast. The doctors then believed your injuries might have been self-inflicted, which is why you were transferred here. That was three days ago."

I envisioned the knife sinking into my stomach several times before breaking her wrist. Damn, curse. It was unfortunate how things played out. I didn't necessarily regret the outcome, but the roommate wasn't my intended victim. If she hadn't broken what was mine, I might have left the little human alive.

"Maryanna, can you recall what happened that night?"

Flippant, I replied, "No."

"Is it because you don't remember or you don't want to?"

"The latter," I mocked.

As though two iced fingers pressed into my left temple, a masculine heated command resonated within my skull. *"Keep talking. I have to figure a way out of this for both of us. You have to keep them occupied."*

At this point, the only way I could keep their attention was to retell my story. I've relived the nightmare time and time again, but listening to the sins of the damned slip between tongue and cheek made each scene etch deeper into my subconscious.

Cautiously, I glanced to the side of the one-way mirror and noticed a micro camera affixed four inches above it. That tiny lens would serve as my focal point. Breathing measured, I made my heart rate sync in rhythm. Remaining calm would keep my true nature contained.

Transfixed on the camera, I started, "The accounts about my life might come across as though I am seeking repentance for my sins, but this is quite the opposite, for I can no longer relate to empathy. I've accepted this existence. The darkness beyond the reflective void is my comfort.

"It has taken many forms of pain, but in the end, I have come to terms with what I am, and now, I embrace the addiction, the challenge, the desire to allure and coax the misinformed souls who believe I can foresee their future. It is somewhat unfortunate because I can see it, but if I choose to disclose this knowledge, it will be my undoing. We can't have that; I love myself too much, and many would miss playing the game if I were gone.

"Throughout the centuries, numerous stories of lore have changed, twisted, and altered to fit some wild tale to spark terror, dread, or anxiety for entertainment or amusement. But, speaking about this sweet torment—so openly—stirring the raw emotional cocktail for me to choke down once again may come at a cost."

The mic hissed before the doctor remarked, "I'm not sure where this is going, but if sharing your past can bring you back to the present, then please continue."

"This narration is from my perspective, but before I share this tale, allow me to start with a warning;

"If you stare into the glass while whispering my name, if a reflection appears, do not gaze directly into those eyes…for I cannot guarantee your life will be spared."

So many bones ached from maintaining the same pose during several flips of the head seamstress's hourglass. The new floor-length gown seemed to be a newfound torture my aunt planned—punishment for my upcoming twentieth birthday.

My mother's older brother was the Duke of Herford, Harold Herford. My uncle and father were childhood friends and spent many summers together. During which my mother, Lillian Hertford, was introduced to my father, Lord Gallen Cambridge. Once his father passed, he inherited the land and the title of Duke of Cambridge. Shortly following, he married Lillian.

After my father's death last winter, my mother's health declined while managing our affairs and the Cambridge estate. When word reached the Duke of Hertford about his sister's grim condition, he insisted I should visit until matters were settled and her health improved.

During this stay, he promised to host a birthday party for me at Hertfordshire. My aunt, the Duchess of Hertford, Serina Hertford, wasn't thrilled given the daunting task. I believed her resentment toward me shifted from a light snowfall to a full-on blizzard.

Uncle Harold seemed to favor me over most of his kin, except his two youngest, Camryn and Kathline. They were twins, a son, and a daughter, almost ten years old. I held them in high regard, for both never treated me with contempt or disdain. Since I did not have siblings, they were pleasant to be around, and I enjoyed their company.

The two older cousins perceived me as the black sheep in the family and were not in good relations. Lady Jane Hertford, their firstborn, was about a year older than me. Her shrewd demeanor and the fact that she disavowed our family's religious beliefs were off-putting. The only subject we could connect on was her upcoming engagement to a Duke from France, Monsieur Jamison Belmont.

Her brother, Lord Sean Hertford, was a few months shy of

turning twenty after me. To describe his character kindly, picture a diseased weasel. Whenever I entered a room, he would immediately covet every move—always making crude comments about a woman's appearance and how her conduct should be.

In the span of a blink, a seamstress appeared behind me to position both arms straight to either side. I huffed in frustration. Another girl measured each arm from wrist to shoulder, rattling off the numbers as one of the helpers wrote down the information. I peered upon the reflection of a half-dressed female scarecrow staring back at me. Daydreaming, I envisioned standing in the middle of the King's royal gardens—crows resting on each arm. But since I couldn't smell the roses or damp earth, the reverie swiftly vanished.

Tresses askew, a few untamed inky curls started to tickle. I blew at two by my nose, but I was unsuccessful in relieving their irritation. At the same time, I slumped forward. The head seamstress, Amithina, clapped to command attention from everyone.

Two neck bones popped as I twisted toward the sound. The relief didn't last long; it was replaced with a dull throb, which exasperated my dark mood.

Using a superior air over a subordinate, I reprimanded the head seamstress. "Excuse me. I am not one of your dogs. You will address me accordingly, or I will have you and your staff removed and hire a new gown designer from Essex or Yorkshire." I started to drop my arms when the girl behind me propped them into position. "You touch me one more time," I threatened.

Blood drained from her face as she backed away, curtsied, and averted her eyes to the ground. It pleased me; she knew her place. Studying the petite girl, I toyed with the idea of adding her on as another personal servant.

A soft sneeze redirected my thoughts. I scanned the room to locate the direction it was from. Two pairs of tiny shoes poked out from under the curtains to the far left of the room. I bit the inside of my cheek, realizing the twins were spying on me again. *'If I didn't establish my position, how would that appear to them?'*

Peeved, I faced Amithina. "How much longer must I endure this mundane torture? I must bathe and dress for dinner. The Duchess is very strict on punctuality, as you are well aware." To affirm the warning, gongs from the cathedral bells resonated on the half an hour mark.

"Lady Maryanna, I beg your forgiveness, but if you want the best fit for your gown, we need you to hold still a bit longer. We've toiled for five nights to keep to your schedule, and please permit me to say that your choice of material complements your fair skin and eyes extremely fine." There was a hint of self-satisfaction behind the swift compliment.

It pained me to admit that she was well-versed in flattery. Temporarily forgetting the little spies, I admired the gown of pale rose and pearl beadwork intricately fashioned in diminutive swirls around the bodice—a square neckline adorned with an inch of silver, eyelet lace. The reflected pink frown sparked an old argument from over a week ago between the Duchess and me. I would have preferred a V-neckline to show off my best features, for I found delight when the frigid women would blush and the tight-leashed males ogled. But to my dismay, Serina was a prude and insisted it wasn't proper for the occasion.

From the low waist to the hem, a sheer pattern of gold-inlaid flowers draped in pinned waves cascaded to the floor, where the material pooled around my stocking feet. From under the dress, I poked out and pointed a toe to inspect the pale white stockings my uncle commissioned with the dress. Temper dissolving, I envisioned the footwear my mother sent as a birthday gift.

Amithina's reflection saddled up to mine in the mirror. "Does the dress please you, my lady?"

I lowered the leg and puffed another curl as a smile widened across my doppelgänger. In defeat, I answered her with an exhale, "Yes." An unexpected giggle escaped, and I slapped both hands over my mouth. Right then, the material down each arm made a tearing hiss from behind.

All four girls moaned in unison as Serina entered the chamber. Collecting their composure, each curtsied, formally greeting the

Duchess of Hertford. Remarkably, the head seamstress mentally commanded them, and their attention shifted toward me as hands fluttered, tucked, pinned, and repaired the mishap.

The elderly woman stepped in between me and the mirror. Two lackluster, black-brown eyes roamed down the dress and back to lock upon mine. I figured she was waiting for me to acknowledge her properly.

With a slight shrug, I used my chin to gesture an informal greeting.

In a curt tone, she responded, "Lady Maryanna."

From years of conditioning, I straightened. "Duchess."

Pivoting to Amithina, she pointed at the sleeve tears. "She will be presentable by tomorrow evening, yes?"

The seamstress bowed with a tight nod. "Yes, my lady, the gown will be ready by sunset and delivered in the morn."

"Good. Once you are done with this task, please see Lady Jane before you and your staff depart. Her bodice is stabbing into her lower back. I believe a pin or two was left in the seam. If there is a speck of blood on her dress, I will not compensate you for your time. Slapdash labor is not rewarded."

With arms folded, she began to pace while inspecting the attendants to scrutinize their work. Serina's last step brought her full circle. The air between us held a slight chill as we mentally threw daggers at one another, during which several hands tugged, tightened, and pinned to the timed beat of possible dismissal.

Drawing attention to herself, the Duchess clasped both hands with a pop. "Well, Maryanna, I do have to say the color suits you well."

Shocked by the compliment, I was about to thank her when she added, "At least the color draws attention from you and more to the gown. It will help you blend in as a conversational piece." She refolded one of the pinned swags of material. "Yes, girls who remain next to walls must have something to discuss."

Dropping her hands, she lifted the side of her dress. With a single nod, she left me with a warning, "Maryanna, do as Amithina says. Natalie will be here shortly to help you change for dinner."

To keep from fighting, I feigned interest in the seamstress's work. Not making eye contact, I took a shaky inhale by masking it as a yawn. "Yes. Five-thirty. I will be there on the chime."

I didn't want to admit it, but each icy remark from her began to fester, deepening my disdain for the woman. Serina's oppressive nature made it hard to breathe at times. I briefly wondered if others felt the same.

The rustle and swish of satin signaled her immediate departure. But, before she reached the doorway, from over a shoulder, she said, "Amithina, do not forget to fix Jane's dress," and then slammed the door.

A set of two frowns appeared in the body-length mirror.

Kathline spoke first. "Mama can be scary at times."

Camryn nodded in agreement and added, "I do believe she means well, sister." He tugged on one of his sleeves. "She does seem ireful most of the time." There was a lack of confidence in his reasoning. "I have to say, sometimes you sound like her, Maryanna."

It stung. He thought his mother and I were similar. Ashamed from my earlier conduct—*'pride be damned'*—I turned to Amithina and apologized. "I'm sorry. It was wrong to demand and not take into account your work." With an airy laugh, I continued, "My parents would have locked me in one of the towers for overstating my place."

The twins bobbed their heads in agreement.

"The Silence Chair has seen my backside many times for that same reason." Camryn flatly stated.

Kathline blushed and then playfully punched her brother's arm.

Amithina's grimace thinned into a softer line. Straightening, she smacked her apron and grumbled, "No need to apologize. I know my station, and my assistants know theirs. We will be done in time. Naomi, Debra, go collect Jane's dress."

Both girls scrambled to gather their tools and sewing boxes. Formality caused them to pause and then curtsy before leaving.

Attention was altered from Amithina, and I saw several long

fingers heading straight for me. An involuntary gasp escaped but was timely matched to the others in the room. Reacting from panic, I lurched backward, which caused the stool to wobble. That's when two hands latched around the neckline, and the adornment of silver eyelet ripped away with a swift yank. After a spell, I watched a scrap of eyelet fall to the floor. Amithina slipped three pins between her lips.

Holding the pins between her teeth, she said, "Now, let's tend to this mishap."

"Subject is displaying signs of schizophrenia."

The blunt statement jarred my subconscious as Amithina's features melted, then whirlpooled down the drain of reminiscence until I was left with an icy numbness.

A disembodied voice, which only I could hear, clipped from behind me. *"You're on a one-way track to getting us committed."*

Exhausted from revisiting the past, I slumped forward, not to draw attention while responding to it. *"Look, I'm doing my best. You know, discussing certain events reopens old wounds, stirs the darkness, which sparks your hunger, and sends me into a frenzy until we're satisfied."*

"You say that like it's a bad thing."

"I honestly don't care either way anymore. But if we split apart and there's bloodshed—I promise you—I'll drag you to the closest church and bathe in the baptistery until we're waterlogged."

He made a terse *'humph'* before diving into my subconsciousness. Like a snake coiling around its prey, he entwined his masculine presence around my core. For the first century, whenever he touched me this way, it felt as though my spirit was being evicted from this body. In the past, he called it our snuggle time. I figured this was his way of distracting under the guise of sulking without losing face.

His presence nuzzled against an ear and joked, *"Maryanna, your confession, if you were truly repentant, would age a priest by a year. Personally, there could be other ways to torture your existence. Besides, when the righteous speak about repentance, it gives me a headache—"*

Aggravated, I lashed out, "What are you doing? Shouldn't you be searching for a way out of here?"

Shocked by the abrupt outburst, I realized the people behind the glass stopped conversing. Filling the pause was air sucking through my fingers and a demon's internal laugh. The object in my sleeve slipped, and to stop the momentum, I calmly placed both hands in my lap.

Teeth grinding, I mentally intertwined anger between each syllable. *"You are purposely trying to rattle me. Stop testing the lock on my composure and find what I need."*

The doctor's words were blunt. "Maryanna, do you need a break?"

Shaking my head, 'no,' I berated myself for losing control.

"Do you want to continue?"

There was a difference in pitch between the males in the small room and the doctor. Once the disagreement quelled, she asked again, "Would you like to continue?"

Seething, the demon gently cooed, *"Go ahead, answer the bitch before she strikes a match and ignites my boredom."* This bout of tolerance he was displaying was out of character and a bit unnerving. He was planning something.

Being stuck in the chair and unable to escape caused my heart rate to spike. The presence beside me dissipated before he left a slideshow of carnage flipping through my consciousness. It lit a chain reaction, and I struggled to contain my true nature.

A crazed bout of laughter resounded that only I could hear. The pressure was so intense I grabbed a handful of hair and slammed myself into the back of the chair. Then his laughter strengthened, shredding my vocal cords. The reaction filled the room with repetitive clicks and airy gagging.

Sweat beaded at the nape of my neck. The air turned stagnant as it mixed with the heat from the hanging bulb which seemed to intensify with each mundane second. Mouth dry, I licked the lower lip until the small wound reopened. Tasting my blood was dissatisfying, like tepid water, but it would help to maintain control.

There was a faint snick of a key. Heavy footfalls accompanied the squeak from a gurney. Hands grabbed my shoulders and upper arms. A light touch of fingers pressed into my left arm for a vein, followed by a sharp prick. The tingle of medication began to fizzle as I used my abilities to counteract it.

Frustrated, I berated the demon. *"You're not helping our situation."*

Phantom fingers traced along my jaw. *"I still enjoy it."*

Ignoring him, I pretended the drug was working and then leaned back until I was facing the hanging light bulb—dark shades of red and orange strobed behind closed eyes. The raw color of red drew me in, along with a soothing calm layered over the weighted memory from my twentieth birthday.

With a hitched intake of air, I softly stated, "This is how the game began…"

I allowed the past to drag me into the depths of my personal hell.

On the night of the party, three more attendants were helping Natalie, and I reveled in the attention. She filled the copper tub with warm water and different colored petals from the Duchesses prized roses. I soaked until the water turned cold while the four women fussed. The basket of petals was a present from Serina and Harold. I would bet my inheritance the gesture was solely made by my uncle, but I gladly accepted them. Today, I was determined that no one would tarnish this day.

Natalie retrieved warm linens from a wooden rack by the fire. When I stood, she draped them around me to dry off. It was heavenly. Two much older women, I believed were Jane's attendants, directed me toward a chair when there was a harsh knuckle tap on the door.

There was a young miss, whom I didn't recognize stopped fluffing the pillows to answer the door. After a brief exchange, she ended the conversation with, "I'll be sure to inform Lady Maryanna. Thank you."

When the girl turned around, a huge wooden box was in her arms, and a smaller one tied with a white ribbon was on top. With a bright smile and words laced with excitement, she exclaimed, "My lady, this is from Amithina." She then placed both boxes on the bed. Lifting the smaller one, she added, "This gift, I was told, is from the Duke of Hertford." Then, she moved it toward the footboard.

Natalie held a robe open as I slipped into it. Bounding over to the bed, I cinched it closed. *My dress had arrived.* A pair of hands came into view to lift the lid. The young servant's eyes sparkled with anticipation, and I found it contagious as we gathered around to see inside.

Firelight glinted off the beadwork, adding to its ethereal beauty. Breathless, I traced the bodice to the neckline. We reached into the box, and with some effort, lifted the heavy fabric and then laid it out on the bed. I squealed. Amithina recreated the gown and added the cut I wanted to the neckline. I jumped like a child receiving their first pony.

"Happy birthday to me. Happy happy birthday to me," I exclaimed in a sing-song, heaving the dress off of the bed to hug it tight.

The women laughed and clapped until the tacky, gold swan statue clock on the end of the table chimed five o'clock. The party started in two hours. A wind of haste swept through the room. Natalie bestowed certain tasks to each servant as I managed to hand the garment over to four outstretched arms.

Another attendant placed a high-back armchair by the mirror

and directed me to it. The hustle and bustle of the evening lifted everyone's mood. Once my hair was pinned and curls placed according to my instructions, it was time to dress.

After squeezing into the corset and gown, Natalie told me to face the mirror. She inserted a spring of lilac into the top of my corset by the left breast and under the lace.

Awestruck, I beheld my form. Twenty agreed with me, even though my cousin, Sean, jabbed that I would forever be an old maid and never find a companion. Secretly, I believed there was more to his comments. Since he blatantly insinuated once, during a small family gathering, that I would be his wife. I recalled that everyone in the dining hall had fallen silent until the Duchess vowed she would not approve of such a union even in death, which caused me to choke on an after-dinner comfit. It was right then that our relationship took a nasty turn five years ago.

With some extra effort, I shoved down the soiled memory. A pair of delicate hands placed the small box on the vanity. Caught off guard, I briefly stared at the petite female as her smile widened. "Pardon, but I was told, per the Duke's instructions, you were to be presented with this today."

It was hard to contain the excitement as my fingers fumbled to untie the ribbon. Surprised, I lifted the silver-etched hand mirror to face level. The servants filled the moment with remarks of splendor, gorgeousness, and thoughtfulness of my uncle. Studying my reflection in the oval-shaped glass, the face from within seemed judgmental.

A light tap pulled me from the mirror's hold. Natalie pointed to the back of it. "Did you see the inscription?"

When I flipped it over, an intricate open rose was in the middle. Five loops of thorny vines encircled it. Written on the edge of the frame,

To: My Maryanna—May the bonds of eternity never break— trap infinity within time's embrace.

A fluttery tension began to build. A tear trailed down the reflected copy of me. Shaking, I whispered, "It's from my father."

A soft knock at the door made us all turn. The girl who answered it earlier hustled to open it and immediately curtsied. In a deep blue satin and lace gown, Jane Hertford pushed the poor girl aside to make her way toward me.

Cold blue eyes met mine before she took in my attire. Aloof, she curtsied before inquiring, "Lady Maryanna, are you almost ready? My father is requesting an audience with you."

Gently, I placed the mirror on the vanity. "Yes, I'm ready." When I stepped beside her, I added, "Your dress is beautiful. Amithina has a remarkable talent with a needle and vision."

Sniffing, she placed some space between us and twirled a few times in the hallway. Long brown curls bounced, adding to her spoiled demure. "Yes, I do believe it compliments me in all the right places." Jane fiddled with something under the neckline of her dress and then noticed mine. Frowning, she tapped a pointed fingernail on her cheek. "You are going to get in trouble when my mother sees what you ordered Amithina to change."

Irritated because I didn't want the seamstress to have a blemish on her reputation, I allowed Jane to believe the change was my doing. "I am twenty. I do not need my attire picked out for me."

Prancing like a peacock, she opened her fan and held it over her mouth. "But I guess at your age, there's no time to practice modesty. Time is ticking, isn't it."

"I don't have my father here to arrange marriages for me." Anger lodged in the place where the words had been. Then I realized my right fist was cramping. Gradually relaxing each finger, I played off the action by readjusting a few creases in the material. On the verge of tears, I marched past her. "You have no founding to boast about your engagement to the Duke of Belmont. It's amazing how he appeared out of thin air. Handsome, titled, rich, and most of all, conveniently available."

Jane puffed out her chest, flesh darkening as she tried to remain composed. "Jamison and I are in love. We've been courting for well over two years."

"Yes, and I'm sure you look lovely from a distance."

The snap of her fan and scuffle of shoes made me pause. I turned to—

Slap!

From the impact, the heat spread like venom. I flinched to return the blow but hesitated. From the east hall, Kathline and Camryn's conversation rose in delight. Instead, I rubbed the other cheek to match the sore one so they wouldn't ask questions and gave her my best watch-your-back glower.

My cousin straightened while pretending to fix her hair. Then an unpleasant aroma wafted down the hall. I started to ask if she detected it, too, when it instantaneously dissipated. Melted candle wax and hollyhocks became overpowering. Her fingers slipped under the lace again to touch an object.

It was a dark-metal cross pendant. When my cousin noticed I was watching, both hands dropped to her sides as she regained her rigid composure—the moment made me uneasy.

Both kids came bounding toward us, singing Happy Birthday. Each grabbed one of my arms and ignored their sister. It gave me a smug sense of satisfaction that I was their favorite. When the kids weren't looking, I stuck out my tongue.

While we walked, Camryn observed that my hair was pinned differently. Kathline admired and patted the beadwork on the bodice. We chatted all the way to the main greeting room. Jane kept her distance, strolling four, or five feet behind us. I reached out to open the door when they tugged me down the hall toward the ballroom.

Camryn saw my confusion and explained, "No, no, father is in the ballroom. Mother is talking to the head of the house about the party. She will join us later." He repositioned to open the door for me and his sisters formally. Jane disapproved of our banter with a little "Tsk," rushing past us. Kathline and I giggled. We then curtsied as Camryn bowed before we entered.

The room was draped in deep red wine and bright ember, with gold as an accessory. Dark curtains hung from ceiling to floor. Table covers in the same shade of Cabernet was decorated with a gold paisley pattern. Next to the cream and gold place settings were orange napkins. We were impressed. The kids left me to gawk at the dessert table.

Uncle Harold was conversing with the musicians. I made my way to stand beside him. The man with the baton briefly acknowledged me while never breaking his articulate thought with the Duke.

Startled, my uncle stepped back, then blinked a few times as he beheld my stature. "Oh, for a second there, you reminded me of Lillian."

Laughing, I replied, "You always say that, Uncle. Do I really look like her that much?"

He grabbed both hands and held my arms out to admire the gown. "Yes, you do. If I believed in doppelgängers, I would say you were hers."

The musicians mumbled for redemption, and a few made crosses over their chests.

"Uncle Harold," I scolded.

In a fatherly side embrace, we laughed. Then he spun me around while pointing to certain party amenities ordered for the occasion. Harold was never one for formality amongst his family unless his wife was around. We stopped at a table with different candied fruits and nuts.

He popped a candied fruit into his mouth. "Go ahead. Try one."

I selected a slice of orange. The sugar-coated treat hit my tongue before the juice exploded. After savoring the last drop, I faced him, overflowing with pleasure. "Thank you for this. It is splendid. And thank you for the new gown."

Wringing my hands together, I felt uneasy all of a sudden. A question needled me, but confronting the bleak subject might cast clouds of sadness on the celebration.

Noticing the shift in my behavior, Harold motioned to the musicians. They fumbled over each other until they settled into their chairs. The first notes drifted into the air as an open hand appeared before me. "Lady Maryanna, shall we take to the floor?"

I gave him a weak smile and slipped my gloved hand into his.

"I would be honored. Thank you."

Dancing to a waltz, he whisked me into circles until my smile became genuine.

Uncle Harold cleared his throat. "Maryanna, I know things have been hard after your father's death. I didn't intend to cause you grief today. But Gallen made me promise to give you his gift if he wasn't able."

Hearing my father's name carved out the hole that was slowly healing. I understood my uncle meant no harm by discussing his wishes. I shifted my stance so he wouldn't see my sorrow.

"We were together when he fashioned the piece."

My head snapped up. "My father made it?"

"Yes. It was our secret. We would sneak away and watch the glassmakers and blacksmiths work. Eventually, some started teaching us how to use the tools of the trade."

I snickered, picturing both of them as impish young lads hiding behind corners to watch the common folk work.

"As you can imagine, it didn't sit with either of your grandparents. So, when we were older, we vowed to follow our passion and created a private workspace. Since I married first and retained this land, I made the workroom here."

Astonished, this was a different side of my father. I wanted to know more. "Pray tell, why a mirror? Surely, he could have fashioned other trinkets."

His eyes crinkled. "You don't like your gift?"

"No-no, the mirror is exquisite. It's just, well, I'm not sure how to explain the sensation. I sense an uncomfortable stir from within when I hold it."

"Oh?"

"Like something is tugging on my heart. Disrupting the rhythm of life." I tried to brush off my explanation with a light chuckle. "Is that normal? Maybe it's because I read the inscription and realized it was from him."

Harold leaned in and whispered, "Maryanna, I have some private information about our family. You must listen with an open mind."

I nodded. "Yes?"

"The mirror was forged with blessed silver, and Gallen used holy water to cool down the metal. It is special. The pull that tugs on you is from the other side. The mirror is a gateway of sorts. If, for any reason, you find yourself without an escape, the mirror will keep you safe."

Out of sync with the music, I stared at him in disbelief. "I do not understand. Gateway? A gateway to where? How does it work? Why would I need protection?"

Hesitant, my uncle sighed. "You are special, like the mirror. I might be able to explain our family's origins but after the party. If I rush through the details, it will sound absurd and hard to understand. Trust me, I stressed to your parents that our family's history was vital to know, even at a young age. And with each passing year, it became harder for them to explain. Eventually, it changed to worry about whether you could handle your future. They feared you wouldn't accept your calling if you found out the truth.

"I cannot discuss the specifics as of yet. But creating the hand mirror was Gallen's way to leave you with some protection if he could no longer keep you safe."

What he was implying couldn't be so. If my father and uncle were practicing what I assumed was against the church, it would ruin our family. I swallowed the dread as I realized that if this hearsay reached the royal courts of nearby kingdoms or even the Church of England, it could hang a death sentence on the House of Hertfordshire.

Alchemy was forbidden. Even if he said, they were using it to help me.

'You are special,' echoed in between my ears. *'Why me? What was so special about me that they would risk everything?'* Teetering, I felt faint. "I need some air."

Uncle Harold harrumphed and stopped dancing. He let go of my right hand to dig into his breast pocket. A smirk grew, which emphasized the crease forming in between his eyebrows. When he withdrew his hand, snaked around four fingers, was a silver chain. Dangling was a purplish-crystal pendant.

His face beamed with pride. "I made you this. It is a Spirit Stone. Think of it as a rare gem, specifically designed for you."

Dumbfounded, I stepped back, hesitant to touch it.

"Maryanna," my name rolled off his tongue in disappointment, "It will not bite you. With this key, you can open a pathway between life and death. Time doesn't exist within this space. One of the books we found the spell in referred to this place as the Holding." His face hardened when he added, "Once I put this on, do not remove it under any circumstances."

"Wh-what? What do you mean I can't take it off?" Instinctively, I raised a gloved hand to my throat.

His eyes glossed over as he asked, "Remember when the birds nested beyond the gardens? You found a baby bird. It had fallen from the nest and broke its neck. Do you recall your reaction?"

A scene from my past filtered in, but the picture was fuzzy and muted. I instantly became parched as the vocal cords tightened. It was getting harder to breathe as the memory roared back to life. The pressure building around my heart made me gasp. An eerie silence swirled from the back of my tongue. I clenched my teeth to the point of grating.

His eyebrows lifted in surprise. "Good-good. It is working."

Dizzy from lack of air, Harold slipped the chain around my neck and fastened the clasp. "Gallen and I found a way to keep your secret safe. Unfortunately, our skills weren't enough to maintain certain safeguards." His eyes filled with unshed tears. "Altering one's nature can come with a cost."

Uncertainties raced, making the walls in the room spin. It was too much to intake as true. He straightened. Doubt rising like bile, our silence was interrupted as a finger tapped my shoulder. I craned to see the Duchess glaring at her husband, lips ready to reprimand.

He interjected, "Darling, I only wanted a dance with my niece before her dance card was filled."

Lifting my hand, Uncle Harold motioned to the tables. "So, eat, drink—enjoy yourself tonight. Happy Birthday, Maryanna."

Aunt Serina scoffed before criticizing one of the servants and directing them toward one of the dining tables.

Once out of earshot, Harold kissed my forehead and in a rush of gibberish, said, "Ayh-na-drutia-blou-trit." Then touched the crystal and whispered, "Sce-cee-fotnia-nok-sleep. This is only temporary."

I was about to protest when he winked at me. Confusion swept over many frightening questions, making the depth of our conversation meaningless.

"For now, forget. We'll finish our talk later. I promise."

The children ran over. "Maryanna, come look at this." In a daze, Kathline grabbed a hand and dragged me to a tower of sweetness. Camryn was right on our heels. The seven-layer cake was decorated with ivory buttercream frosting and chocolate shavings as a garnish. It was simple and perfect. Saliva pooled as I imagined the first bite. Tempted, I resisted swiping a finger along the bottom.

An argument in the far corner distracted me from the tasty treat. Jane and a well-dressed man were in a heated discussion. I frowned while straining to hear one word. My determination was rewarded with a sentence. "We have an agreement—I own you," she sneered.

Lips quivering, I spun to grab the kids' hands. *'I own you,'* echoed on playback as the emotions building between them overwhelmed my senses. In a haze, the children's protest from our abrupt departure sounded far away. The only response registering was flight. I didn't want to know about the agreement between that man and my cousin.

"Maryanna, where are we going?" Kathline's cry snapped me out of thought.

Oblivious to the fact I had marched us into the hallway, Camryn pulled his hand from mine. "What did we do wrong?"

"Nothing. I'm sorry. I needed some air and didn't want to go by myself."

Kathline stood before me and meekly asked, "Mary, why are you crying?" It was their nickname for me when we were alone.

"I—I didn't know I was. Sorry."

From either side, small arms wrapped around my waist. Camryn looked worried. "I didn't mean to upset you."

Wiping the tears away, I reassured them. "You didn't. I'm merely overcome by the splendor, and honestly, I'm missing my parents." Their concern made me smile. "I wish my mother could be here."

A flood of emotions churned. Everything from the mirror, the hazy conversation with Uncle Harold, the present from my father, Jane's behavior, and the mysterious man fighting with her. I wasn't sure if I could take any more unwelcome surprises.

Remembering the heated argument between Jane and the man, I asked the kids, "Do you know who your sister was talking to earlier?"

Kathline wrinkled her nose, and Camryn mimicked the gesture. She spoke first. "That's sister's fiancé."

Pivoting on a heel, I whirled around to the door and peered into the room. A few more people were busying themselves with their duties. Finally, I spotted the Duke of Belmont. He had a horsemanship build, wide shoulders, a trim waist, wavy raven locks pulled back, angled features, and a natural blush that enhanced his dark eyes.

He was talking with my uncle and one of the musicians. But every now and then, he would glance at me. When our eyes met the third time, a zing of fervor brought warmth to my extremities. Phantom fingers skating over my skin left me wondering what stirred within Jane when she kissed him.

Internally, a masculine voice said, *"Would you like to know as well?"*

Disbelief swam in between my ears. This couldn't be. I left the kids and stepped into the ballroom. Mesmerized, I found myself drawn to him. This man couldn't have known what I was thinking. *'But how did I hear him from such a distance?'*

Something was off about him, yet with all my senses screaming to get away, I found myself standing two feet before him.

Glancing down at me, Uncle coughed and then pardoned himself. He paused before introducing Jane's fiancé. "Lady Maryanna, this is Monsieur Belmont, or recently titled the Duke of Belmont."

I held out my hand to him. "It is a pleasure to meet you."

In one swift movement, he latched onto four gloved fingers and feather-kissed the material. When his lips grazed my glove, it was as though he pushed his presence against my space. He then squeezed, a little too hard, for half a second before releasing.

My uncle smacked the young man on the back in a friendly gesture, breaking the awkward greeting between us. His once soft demure changed instantly to appear guarded as Jane looped her arm over his. As their hands met, she intertwined their fingers. He stiffened.

Interesting.

I compared my cousin's pale, flawless skin to his slightly warmer tones. Her mousy hair, as opposed to his dark as a crow's after a rain. Jane's hardened blue eyes to his intense midnight blue. It struck a chord, *'How bizarre,'* I thought. From the door, they appeared black and lifeless. Their pull was similar to how the darkness absorbs a star's light on a moonless night. Both were portrayed to be from different worlds, and yet, I loathed to admit they did appear to be perfect for each other.

"Maryanna, it's time to take your place in the greeting line."

"Please excuse me." I followed Aunt Serina to the door while fixing a few stray curls.

"Stop fidgeting; your hair is fine." The sentence knocked me off balance, and I bumped into my aunt.

After I straightened my stance, I prepared myself to welcome the guests. Once in a while, I found myself searching the crowd for the Duke of Belmont. He patted Jane's hand in the curvature of his arm while conversing with a small group. Right before I lost sight of him, he winked at me but never missed the momentum of their conversation.

"Maryanna, whatever is the matter with you?" Serina waited for an answer.

"It's the excitement for the party, I guess."

"Well, try to contain yourself. It may be your party, but actions and manners reflect on the family. Do not forget that."

"Yes, Ma'am."

Eyebrows pinched, she noticed the alteration. "You went behind my back and changed the neckline, I see."

I avoided her chastising me for a moment as she instructed the twins where to stand.

When the ballroom's doors opened, under her breath, she vowed, "We will discuss this later—with Amithina."

The party was amazing. People I didn't even know were attentive, wishing me health, happiness, and many more birthdays to come. By the half-hour chime, my dance card was filled. Several partners conversed about mundane subjects, keeping it to the weather, fashion, and what music I preferred. It was pleasant except for one thing: the Duke of Belmont had not asked me to dance.

As the night lingered on, the rich food and wine altered my reasoning a bit. I wasn't sick, but both my vision and mouth were affected. Everything had a haze, and the inside of my mouth tingled. Concerned I would make a fool of myself, I stopped talking. So, I resorted to adding to the conversations with a head bob, a smile, or a mumbled "Mmm-hmm."

Pain stabbed me in the stomach, and I excused myself to get some air. My cousin, Sean, was in the corner, nursing his foul mood with a drink. I stayed in the shadows, praying he wouldn't acknowledge me.

It didn't work.

Slurring, he said, "And how's the little debutante tonight? Enjoying yourself, I see. Who's your new conquest?" He motioned with the goblet toward my neck.

I didn't bother with an explanation, not that he would care. Instead, I left my answer short. "Yes, I am. Now, if you'll pardon me."

In a flash of color, I was grabbed and pulled behind a curtain. Liquid splattered around my new shoes, followed by the metal clanging from his goblet hitting the floor. Sean's breath trailed down my neck like a musty fog. He sniffed my hair. Inwardly, I cringed and tried to step out of his grip. His coil on me grew tighter.

"I don't understand you, Mary…," he took a drunken pause, "…anna." Reforming his words, he continued to rant. "You tease and flaunt. You giggle and smile at everyone but me." He belched a cloud of rancid wine in my face.

Gagging, I used both hands to press against him to create some space.

"The wine has impaired your judgment. Stop this, Sean."

"You're only allowed to address me as Lord Sean." Teeth clenched, he leaned closer.

Unfortunately, I was physically impaired since the last glass of wine. Mind reeling, I had to think fast. Using my right arm, I wedged it until an elbow was pressed between two ribs. Sliding his hand to the back of my skull, he intertwined his fingers in some locks of hair and yanked. I yelped, and then he slammed me into the wall and then covered another protest from me with the opposite hand.

He left soggy "sh-sh-sh's" across my face and neck. He pressed his body against the side of my dress. Moving his hips seductively, he buried his face in the clump of curls until he found skin. His tongue traced sloppy circles to my collarbone while constantly murmuring my nickname. "Mary, you whore. Mary, you tease. Mary, touch me. Mary, I want you."

The name would be etched into this nightmare permanently.

With a hitched sob, I reared back, opened my mouth, and bit down on his index finger. He ripped his hand away in haste as I grounded my heel on the top of his boot. Now, it was his turn to cry out. Hopping on one foot, his hand flung out to stop his fall with the curtain.

Between my breasts, the Spirit Stone glittered in the window's reflection. My vision blurred with smears of red, vexed. Teeth chattering, my words gushed forth, riding on waves of fury. "You want to call my name. You want to play this game. I'll kill you for touching me."

Without realizing it, I stumbled forward with enough strength to knock him backward. His head snapped back from the force and hit the corner of the nook. It connected with a sick *'thwack.'* Eyes fluttering, he fell like a stone. Blood oozed from under his hair, leaving a halo of crimson.

Breath held, I kicked under his ribs, then whispered, "Sean?"

Amazingly, no one heard our scuffle nor came to my aid. Not sure if he passed out, knocked senseless, or worse, I fled out of the first open door. Racing past guests and into the garden, I passed the gazebo, allowing the apprehension of him retaliating to push me further into the night. My skirts were heavy but open enough to lengthen my stride. Heart pounding and feverish, I removed the gloves, tossing them on the ground. Next came the combs containing what was still pinned. The wind was liberating as it played with my hair. Long curls, loose and flowing, felt freeing, especially after Sean's ugly nature.

The hedge maze was up ahead. It was my sanctuary. I would hide out there until Sean was found, declared drunk, and taken back to his chambers. If he died in his state, the family would assume it was from the alcohol. I hoped.

Walls of vegetation and the crisp night air enveloped me as I flew into the maze's open mouth. I knew this place blindfolded and welcomed the cover of darkness. Even the sky seemed low enough to touch. Years of playing hide-and-seek with the twins engraved its secrets into a mental map I kept locked away.

My sprint altered to a steady pace as I held out my hands, running out of steam. The velvet leaves slapped against my palms. Right as I turned into the bend toward the inner ring, a twig caught and slit the tip of my small finger. Reacting with an "Ouch," and then I sucked on the wound.

Irritated, I expressed my woes out loud: "Why did Sean do that? He deserved my anger. I shouldn't feel guilty." Feet cramping, I lifted a foot, admiring my grass-stained shoes. I thought, *'Not the best footwear to be running in.'*

"No, not the best for running." The speech was so clear that I couldn't tell if the sentence was in my head or if I heard it vocally.

Startled, I pressed the ball of my right foot into the pebbles. Holding a swordsman's stance, with both fists prepared to strike, I faced the outline of a birdbath. I was in the middle of the maze.

Lowering my hands, I panned the area. "Who's there?"

Crickets, nightingales, and owls filled the air, breaking the silence. I imagined Jane's fiancé. "Like he would be here," I grumbled, feeling dumb.

Nature quit talking. Then, the Duke of Belmont's French accent curved around my name. "Maryanna, what are you doing here?" From one of the adjacent pathways, he emerged.

Jaw unhinged, I stood there gawking at the man who occupied so many thoughts with heavenly and sinful ideas. Then, like a bad nightmare, the memory of Sean tarnished the images. Lost in the moment, I whimpered, and as fate would have it, it cascaded to a full-blown sob.

Within seconds, a gorgeous male on one knee knelt before me. Cautiously, he took my trembling hand in his. There was no sense of physical desire—no emotion—only the coolness of his touch as he gently caressed each finger until he came upon the one with the cut.

Using his thumb to brush against it. "You are hurt."

I withdrew from his touch and curled my fingers. "It's fine. I'm fine."

He sulked. "You don't trust me?"

"No, it's not that. I..." His stare was so intense that I backed away.

"Not all males act that way."

Mortified, I cried, "Oh God, did you see?" Before he could answer, I was poised, ready to run.

In a flash, my cousin's fiancé was next to me. The man seized an arm. Anger tipped me over as I faced my captor.

Frowning, he gently wiped a tear.

Lips parted to protest. I'd had enough groping from men for one evening. He placed a finger over my mouth. With a grimace, he removed it to retrieve a hand. The Duke of Belmont tugged me toward the birdbath. A white and crimson marbled carnation clipped onto his lapel caught my attention.

Nervous, I asked, "What are you doing?"

"Well, how do I say this without offending you, but you smell."

"What?" I shrieked.

"See, offended."

I turned to storm off when the spaced filled with his laughter.

"I don't see how this is funny."

"No, Maryanna, I guess you wouldn't. And do me a favor, call me Jamison," he said while tearing the petals from the flower's stem.

"That wouldn't be right. We barely know each other, and you are my cousin's fiancé. How would that look?"

Jamison dipped the petals in the water and approached me with his hands in surrender before pointing to my neck with the flower stem. "Please, allow me."

I angled to expose the area Sean touched. He placed a damp petal on the skin and then softly rubbed it back and forth. His voice was tender when he asked permission to touch certain spots. Then he whispered, "Vous êtes si belle, ma chérie."

Shocked, I turned to meet him face to face. "Why did you say that?"

"Because you are. I was merely stating a fact."

"But, I'm not yours. Lady Jane, she is your love and the one you are supposed to marry. Maybe the wine has gotten you confused."

Voice laced with yearning, he leaned in and said, "It's an

agreement with Lady Jane, nothing more. Besides, words like, love have no hold over me." His fingers trailed across my face and into my hair. He continued, "That is unless I consent to the one I claim. Maryanna, you may find there is more to me than what you see. But for now, let us give in to the attraction; emotions only complicate what is natural."

Lightheaded, I could feel the will to fight him breaking.

Jamison purred my name. "Maryanna, be mine."

"Only if I can claim you?" I blurted the question without thinking.

His answer was a light breath against my lips. "Deal."

And like a moth to a flame, Jamison kissed me. The touch was gentle at first, fanning the first sparks of desire. This emotional and physical connection didn't compare to how Sean tried to seduce me.

As his touch became demanding, I fantasized about him lowering me to the ground. I worked feverishly to remove his clothes. Heat danced across my skin as his teeth lightly grazed over unthinkable places. Areas, where he passed over, were quickly replaced by an icy chill wherever the silver links touched in the same spots. My senses heightened; I wanted to scream, *"mine,"* over and over.

Remembering what Jane said to him earlier, I pulled away and jested, "Does this mean I own you now, too?"

With my fingertips pressed into his chest, I detected a deep rumble before he quipped, "You can try."

I parted my lips to let him taste what I had to give. His tongue grazed over mine, and it kick-started a zeal of passion between us. I pulled on his lower lip. Jamison sucked on my tongue hard before he shuddered, breaking our kiss. Wiping his lips, he spat and then hissed at me, "Blood."

Horrified, I backed away, remembering the cut. "I'm sorry. This never happened. This never happened," I screamed.

"No, wait, Maryanna. Come back; you need to know something."

I knew enough for one day: I was twenty and discovered my

father and uncle dabbled in forbidden arts. Half of the extended family detested my existence. Two men tried to seduce me. And now, I allowed myself to care for one of those betrothed men.

'Could this day get any worse?'

Tears blurred the night landscape. At first, it appeared on fire, but when my vision cleared, flames wavered to dancing points of light. The night torches cast their flickering firelight against the outer walls of the manor. A peculiar emotion pressed against my moral compass. Part of me wished the area was engulfed in fire—holy fire.

Guests were trickling out the front door. Not wanting to draw attention to myself, I skirted by the stables. Grumbles and harsh exhales from the animals warned me to work on my eluding skills. Edging around the corner, I managed to stay concealed within the building's shadow.

Two footmen patrolling the grounds began to walk toward the path to the stables, likely to retrieve one of the guests' means of travel. Hoisting my gown, I kicked off my shoes so they wouldn't alert them to my presence. Using the building's shadow, I rushed to the other side. Breathing shallowly, I crept past an open window. Upon reaching the corner, I heard the men conversing. Their words were hushed and fast. Eavesdropping, I moved closer.

The first footmen lead into the conversation. "It's too bad they had to end the celebration so soon. It was such a splendid event."

"Well, I'm sure they didn't want a scandal on their hands. After they found Lord Sean in his condition," he paused to add a drawn-out, *tsk-tsk,* "Lady Jane was furious. I could not tell if her reaction was from hearing about her brother or when someone claimed they had seen the Duke of Belmont leave right after the Duchess found her son." The second man grumbled, adding, "I would assume the two must have quarreled."

"I concur, but 'over what' is the burning question."

"Oh, God." The comment slipped out in haste, and I prayed they wouldn't hear it.

A horse whinnied.

Inwardly, I thanked the animal for concealing the blunder.

The first male continued. "I have my suspicions."

Protests from the horses layered over his words as I strained to hear the rest.

"…and since Lady Maryanna is missing, the Duke of Belmont cannot leave without drawing questions," said the second man.

Tears threatened to release an emotional poison, infecting my heart. Standing in the wet dirt made specific muscles cramp, but I remained grounded.

Then one of them added, "After the fit Lady Jane made before heading off to find her fiancé, I'm sure someone will be paying the toll to Hell tonight." The last of his words wafted into the night air.

Fatigued and alone, I sank alongside the wall and took a moment to collect myself—a headache threatened since the last traces of wine were burned away from the run. I would surely be cast into the center of this web of incidents. Nerves raw, I scanned the grounds for a safe haven. The servants' entrance was my target, but nothing happened.

Fear froze me in place. "Dammit, Maryanna, you can do this," I chided.

Hiking the skirt, I inhaled before sprinting across the yard in stockings. Within seconds, I made it to the bricked steps, taking two at a time. Muscles burned, and lack of air sparked a swooshing sensation in both ears as I grabbed the handle.

Taking in a fist full of air as a servant opened the door triggered a conundrum when my momentum continued through the threshold. Feet muddy, I slipped on the stone floor, causing me to slam into a long table. Screaming from the impact, I puddled to the floor, holding myself in anguish as people scattered, yelled, and swore.

I rolled to position my knees under me while protecting my ribs and then used the table's edge to stand.

When the commotion fell silent, someone recognized me. It

immediately spurred an onslaught of questions, ranging from concerned inquiries to scandalous accusations.

Darkness threatened as I wheezed and coughed from forcing myself to breathe. One of my ribs had to be bruised or possibly broken. I motioned for something to drink.

A male by the open hearth understood the hand gestures and ladled water into a cup. Lunging his lanky body across the table to hand it to me was comical. But to laugh would've been unwise. At least, that much I knew.

Rust and grit swished in my cheeks before I gulped the concoction down. Thirst sated, my voice croaked like a crow's. "Could someone please help me back to my chambers?" Lungs quivering, I continued, "I don't believe I can make it."

One of the cooks came rushing in with my attendant and the head seamstress.

Natalie made an 'o' face and was promptly by my side.

Amithina exclaimed, "Oh, my lady!"

Using my forearm as a shield, I leaned into Natalie's one-sided embrace as she balanced our weight so Amithina could slip in on the other side.

My servant whispered, "Where have you been?"

The head seamstress spoke in a rush, "Did someone hurt you? Oh, no, your dress."

Losing my footing a few times, Natalie asked, "Where are your shoes?" She turned her head to look for them.

I tried to answer, but my tongue wouldn't cooperate. After several short coughs and whimpers, I managed, "Later." After another inhale, I used the last bit of strength to mutter, "Please, get my uncle."

An oppressed weight of darkness crashed over me. My body buckled forward. The women responded in cries of fright and worry before I blacked out.

The two ladies managed to reach the bedroom wing with me in tow. Upon entering, the fireplace was lit, but it felt as though the windows were open. Eyes adjusting to the flickering glow, I noticed chalk-like lines by the hearth. Natalie directed me toward the bed.

I backpedaled, but my body wouldn't obey. With an airy voice, I pleaded, "No. Need to leave." Trying to catch my breath, I huffed, "Must leave. The air…" I paused, "feels wrong."

Natalie urged me to lean over the bed. "You're delirious and probably feverish from the injuries." She left to retrieve the tools to undress me. Then, she tried to sound reassuring, "Let us take care of you. But first, I will fetch you some water."

Amithina took the tools from the chambermaid and began to unbutton the back of my dress. "My apologies, Lady Maryanna, but we must get you out of these soaked dressings and assess your injuries."

A splash of water.

Glass shattering.

A scream from behind.

Amithina jerked from me. Panic was a temporary balm, and it managed to mask the pain as I twisted to see what happened.

The outline of two men stood on either side of a short, cloaked figure in front of the fireplace. It appeared that the three of them stepped out of the flames. The blaze grew and danced higher, adding to the assumption.

Petrified, I noticed the tall male holding Natalie in an awkward one-handed hold by the neck. Feet kicking in the air, she struggled to free herself but was rewarded with a harsh shake.

Unspeaking, the tall figure paused briefly to capture the attention of the person standing in the middle. The figure moved with an approval gesture and answered, "You may feed."

My heart stopped. It was Jane.

I could tell he was straining to squeeze even in the dim light. A sickening pop came from Natalie's mouth before going limp. Pitch-black tears oozed from the corners of her unblinking eyes. A shimmery mist of gold and caerulean gushed from her nose and mouth. He started to inhale.

Frozen in horror, I processed the day's events—from our family's secrets to accepting that Uncle Harold thought there could be something different about me that was special. This reality became surreal. My heart rate slowed until the conscious state bridged to the subconscious. Something inhuman crawled out from below my subconscious. In the recesses of my soul, a single note chimed. It grew in pitch until the bond confining what I was fragmented like glass. *'I'm free,'* it hissed, filling me with a flood of information.

Questions bubbled, but the voice from within quickly popped each one with a direct answer. This foreign awareness meshed with me as I watched the man consume Natalie's life essence. This was wrong. I wasn't sure about the how or why of it, but it was wrong. Souls were meant to be summoned and then ferried to the Land of the Dead, where they would remain until their spirit moved on to Heaven or Hell.

'Mine,' the voice grew louder. *'Mine,'* the word tightened my vocal cords.

Beyond the darkness, the presence I detected tore from the emptiness. This inhuman creature was taking over my body, and it chilled me to the bone. An excruciating throb grew, and my teeth began to chatter so violently that I physically thought I was being split into two people. A peculiar awareness of greed, jealousy, and rage possessed me.

The necklace gave off an eerie glow. I snarled, "That was mine!" Pointing an accusing finger, I inhaled past my normal capacity.

The wail released into the world was deafening.

A small row of teeth formed into a tiny, tight smile from under the shroud. "Yes, my little waif. Sing for the dead, She-devil. Sing until your lungs bleed and your soul slips into oblivion."

Clutching at my neck, I intertwined my fingers through the

necklace and tightened, hoping to choke myself into silence. My human form started to unravel. It was as though hundreds of needles were being yanked from my airway. *'Natalie—Natalie—dead.'* Those words echoed from within. I continued to scream.

Several ribs reminded me I was broken as pain flooded into my extremities. Lungs deflating, head pounding, Amithina seized my face, making me focus on her. Unable to retrieve what was rightfully mine, my jaw unhinged, increasing the octave of demand. Small pulsating lights drifted across the room. Panic consumed me as greed turned to need. If I didn't take a breath soon, I was surely going to die.

The seamstress shouted over her shoulder, "What have you done? Maryanna's father paid the ultimate price to keep her sealed. You've unlocked her human form. How will you contain this power?"

A male's maniacal laughter erupted from under my continuous shattering note. "Watching her suffer is most gratifying. We are going to play with our new toy until she breaks," it was Sean. "Besides, my sister knows a trick or two to keep her in check." He pointed down at the white markings on the floor.

Seeing him spiked both fury and dread. The rancid mix of emotions energized the volume of my wail.

This time, Amithina's fingers traveled to the back of my skull. Her nails dug in with urgency. She demanded, "Where is it?"

Unable to communicate, my face went slack, indicating confusion. Tears pulled me deeper into despair. Amithina wiped my face and showed me her palm. It was smeared in black, like Natalie's.

I fought against death's abyss. A pinpoint of light became a focal point.

"Your life is in danger. We must contain you. Where is it? The gift from your father."

My eyes darted to the vanity.

Acknowledging the hint, she said in earnest, "You must use it."

Compelled, I refocused on Natalie and kept screaming.

She left to retrieve it, but Sean blocked her path. He raised his hand. A flash of metal caught my eye. Amithina screamed.

Then, Natalie's dead weight hit the floor.

The second male spoke from the shadows. "Are you mad? Don't kill the woman while Maryanna cries for another. If you value yours and your sister's life, don't do anything rash."

Sean dismissed his warning while aggressively swinging the blade in the air. "Demon, stand down. You are no different than this screeching whore. If it wasn't for my sister's devotion to the dark arts and her promise that Maryanna would be mine after the ritual, I would have already sent you back to Hell."

An ungodly snarl rose over the wailing. Time sped forward as the man rushed Sean. They argued and grappled, yelling obscenities. Amithina dodged the two men to run toward the vanity. Jane started chanting as an object formed in her hand, then she attacked the seamstress. It was utter chaos.

Amithina pinned Jane underneath her body, grabbed her cloak, and started to slam her head against the floor. In a panic, my cousin cried out. "Jamison, kill Maryanna."

His growl filled me with defiance. "No!"

Jane struggled against Amithina's hold as the seamstress tried to smack her again. Jane's voice turned hollow and commanding. "Bond by blood. Pact sealed by rite. By vow, you're mine for life. *I own you!* Kill her now."

The roar he released cracked the stained-glass windows. A body was thrown against the door. It was Sean's. Wheezing, he slid down to his knees. Next, the smack of flesh, a woman cried out, and then a crash. Amithina's body broke the towel rack by the hearth. She cradled an object protectively. On her last breath, I watched her head loll in my direction, eyes wide open, blood dripped from her nose and mouth.

"Not her," Jane shrieked.

At this moment, I could sense the rhythm of a dying heartbeat. My knees started to buckle, but I forced myself to remain upright and fought the urge to scream against the unnatural pressure building in my chest.

Streaks of onyx slithered over Amithina's lifeless body. Then I realized her soul was drifting in my direction. I fought against the desire to call for her.

A glint of silver pulled me forward. The image in the mirror was supposed to be me. Except, it wasn't. It couldn't. Wild strands of hair coiled and straightened like a nest of snakes. The coloring of the skin was almost transparent. Lips dry, cracked, and agape. But what shocked me was the two empty holes leaking inky streaks down pale cheeks.

The stone Uncle Harold gave me defied gravity. It levitated, tugging toward the mirror. A deep purplish glow emanated from the pendant. The two were linked.

From the right, a warm current invaded the space. I barely felt the light touch of a hand, accompanied by a familiar scent. Carnations…

A faint masculine whisper entered my thoughts. *"Trust me."*

Jamison stood before me. "Don't waste Amithina's sacrifice." Using a brazen tone. "Accept it. This is your fate."

He snatched a hand and wrapped my fingers around the silver handle. Cool air swirled into my chest; I could breathe again as the stone landed in between my breasts. The ghostly image in the mirror vanished and was replaced with a bruised and marred version of me.

Jamison's eyes shimmered like heat vapors rolling off of burning embers. The color pulsed around each black, horizontal pupil. They were shaped like a goat's.

A single tear trailed down his cheek. In my head, I heard his regret. *"I wanted to tell you."*

"You fool." Jane used the vanity to stand. "You cannot disobey me. I'll send you back if you do that again."

"Requests must be specific." He snarled.

"You are a spell away from being banished."

He grimaced before taking my face in his hands. "Maryanna, breathe. Collect yourself. You'll have to fight. I cannot save you again. Je suis ici pour te tuer, mon amour."

Regaining my bearings, I blinked at him in confusion.

He sighed and dropped his hands. "I was summoned to kill you, my love."

A whimper of betrayal escaped as I backed away, clutching the mirror. I imagined my father and forced myself to believe it would work.

"What? Unacceptable. You can't!" Jane's spoiled demure echoed throughout the room. "You swore your devotion to me—love only me."

Jamison's stance turned protective as he faced Jane. "Devotion, yes, but never love. I may be a demon, but certain powers, like love, are non-negotiable," sarcastically adding, "Master."

Firelight outlined her figure as she stepped forward. "Jamison, I command you to kill–."

"Sister, you promised that the succubus would be mine since we were little." Sean's swift interruption was emphasized while threateningly waving his blade.

Affronted by his interruption, Jane screamed, "I saw your precious Maryanna with her tongue down his throat. He's mine—by blood—I will not lose his hold to the likes of her." She spat. "Maryanna cannot live, Brother. This banshee will ruin our family." Her hands swung from Natalie to Amithina as proof of her claim. "She will only bring death's swift touch to our door."

Flames rolled out of the fireplace. Orange and yellow flickers engulfed the furniture, leaving angry streaks of red. Sparks rained down, landing on the rug and the bed canopy. Even the curtains twisted as if they were in pain.

My gaze latched onto Jamison's. The color in his eyes burned with the same intensity as the room's.

This time, I was the moth.

Jane seductively touched his shoulder and whispered, "Kill Maryanna."

The love he held behind those burning orbs vanished.

Clutching the mirror, I bounced off my toes toward the door. He was in front of me so fast that I crashed into him. It was like hitting a stone wall. Warm liquid dripped from my nose. I stumbled backward, then swung my weight in the opposite direction. It was a failed attempt. I fell into his outstretched arms.

The fire's heat made me dizzy. Jamison gathered me into a tight embrace, then pressed his full length against me. Lowering his mouth to mine, he brazenly kissed me. Mind spinning, I felt his desire for me, not physically, but on an altered level of control. When his tongue slid over mine, I tasted honey and spiced wine. He did the same action again. His muscles hardened like two vices as he lifted my body. Beads from my torn bodice began to pop off in a shower of color. Breaking our kiss, he heaved me higher into the air and then flung me across the room.

I rag-dolled into the vanity. Broken glass sprayed all around me. Searing pain exploded from the areas where my spine had snapped. The hand mirror fell to the floor before gravity dropped me onto the stone floor. Horror gripped me when I saw the mirror lying unbroken, mere inches from my fingertips. Not that it mattered. I couldn't move.

Jane coughed and gagged a few times from the heat and smoke. "Well done, Jamison, now put the fires out." She fanned herself. "I can't think in this heat."

Instantly, the room grew cold, but the smell of sulfur and charred wood lingered.

Pieces from the vanity's mirror crunched under the demon's shoes. Internally, I sobbed, for he wasn't Jamison anymore. He was Jane's means to an end—my death.

Numerous tiny cuts and a few gashes were dripping blood from slivers of embedded glass. It pooled under my outstretched arm. Another set of boots stopped beside me. I lay there, unmoving, when several fingers grabbed a fist full of hair and forcefully lifted my head from the floor.

Sean rested on one knee while he studied me and then turned to his sister. "Your demon broke my Mary. You said I could have a demon, too, if I gave you some of my blood for the ritual." His words fell flat, and I wondered if I could scream for my soul.

Jane tussled her brother's hair playfully. "It's okay, my dear; you'll see her soon enough."

Taken aback by his sister's acclaim, Sean dropped my head to pivot around and unsheathed his dagger wildly. The tip of a short sword was plunged between his lips and broke through the back of his skull.

Splattered in blood and bone, I listened to him gag involuntarily on the blade.

Lady Jane withdrew the sword with force. "Say 'hi' to your beloved Maryanna, and no hard feelings, Brother. I couldn't have done this without you."

Sean's body slumped forward in Jamison's path, releasing a death rattle before going limp. The demon shoved Sean's body away and knelt before me. His eyes transformed back to the midnight blue I remembered.

Jane took two steps back to assess the room.

He removed a few blood-soaked curls from my eyelashes.

Jane yammered about what to do next and wasn't paying attention to her demon.

He was in my head again. *"I feel you slipping away. Don't give up now. Maryanna, embrace your banshee nature and free me; free us. We can work together. Live eternally; together."*

Leaning forward, he whispered, "The woman believes you are dead. She foolishly killed the only link keeping me from disobeying her. Jane used her brother's soul to conjure me and his blood to bind me. I am no longer hers to command, and because of that, I will be pulled back into Hell if I do not link with another."

Sean's lifeless body came into view.

Jamison touched my cheek. "I've tasted your soul, and you've tasted mine. Claim me, Maryanna. Make me yours. I promise you'll love it and possibly regret it at times, but it is the price we pay to play as demons."

Using what air was left in me, I muttered, "How?"

"Let me consume your soul."

A wheeze was all I could muster as my throat strained to sob.

Internally, I replied, *"Either way, I'm dead."*

"You are dying. Look, Jane told me about the mirror, the Spirit Stone, and your banshee abilities. I can teach you how to slip in and out of the Holding, enlighten you about your family's history, and the Land of the Dead. Plus, you will have me at your beck and call. Does the price of one's soul seem so much?"

The world went dark for a brief moment, sluggishly mulling over the pros and cons. Then, the coolness of smooth glass was under two fingertips. The stone began to burn.

"First, you must agree to release your soul to me. Then we'll work together to unlock your true power."

Bloody fingers smeared trails across the mirror. Weak from blood loss, I uttered, "You may have all of me. I claim you, Jamison."

He disappeared from the room, filling it with his boisterous laughter. Jane stopped in midsentence and spun around to see me on the floor and bleeding out, but her demon was nowhere in sight.

She yelled toward the ceiling. "All right, enough games; come back and help me get rid of the bodies before others come to investigate. We've had enough bloodshed for one night."

When my heart stopped beating with the final exhale, agony didn't scratch the surface. There was an inward pull, and my presence turned inside out before splintering into nothingness.

Opening my eyes to death was a never-ending nightmare. The gates to the Land of the Dead materialized on the jagged rock path. Dry columns of air whipped around. I tasted grit, followed by an intense need to drink. The demand to be sated was unmeasurable. Beyond the iron gates was the lingering essence of the departed. They wandered about, bumping into each other.

My insides blazed, fueled by an empty ache; I opened my mouth to call for them.

A hand appeared over my mouth. "Do not cry for them, my love. They have found their peace. Your kind only calls to those who cannot find their path to the gates. But, now that I have consumed your succulent soul, you will cry only for the lost and to feed our needs."

Removing his hand, I shouted, "Demon, what have you done?"

Overpowering my space, he took my mouth until his touch consumed every thought. When he released me, I was back in my chambers and still on the floor. Jane loomed over me, kicked my hand away, and snatched the mirror.

Holding it to her face, she cooed, "Mary, Mary, Mary, your new dress is ruined. Covered in your blood, Mary. Look at you now, Bloody Mary."

Removing the cloak's hood to free her hair, she spun, saying, "Your father was a fraud, Maryanna." Jane flipped the mirror over and read the inscription out loud. "May the bonds of eternity never break—trap infinity within time's embrace."

There was a surge of power followed by the inhuman purrs of the creature I shared this space with and time upended as I disappeared from our reality to reappear in the mirror. I was slightly alarmed, until I realized Jane's face was on the other side of the reflective surface. My father fashioned it to work as a gateway. I fanned out to display five digits against the freezing glass, pleading with her to say my name, to acknowledge me.

Her face twisted in disbelief. "Maryanna?"

The pendant became hot.

Lips quivering, she uttered, "Maryanna, is that you?" She whipped her head around, looking for me in the room. "Jamison, if this is one of your spells."

"Make her say your name one more time." Jamison's desperation to execute some revenge spiked my hunger.

With urgency, I pounded against the mirror. Jane yelped, "Maryanna," and released the handle.

I caught it inches from the floor.

Hovering, I lifted the mirror to eye level and was met with the banshee's face—no, mine. My uncle's words held more meaning, *"Accept your calling."* I lowered the mirror and counted each corpse and gave her a wide smile, one I would only bestow upon the damned.

I clutched the stone around my neck, flipped the mirror, and held the reflective side for my cousin to see the demon standing behind her.

The first pains of hunger hit. "Jamison, let's play."

"Let's play," repeated until it replaced the screams and pleas from the servants and the members of my uncle's family. Kathline's and Camryn's empty eyes and broken husks tugged on old emotions.

I sniffed.

It was followed by Jamison's smug accusation. *"After hundreds of years, I see you're still burning a candle for them."* He was pressing his emotions against my soul.

Face dampened from emotions, I was hit with an excruciating white light. In a rush, I whispered, "Where are we?"

"Examination room. You almost depleted our energy counteracting the toxins they pumped into your veins. But the charm I used kept you from letting the cat out of the bag."

Edgy, I stated, "That's because you were only provoking me to change." Displeased, I tugged on the handcuffs on either side of me. "Great. At least they didn't find the stone. After we get out of here, I want a new necklace. Did you find my mirror?"

His silence was an unfortunate answer.

"And that's a solid 'no'." I tugged hard on the right cuff in frustration.

"Maryanna, a demon has to eat. I can't turn solid without it, and you can't change unless we've been charged. We are the equivalent of a poltergeist and a normal human."

Irritated, I smacked my head against the gurney and huffed. "Give me some credit, four-hundred and sixty-something years we've been together."

Jamison purred, *"You are still as beautiful as the day I saw you."*

Testy and not feeling overly romantic, I clipped, "Charmer."

The insertion of a key drew attention to the door. Heart racing, I inwardly spoke to the demon. *"Plan?"*

"Yes. Give them all the crazy you can muster. Don't hold back."

Ben came in carrying a box. 'Maryanna' was taped above the handle. "Well, little missy, the doctor's cleared you for temporary residency."

The stone by my elbow grew warm. Anxious, I scanned the countertops. Ben's comment would be the spark to ignite my acting. "What?" I shrieked and then kicked frantically, pretending to throw a fit. I fell into character. This would buy Jamison a little more time.

The guard approached as I twisted myself so my foot would clip his jaw. Fuming, he used his mic to call for reinforcements and leg restraints.

Soon, the gang was all here. Cecil and Ben were fighting to hold a leg. Dr. Worthington flew through the door with a clipboard, barking medical instructions.

Franklin retrieved a vile from his table and grumbled, "She needs to be punched in the mouth, not sedated."

Jamison yelled in my head. *"I found it."*

"I'm a little busy," I answered, continuing to thrash.

"It's in the box."

Comprehending the mirror was close, I amped up the acting and shouted in Latin for all of them to burn in Hell as an added flourish.

Jamison coined, *"Nice touch."*

The male nurse pushed past Ben. As he bent down to swab my arm, I jutted forward, breaking his nose with my head. He cried out as blood gushed everywhere, crimson splattered in different patterns on the bed, him, the doctor, and me. It was beautiful.

Sounding a bit deflated, the doctor ordered, "Franklin, go to the infirmary."

She turned to me, wiping her hands on a used towel. "Really? If this continues, we might have to change things to a more permanent future." Heading toward the sink, she paused after noticing the box containing my things.

When she exclaimed, "This is beautiful, Maryanna," I smiled in anticipation. With a bloody hand, the doctor lifted the mirror out of the box. Admiring her reflection, she added, "Maryanna, is this yours? It seems to be very old."

The stone was on fire next to my skin. The key was primed as my demonic nature was summoned into the mirror. Both men hollered in hysterics when they found themselves grasping for air.

Dumbfounded, Dr. Worthington scanned from the empty bed to the guards and then down at the mirror, where I was waiting for her. I placed a hand on the reflective surface, anxious with anticipation. The doctor squinted, clearly questioning her sanity. "Maryanna, is that you?"

My demon appeared behind her and gave me a wink as I reappeared on the bed. The banshee only had one purpose in order to embrace their nature, and that was to summon the damned. Picturing her throat torn out, I licked my lips, waiting for the first traces of the doctor's soul to slip past her lips.

"Jamison, let's play."

Tainted Currents
By Kathy-Lynn Cross
Beware of what lies
beneath the waters; for
even time cannot erase
what the river remembers.

Copyright

Tainted Currents

Tainted Currents

May 1879

Pa told me not to wander off this morning before he left to pan in the nearby river. He kept strict rules, which was suffocating at times, but ever since our family's tragedy, I understood why. His fears were well-founded after his brother was killed over a small sack of dried gold dust. My uncle's death caused a deep-rooted distrust for drifters who passed through Mammoth's trails searching for a quick fortune. After our family laid claim to an area near Skelton Lake, he thought it would be best to keep the family grounded by joining the Mammoth Mining Company. Being part of a community would be safer than striking out on our own.

Spring flowers filled the air with their scent, mixing with the midday sun. Their aroma led my sister, Kari, our cousin Emmie, and me deeper into the forest. The combination cast a spell on us as we skipped and chased each other in zigzag patterns across the rocks along the open area near the creek's edge. We were overdue for a break from our daily chores and needed the exercise.

Kari's blonde braids turned butter gold from the sun's artistry. Every time she spun, I couldn't tell what was brighter, her hair or smile. She shared our mother's natural beauty but never allowed the compliments to go to her head. There was a contagious humbleness and gentle manner about her that sent waves of happiness over anyone in her presence. Even though she was younger than me by fourteen months, I enjoyed teasing her about minding me since my eighteenth birthday was in a few months.

I untied the lace ribbons from my ebony braid. A dense pine breeze fingered through the wispy strands. My features were similar to Pa's younger sister, Millie, who passed away at fourteen from yellow fever. I saw myself as a spindly creature with lanky legs and cream-tinted skin that turned a light shade of blue during winter. The only feature I found pleasing was my hair and dark green eyes. Ma always told me their color reminded her of growing things—a symbol of life.

Emmie was my pa's niece, and since my uncle wasn't here to care for her and my aunt Fern, he included them in our immediate family. My cousin and sister were very close in age, being born in the same year and season. Watching them together, one would believe they were twins. Their similarities ranged from clothes and mannerisms, to their favorite pastimes, storytelling. It brought me joy when they would insist on one of my outlandish tales. I would pretend their request was childish just to mess with them.

This afternoon was no different. Once they lost interest in skipping stones, there was an endless demand for verbal entertainment. Coyly, I snaked the chain to my locket around my fingers as I thought of an alternative. "I'll tell you what; I promise you a story if you can catch me." I released the silver chain and touched the oval, floral pattern of the locket to ensure it was there. Ma said it was her ma's before, and it was left to her when she passed. It was only one of the few pieces of worth we had yet she gave it to me on my sixteenth birthday.

My attention was back on the girls as they eyed one another. The two were in silent conversation, holding my time hostage while I waited for an answer. Kari shrugged, followed by Emmie, nodding her short brown tresses. Mischievous smirks grew as they turned to face me. In the same stance, their voices worked together, first Emmie's. "All right, Hazel, we agree, but story first."

My sister chimed, "And we get to pick the game."

I thought about it while shielding the sun. A story could be told anytime, but we could enjoy a few hours before the shadows lengthened, indicating our time to head home. I had to barter.

"How about a long tale after dinner? I promise to finish it before bed."

Kari's lips pursed while toying with the idea. Emmie made an inner throat cough. Impatient, she said, "I'm thinking, Em."

Using Ma's judgment glower, I eyed her, both hands on my hips.

Mimicking my movements and tone, she raised one eyebrow, "Hazel, let me think."

Emmie skipped away from my sister and hopped in front of me, splashing mud on my shoes. "Can we pick the game?"

I felt the mud soaking through my socks. "Yes, you can pick the game."

Off in the distance, we heard hollering. It echoed delight. Someone must have found a nugget instead of flakes. We giggled and joined in the excitement.

Once we stopped jumping around, I brought us back to our discussion. "Well, what do you want to do?"

Kari's braids bounced as she sang. "Tag?"

"Yes, yes, tag." Emmie bubbled with anticipation. "Is it okay with you, Hazel?"

Laughing, I lunged forward. "You're it." Then, I punched Kari's shoulder.

Unblinking blue eyes, she exclaimed, "No, no, not me!"

An explosion pierced the air, its shock wave sending birds into the skies. It came from the lake's direction, making me nervous. Pa's crew was in the area, panning the river flowing to Skelton Lake. A rumbling in the distance followed. We scanned the area for frightened deer or possibly a black bear.

An eerie quiet settled in our surroundings. Emmie shot me a shocked expression. Kari stepped closer and placed the tip of her right braid into her mouth. A telltale sign she was nervous.

Several angry male voices rose yonder.

Shots fired. We jumped with each hefty blast. I swallowed my heart, forcing it back into place.

Kari screamed, "Pa." This action spurred her into motion. All I saw were two blurred streaks as Emmie trailed behind her. Instantly, their shouts turned to wails of dread. Alarmed, I joined in the chase to catch up with them. A caustic odor of burnt black powder singed my nose and throat. Uneasiness turned to horror when thick, pale smoke snaked around us in a peculiar fog. An unnatural sensation slithered up my spine. We needed to head back to camp and warn Ma.

Taking in a few gulps of air, I called out, "Kari? Emmie?" Gasping, I stumbled on a fallen log. Twisting my ankle, I landed with a soft thud—the hand I used to stop my momentum fell against something tepid and sticky. A hint of wet earth, charred woods, and a metallic odor tinted the air.

Wiping the sweat from my forehead onto the back of my hand, I called out. "Emmie? Kari...Pa?" I coughed and called out for Pa's mining buddy, Brett. Hearing no reply, not even from my sister or cousin, I screamed, "Anyone?" It was too quiet for all the commotion we heard in the woods, but the only response I received was the river's babbling.

I tried to stand, but my hands lost traction. In front of me, Brett's empty face stared at the sky. One eye lacked emotion, and the other was gone. Blood oozed from the open hole. Terror choked me from screaming.

Scrambling away from the dead body, I heard an ear-piercing shrill of panic. Emmie's pleas for help magnified my horror. An ache crested in my chest as I struggled to peer through the smoke.

Eyes stinging, I attempted to stand, but pain raced up my left leg, causing the morning meal to reappear. Through the retching, I heard Kari scream from behind me. "Pa!" The crack of a cupped hand striking skin made me heave a second time.

"Shut your mouth, missy." A male's voice threatened.

I wiped the spittle from my lips. "Who's there?" My voice was barely audible. I shifted my weight to straighten to my full height and side-hopped to avoid falling onto Brett's lifeless body. Fear strained my voice. "Who is out there?"

"There's another, Al." This man's complaint came from farther away.

The man's menacing voice asked, "Neal, where are you?"

Apprehension forced me down. They knew I was here but couldn't see me. Crawling toward the rippling water, a prayer for someone to save us slipped past my lips. This must be the place where my pa was panning. I needed to find Pa and the girls.

A demanding tone kept me rooted in place when I heard. "Frank. Neal. Shut up! The blast will have stirred curiosity in the camp nearby. We need to move fast. Gather the gold and take care of the females."

"Give. Me. A. Minute." A strained, back throat groan came from a man downriver.

There were three men? 'Lord Almighty, help us.' I started praying in my head when a repetitive grunting and splashing tore me from my entreaty.

By the river's edge, the smoke lifted from the rushing waters. There, a man hunched over Emmie as her arms flailed, struggling to live. He secured his hands on either side of her neck while driving her under the water. I wanted to rush to Emmie, but my ankle reminded me I wouldn't get to her fast enough. Watching in horror as the movement in her limbs went slack until she was a motionless doll. Pale pink lips parted; her vacant gaze faced in my direction. Wet hair draped across half of it. A surge of water flowed over her head, but she didn't gasp for air or thrash.

Using the back of my hand, I wiped the tears away as realization sank in. Emmie was dead. My stomach wanted to lurch, but I used restraint to prevent it from doing so.

How am I going to tell Aunt Fern her daughter is dead after losing her husband mere weeks ago? Digging my fingers into the ground, I pushed slowly away from the swift-moving water. I needed to rescue Kari and find Pa, then get help.

"Hold, little missy."

"Emmie? Hazel?" Kari shrieked, "Pa!"

The male's voice commanded, "Stop struggling," the word "Now" echoed through the forest.

Fear, anger, and frustration tinted in her voice. "Hazel? Pa!"

"Your pa can't save your pretty little–" His comment cut off as a muffled gripe came through clamped teeth. I heard Kari wrestle the man, and I felt a ping of pride that she was fighting for her life. I had to find a way to save her.

Ankle protesting, I crawled backward. My good leg hit something hard, and I hoped it was a log, rock, or even Brett's body, but a hand snatched a fist full of my hair instead, lifting me until I was on my knees. Back arching, I used the position to reach the part of my head on fire. I used my nails to claw at the gold thief's hand, making him swear under his breath. Craning my neck to the side, he leaned down to get my attention.

"Well, little missy, you and your friends must be searching for a cat named Curiosity."

I tried to stare at the ground, but he jerked me back and used his other hand to grasp my chin. "And you know what happened to the cat, right?" He clicked his tongue several times in a condescending mock pity. "It's too bad you don't have eight lives to throw away." The harsh sounds from the water's edge warned me that I might not live through this. His hand moved from my chin to clamp onto my upper arm. Squeezing tight, the man heaved me toward him, and my ankle buckled.

I screamed.

He punched me.

Below my left eye, a crunch echoed in my head. The negative sensations from my ankle and scalp were replaced by stars that spun in my vision and mixed with unspent tears. The combination blurred the world around me. Losing the ability to control my body, it crumbled in on itself.

"Al, did you catch a mouse?"

My attacker was Al, so I made a mental note to tell my pa when he found me. I tried to work my jaw, but my tongue was swollen. The blood in my mouth became pasty.

He leaned in close, sniffing the side of my neck and wet hair. Al almost purred. "No, I found a cat."

Footsteps splashed as two blurry shapes came closer. One of them spoke, "You've got a live one, huh?"

"For now," my captor turned and motioned his chin so he could keep me bound by his hands. "What about the others?"

"Taken care of, Boss." He shook a bag. "We'd done what you said–collected from the trays, pans, and the bodies."

Al released my hair to trail his fingers down my neck. I quivered, trying to recoil from his touch. He chuckled at my attempt.

My face started to feel puffy from where he punched me—pressure behind the eye building. My right eye recovered, though, as his bemused expression replaced carnal want. The lines around his eyes and mouth hardened.

Shuddering, I uttered, "Leave me alone," through half-swollen lips.

The wickedness in Al's black eyes burned the chance of hope away. He licked his trembling lips before barking an order. "Neal, Frank, change of plans. Collect the bodies and arrange them around the blast creator."

The man who blemished the last memory of my cousin spoke, "What if they aren't dead yet?"

The smolder in his eyes never wavered as Al growled, "Take care of it. Go, now." His brow creased while staring at me. "I have some questions for the young lady and I would like some privacy."

Both men continued to hover.

"Get going." He hissed.

Once they turned around, Al leaned into my space. "Sorry about them, sweetheart; they don't know how to treat a lady."

Tilting to watch them go broke my moral compass. As much as I despised his lackeys, I didn't think he would touch me if they were watching. Tears leaked from my undamaged eye, and I punched his chest. He took it to mean something entirely different.

The corners of the man's smirk twitched. "You have some fight in you? That's even better. I promise it won't hurt…much."

Using my other arm, I pushed my body away from his and dug my good foot into the earth to gain traction. *'Get away. Get away. Get away,'* a voice screamed in my head. Those two words were a plea…a command…a need.

I kicked out and connected with his shin. He swore and then tackled me. This was Hell, and I was fighting a demon. All the strength I could muster, I willed into my arms and legs.

Al tried to pin me down but misplaced one hand, seizing a handful of my dress. I lifted my shoulder and strained the muscles in my arm. He lost his balance and fell forward. Survival instincts kicking in, I swung. Dirt and debris went into the air. I heard my dress tear as my elbow connected with Al's chin.

The impact made his teeth crunch together. Al's surprised expression turned to a blaze of hate, fanned by my will to escape him.

Saying nothing, he clamped onto both shoulders and shook me. I popped up my knee, missed his manhood, but connected with Al's gut. He grunted, pushed his face into my neck, and bit me.

I screamed in his ear.

A rancid, tobacco-filled exhale lingered as his fingers bore into my skin. "You know, I like my women young."

His mannerisms sparked me to thrash harder. "You may take this body, but you will not slake your lust." Thinking I would rather die than have this monster ruin what I held pure. Instead of 'Getaway,' my new plan was 'Kill me.'

I did everything physically in my power to heighten his wrath. It only spurred his need. Exhausted, he overpowered me. Limbs weak, I couldn't stop him from tearing off my dress. I heard the clink of a belt. Al pressed his weight on me, making it hard to breathe.

The string of words that came from me would've shocked my ma into serving me a plate of soap for dinner. Traumatized, I didn't move as he deflowered me. I cursed myself for not being strong enough to protect those I loved. I cursed this place and those who came here. Men were evil, greedy creatures.

"You are so sweet, my kitty." Huffing empty praises made me want to will my heart to stop. His hands roamed, but their final resting place was around my neck. Fingering my birthday present, he yanked on it until the bite of the chain left me a stinging reminder. "Thank you for this." Using his knees to keep me pinned to the ground, Al gradually rocked to a sitting position. Patting his pants, he found the pocket he wanted and retrieved a small leather pouch.

He placed the locket in his chew bag.

I cried.

My sobbing must have infuriated him enough to silence me. His hands found my throat again, and he squeezed, cutting off my air. Blood roared in my ears. I stiffened under my attacker, trying to suck in one more breath. Hatred wrapped around my dying heart. I wanted to kill them.

Abruptly, his presence was gone. I found myself floating as my extremities dangled, then began to sway with each of his steps. I cracked an eye to see where we were going. *'Am I alive? Why would the Almighty keep me from Heaven? Was my soul so tainted that I wasn't allowed to enter?'*

Detached, I thought, *'So, be it.'*

"It's about time." A raspy voice said.

"She was worth it." Al's oily statement covered me in shame.

My head rotated with his movements, and I was now looking at my sister's upside-down, vacant stare. Her head hung grotesquely as the man struggled with her dead weight.

Rage burned. I wanted revenge. I wanted them to pay.

"What should we do with them, Boss? They're not part of the crew, and there'll be questions if they're found."

"Toss them into the eddy."

It was the last thing I heard.

Chapter: 1

Present Day

'*Breaking up was the right thing to do,*' I thought while scraping the bottom of a Ben & Jerry's container. Keeping myself from crying, I focused on enjoying the last spoonful of Half Baked while assessing the apartment. Forlorn and dejected, I leaned against the counter. TK protectively rubbed against my calf. He shook out his soft, light-gray coat and circled twice.

'*Has it only been two weeks?*' I sucked on the spoon.

I didn't comply with his subtle demands. Ears slanted and eyes narrowed, TK meowed to reprimand me. Sighing, I scraped the sides. Sparkling sapphire eyes emphasized his silent demand for ice cream. With a huff, I threw the container in the trash and lowered the spoon. He licked it twice and then cleaned his mouth in dissatisfaction. Matching my humdrum mood, he moseyed to a nearby sunbeam for his mid-morning nap.

Turning to the sink, I dropped the spoon into a dirty coffee cup. The air conditioner kicked on. Cool air hit my damp cheeks. '*Great, I'm leaking again.*' The old sweatshirt sleeves came in handy removing the moisture. A light scent of cologne mixed with the lingering aromas of vanilla, cookie dough, and chocolate. Seth's faint scent from his KRave sweatshirt sparked several good memories. It was two sizes too big for me, but comfortable to sleep in. I pulled on the hem and scrutinized why I was wearing it. A few more tears fell on the material.

I missed the man from six months ago.

During the first two months, I was his princess. Things began to sour going into our third month. Seth's growing hostility and jealousy caused me to steel my nerves and rethink our future. We hid our problems well. But the plastic smile I screwed on before leaving the apartment was demoralizing. His outbursts became unpredictable. I never knew what would trip his mood. Although his dimples made my heart race, and his lips tempted me to stay in my heart, I knew it was a one-sided relationship.

After five weeks into our relationship, I introduced Seth to my foster parents. He delighted my mother by openly showering me with affection and praise, impressed my father with his career choice, and dropped hints of 'future us' living a comfortable life. After finishing school and passing the bar exam Seth had a position waiting for him at his father's law firm. He appeared to be perfect to everyone, even our friends, but to me, he was perfectly flawed.

'He shouldn't have hit me.'

Our fights were never physical, but at times, there was an unsettling emotion behind his milk chocolate eyes. An overwhelming possessiveness that instantly transformed him into Mr. Hyde. I remember the night he exploded through the front door. Waving his phone while shouting accusations of cheating, and before I could defend myself, Seth's curled hand connected under my left eye. The bruise was minor since I flinched in time to deflect the blow. Two weeks later, the mark was gone, but the crack Seth had left in my heart felt permanent. At least I wouldn't have to fabricate an explanation. Hiding out in the apartment couldn't last much longer. I used most of the sick hours, and my vacation time was down to three days.

"A Pocket Full of Sunshine" filled the noiseless room. I wandered to the coffee table. I couldn't explain how this infectious tune always lightened my mood. Not even bothering to check the number, I knew it was Trey's ringtone. Like clockwork, he was probably checking in on me. Swiping the screen, I answered, "Yellow."

"Hey, Ceanna. When was the last time you showered?" It was Trey's twin sister, Kailee.

Caught off guard, I laughed. "Who would I shower for?" It was apparent she wasn't going to allow me to soak in my breakup pool.

"A little Trey bird said you needed a good butt-kicking. So, I packed a get-over-him breakup kit. It includes actual food, and your new roommates, Ben and Jerry, are getting evicted."

"I don't know, Kay. Moping is part of the ritual." I collapsed onto the couch. "And I broke up with him…a few days ago." Leaning into a throw pillow, I noticed a dried stain of melted chocolate. Absentmindedly, I picked at the brown spot.

A snort came through the mic. "Yeah, it's been two weeks and four days. I know because I've been covering someone's work schedule. You're lucky Mason has a soft spot for emotional charity cases. If I asked for two weeks off, he would've signed over my soul to the company." Two seconds of different songs were coming through the phone. She was channel surfing. Kailee softly grouched about her inability to commit to a station. A muffled argument followed.

"Hold on, let a girl talk here." Then she blurted, "No, she doesn't sound okay."

Being ignored, I coughed into the receiver.

"Hey, you don't have to throat beckon me. Be patient, or I'll make you take a number." Kailee playfully threatened.

"Ah, you called me."

"You want me to place the phone by the speaker for some hold music?"

I could hear Adele singing "Hello" and didn't think it would help our situation. "Not really."

Completely dismissive, she clipped curtly, "Bro, keep your eyes on the road. I want to get there in one piece."

Slightly curious, I asked, "Where are you going?" Before Kay could respond, my cell beeped twice, displaying a picture of my parents. Inwardly, I cringed. "Hey, my parents are on the other line; I'll call you back."

"Sure. We'll see you soon. Oh, and we have a surprise for you."

Only half listening, I said, "Um, surprise? Yeah, I'll call you later."

I switched over. "Hi, Mom-Dad," acknowledging both at the same time.

In a boisterous greeting, they sang, "Hello, Ceanna." Gritting my teeth, I held the phone away from my ear.

Inquiring about the unexpected call, I asked, "What's new? It's not Saturday already, is it?"

Dad spoke over Mom, "We wanted to hear about your grades."

'Oh, love a duck.' I honestly forgot all about them. Partially because I knew they weren't ideal. For the past two months, I have played the part of the devoted girlfriend to quell Seth's mood. Saying 'yes' to him meant saying 'no' to schoolwork most of the time. My grades were going to reflect the mismanaged time.

Quickly, I attempted to stall. "Um, I can't find the laptop charger, but I'll text you what they are when I do." With an inward promise to myself to become more focused on school, I hoped karma would give me a pass.

"You haven't been able to check?" Mom dramatized her disappointment.

Before they had time to reconsider, I added, "The laptop's been giving me trouble charging. The last time I tried to log in, it accidentally locked the school account when it powdered down." With a Cheshire cat grin, I congratulated myself for my fast ingenuity.

It was short-lived when Dad offered, "You can give me your password. I'll turn on the desktop."

Alarmed, I sat up too fast. Racking my brain, I countered, "I'm waiting for someone in the registration office to call me back with a new passcode."

My mother interjected a "tsk-tsk." "Oh, that's too bad."

Dad wasn't convinced and challenged. "Did they give you an estimate of when your account would be unlocked?"

Darn, stacking the lies wasn't paying off. "After Memorial weekend," I blurted. "I guess they're short on staff because of the holiday."

"We'll call you on Tuesday then. What time is good to catch you?" Dad sounded suspicious.

"Can you call on Wednesday? I have classes in the morning and work that night; Wednesday is better."

He gave in this time. "We'll call you on Wednesday."

Mom prodded, "Honey, how is everything? Are you doing anything this weekend, maybe with Seth?"

Irritated, I snipped, "You know, I could be doing something with my friends this weekend. I have other friends."

"I know, Ceanna. I only meant…"

"I need to get ready for work." Tossing in one last lie, strictly for selfish reasons, and thought, *'Why not? What's one more?'* I peeled myself from the couch to cross the room for a tissue and then used it to stop the new leaks. In my cup of sorrows, guilt floated to the top like curdled cream. *'Damn emotions.'*

After exchanging "goodbyes" and "love you's," I tossed the cell onto the desk and turned on the laptop. The website for California State University, Sacramento login screen queried for the username and password. The grade screen blinded me for a second. Squinting until the letters became clearer, there was an A, a B-, and a B, and then my heart sank when the last two came into focus…two F's.

With all of the emotional tumbling I'd done, going through a breakup should be an Olympic sport. Crushing failure amplified the waterworks as I turned off the computer. I sank into the sands of 'what if,' ashamed of how I mishandled everything, and all because of a guy. *'Which was also my decision,'* I thought callously.

This Wednesday, I'm going to inform the two most important people that I failed two classes. Anxiety slithered through the door and joined the pity party. Nothing right now seemed stable. *'How did I become so weak?'*

TK jumped on the keyboard and head-bonked my chin. "Well, I can always count on you." The sentence reaffirmed my loneliness. The fluffball answered with a reassuring purr. I hugged my cat close and cried.

Chapter: 2

'Camping,' I thought with repulsion.

The crinkle above my nose emphasized what I thought while wiping the condensation from the slick surface. Dark-ringed, puffy eyes scowled back at me through the first swipe on the reflective surface. I didn't recognize the woman who filled the oval mirror. Instinctively, I removed the damp towel and ran four fingers through my straight, black hair a few times to air dry before adding some leave-in conditioner. Once dried, I opted out of styling it, blew it straight, and secured the long strands in a relaxed ponytail.

Kailee insisted on a shower. Parting my lips to inspect my teeth, I uncapped the toothpaste. After a few minutes of removing the sugar residue, I called it good.

Self-consciously, I gave myself one last check before honestly asking, "Do you really want to go camping?"

Approximately thirty minutes ago, Kailee burst into the apartment, carrying a bag of what she considered real food and camping paraphernalia. Kay instructed her brother to put the food away as she dropped the brochures on the couch and then placed my laptop on the coffee table. They came up with the crazy idea that I needed an intervention and planned a camping trip for Memorial weekend.

Trey went into the freezer and tossed all five unopened containers of ice cream. I screeched that he was going to reimburse me for those. He masked his laughter behind the freezer door as Kailee pushed me into the bathroom to scrub off my boohoo scum. The shower did help, but I fumed about all that comfort food melting in the trash.

Cracking the door, I could see the empty computer chair. The two had argued about where to go since the majority of camping sites were reserved. They moved to the living room, and since I couldn't get a visual, I left the bathroom in haste.

Trey sat on the couch, teasing his sister as she typed the wrong camping sites into the search engine. Kay sat cross-legged on the floor in front of the coffee table, tersely insulting the laptop. She pressed the keys with extra force. If I didn't recover soon, I would have to work extra shifts to pay for a new one.

Hands on my hips, I stomped toward them, and in a fluid motion, used two fingers to close the screen until there was a light click. Trey's mouth opened to protest but froze once he locked onto me. A slight tingle of heat settled in my cheeks. Normally, his eyes were brown, but today, they reminded me of melted caramel, closer to his sister's bright amber.

I've known them since our junior year of high school when Kailee and I had two classes together. She was a no-nonsense, partially guarded person with a big heart. It took about a month for her to size me up until one day, she invited me to lunch. Little did I know there was someone she wanted to introduce me to. The second we sat down, Trey slid in beside her, glimpsed at me, and said, "Hey, Ceanna, what's up?" Right then, he became my brother, too.

But, at that moment, I was seeing him for the first time in four years. Trey's expression softened, and it stirred an unusual sense of shyness. Kailee squinted at her twin and smacked his mouth shut with a chin pop. Her purple nails snapped in succession to get my attention. The repetitive action worked. Satisfied she had our attention, she raised the screen and went back to searching.

Sweeping the moment under the mental rug, I took advantage of the awkward pause to set them straight. Finger pointed, I said, "First, I would like to say 'thanks' for thinking of me, but I'm fine. Second, I need to go back to work. Third, I'm not sure I want to go camping, hiking, or whatever fresh air-related activity you're planning."

She huffed and rolled her eyes. "Ceanna, I've known you long enough to know you're not fine." Aimed to protest, she held up a hand. "I think we all could use some time away from the city." Her face became smug. "Besides, Mason owes me."

My finger lost its power and curled in from her presumption. "You spoke to the manager? Kay, I never said 'yes' to the idea. Heck, I didn't even know about it until forty minutes ago. How could you?" The plea in her eyes fizzled the argument.

"We need this, you more than any of us. Plus, Mason already has extras on the schedule for sick calls." Kailee went back to clicking the mouse.

"I need my job," I said, upset, not believing our manager gave us both the holiday weekend off. *'Maybe if I called him back, he would put me on the schedule,'* I thought.

Tongue in cheek, Kay spoke slowly, "Stop fussing; I took care of it."

A deep snicker swayed my ire. Trey was back on the couch, staring at the ceiling. "Kay-Kay, tell her the good part," He mocked.

With a huff, she stopped scrolling. "I'm going to watch his kids the following weekend."

Her brother coughed.

Rolling irises met mine. "We are going to watch his kids."

I took two steps back. "What? We? As in, you and me?" Being an only child, I knew nothing about kids.

"Don't get your quills in a knot. They are six and eight. It'll be a weekend of pizza, video games, and cartoons. And if all else fails, we'll let them abuse Trey."

"Hey," Trey smacked her arm.

I reconsidered the idea. Getting away and soaking up some sun might not be such a bad plan. I was about to ask Kay a question, but Trey changed the subject. "Mat said he has two tents and a grill." He pressed into the cushions.

Stunned and a bit peeved, of all people for them to invite, why him? "Mathew's coming?"

Sliding behind his sister, he mouthed, 'She invited him.' Now, I am torn. Their plan sounded low-key, but now I wasn't so sure with

Mat coming.

Kailee had a secret crush on the guy for about a year but played it off as strictly a lust phase. Trey and I were not convinced. It had been eight months since her last serious relationship. But my hesitation stemmed from the simple fact he was one of Seth's friends. It would be awkward seeing him and would remind me of my ex.

"Kay?"

"Yeah?"

"Why would you invite Mathew if this is an intervention weekend for me to not think about Seth? Mat hangs with him. I'm not digging the idea of having to work out my issues with him nearby." I closed the gap and lowered to the floor to sit next to Kailee. Not thinking about my actions, I used my shoulder to shove Trey's legs apart so I could sit closer to his sister and see the screen.

Pictures of camping sites, rivers, trees, blue skies, and people hiking or fishing were plastered on the screen. The lake, surrounded by a row of trees and a worn boat dock, caught my attention. I took the mouse from her and clicked on the picture. Briefly forgetting about Mathew, I asked, "Where's this?"

"It's one of the Mammoth Lakes," Trey said from behind us. He pushed my head to the side to see the screen better. "That's Skelton Lake. It might take us an hour longer than one of the other camping sites I was considering. Let's see if they have a few spots open." He took the mouse from me and clicked a few tabs. "The rates are cheaper." He paused. "I wonder why? They have fishing, hiking, boating, and everything the other camping sites offer. They even have some cabins available to rent by the lake."

Excited, Kailee playfully smacked her brother's hand and grabbed the mouse to click the rental link for the lodges. "Cabins?"

Trey, clearly satisfied, snickered while saying, "Hey, you said you wanted to rough it. We're roughing it. Or should I ask for my two hundred back and reserve the cabin?" He opened his hand.

Kailee stuck out her tongue.

Since she was distracted, I reclaimed the mouse to expand the picture. Mesmerized by the blueness of the water, Kay heaved a sigh. "Listen, I know Mathew and your ex-man are friends, but come on, it's Mat. He's funny, sweet, tall..." She drifted into one of her fantasies.

Recognizing Kay's reaction, Trey groaned. He kicked a leg above my head so he could stand before proceeding to the kitchen. "Who wants a drink," he asked, "I think we're going to be here for a while." He stopped to pet TK and then continued to the kitchen.

Kailee jolted from her daydream, and without missing a beat, said, "And don't worry about entertaining Mathew, leave it to me. Besides, we're going as a group." She took the mouse from me.

"I'm going to call Jaci and see if she wants to help pick out a spot with us," Trey ducked his head to study the refrigerator's contents.

"Jaci's coming too?" I whined. Nothing was going on between Trey and Jaci, but this was turning into a couples' mini-vacation. "Kay, I don't even know her that well. I thought it was going to be just us?"

Kay's face betrayed there was something more to our get-away agenda. Pressing her, "Kailee Ann..." I used her name the way their mom did. She hated it. For extra measure, I gave her the Puss-N-Boot eyes, trying my darnedest to guilt-trip her.

Acting as though we were in a confessional, she leaned in and said, "Don't tell Trey."

The urge to smirk tugged at the corners of my mouth.

She whispered, "I told him to invite Jaci because she'll be a good distraction. Plus, she's nice; you just need to hang around her more."

"Distraction?" I arched an eyebrow.

"I know it sounds bad, but I've been fooling myself for far too long." In earnest, she said, "I like Mat a lot. I thought, if we spent some time together alone..." She beamed with hope. "Trey is always on my heels, and I figured she would be a companionable company for all of us. Plus. I didn't want to dump my brother on you because I know," she squeezed my hand, "you're hurting. Please, Ceanna."

Not able to deny her this chance to see if she could strike sparks between her and Mat. With all of my excuses evaporated, I gave in. "Okay, let's go camping. Who knows, maybe I'll get lucky and lose myself for a few days."

Chapter: 3

I made arrangements for TK's stay at a five-star kitty hotel. He wasn't thrilled, but neither was I. The camping idea remained on the surface and hadn't soaked in. Now, two days later, we were heading for Mammoth, specifically, Skelton Lake.

Surprisingly, we argued for a bit until we decided to stop in Bishop for dinner. After finding a parking spot, I got out to stretch and retrieved my purse before joining the group.

The clouds blushed from the sun's last goodnight kiss. We stood in the parking lot of a little coffee shop that doubled as the general store. A small part of me wished Seth was here to enjoy the sunset with me. The tips of the trees darkened, and the once peaceful scene turned slightly baleful.

With the first drop in temperature, I hugged the purse for warmth. Loneliness began to creep in until a hand reassuringly rested upon my shoulder. Not realizing someone had slid up next to me and said, "That's pretty amazing."

Trey startled me by his comment and touch for half a second, I reproved myself for being so jumpy. He made his way to stand next to Mathew, who was on his phone, nodding as if the person he spoke to could see. It was amusing to watch his animated responses. Their stealthy approach amazed me.

Mathew ended the call and draped an arm across Kailee's shoulders. Her surprise was subtle. It pulled on a few heartstrings as she hid her happiness almost too well.

Jaci surprised me by looping her arm around mine. "I'm starving. Let's go inside. My stomach is starting to eat itself."

Once seated at a coffee-stained oak table, I ordered breakfast from the back of the menu, salivating at the twenty-four-hour specials. The pancakes were buttery, fluffy, and turned golden brown from the maple syrup. I could only finish two because of their size, and the coffee was surprisingly good. Breakfast for dinner was a comfort food of mine.

Placing the cup on the saucer, I tapped Kailee on the shoulder. "If we are going hiking tomorrow, I would like to stop at the store for a few things." I left my portion of the tip on the table. The others added to the pile of money while they continued to debate on what to do for the next three days.

Kailee's face fell as we both watched Mat wink at Jaci. I gave my friend's arm a reassuring squeeze before everyone fanned out. Kay followed me into the store, Jaci excused herself to head for the restroom, and Trey and Mat made a beeline to the cashier.

As we walked through the wooden threshold, goose skin rippled down both arms. Tugging Kailee closer, I used her warmth to chase away the frosty sensation as we approached the racks of postcards with different nature scenes from around the area. Next to it, another rack of maps and pamphlets, mini books, and brochures on Mammoth filled the slots.

My friend fumed while she fingered some of the postcards in silence.

"Kailee, I'm sure it didn't mean anything. You know Mathew's a flirt."

"I know, but she's supposed to be Trey's distraction, not Mat's," she said, irritated.

I snickered at her response while selecting a postcard with Skelton Lake written in the corner. It was an old picture of miners panning for gold. I flipped it to the back and read the blurb about the Mammoth Mining Company.

A presence overshadowed me as I read it. Smiling, I turned, assuming it was one of the guys. Instead, I was met with a vacant gawk through thick glasses. The man was almost six feet and roughly in his seventies.

"You going to buy it?" He grumbled.

"I might. Do you have any more maps of the area?"

The man adjusted his glasses. "Curious about the area, are you?

Kailee walked to the display of tourist shirts to join Jaci, who was already combing through the different styles. I telepathically tried to signal them to return and save me from this man's emanating creepiness. But not wanting to be rude, I answered, "We're staying near Skelton Lake for a few days. I wanted to know the best hiking trails." I slipped the postcard back into its slot.

He turned, revealing his name tag with Manager written in the block script. Hand shaking, he reached for a folded map. He offered it and said, "I think this one will suit your needs." Then, the manager extended the same hand and introduced himself. "Mr. Owens, Albert Owens. If you want to know more about the lakes, check out the store's back wall." He left me, shifted behind the counter, and situated himself next to the register.

Kay held up a shirt to Mat's chest. It had a big woolly mammoth reeling in a fish on the front. Jaci and Trey laughed.

I slipped away from view and wandered to the back. The whole wall was covered in framed clippings of local history. Skimming the dusty frames of faded portraits and obituaries held an intriguing calm. Pictures and news articles of the miners, how Mammoth was founded, and the faces of their families frozen in a mix of emotions seemed to stare past me, possibly searching for something more filled the space.

Taking a step forward, I kicked a stack of frames. One fell forward on its face. The glass cracked. Grimacing, I picked up the picture to check the damage. Holding it in one hand, I ran my finger under the heading; Tragedy Rocks Town. Featured under the header were the individual pictures of the miners.

Constable Deller is calling in for reinforcements to help with a double investigation. Unsure if both tragedies are related, Constable Deller is forming a list of suspects, and interviews will be held shortly. The first pertains to the blast that took the lives of four miners. The Constable believes the misuse of explosives might be to blame. The second investigation involves the disappearance of three female

My brain stopped at the word missing and started to fill in the
possibilities of what could have happened to them.

At the bottom of the paragraph were the pictures of the missing
girls. The one on the left caught my attention. Her hair was long and
close to the same style as mine. On the glass, there was a smudge
across part of her face. I used my thumbnail to rid the area of the
spot and revealed her name. Hazel Fritzen's timeless expression
made the hairs on my arms raise. Underneath my thumb, the glass
splintered. I quickly dropped the frame and checked the skin.

The owner's presence was back. I prepared to apologize while
retrieving the broken picture from the floor.

Albert cut me off. "Find something interesting?"

My friends were standing behind him. Kailee and Jaci held
several paper shopping bags. Mathew jingled his keys and smirked.
Trey held a fixed stare, glancing from the store manager to me.

Mr. Owens took the frame. Magnified eyes skimmed the
damage. He focused on the smeared blood. "Did you hurt yourself,
miss?"

"It's nothing."

Mr. Owens regarded me before interjecting, "You know, they
never found them."

I frowned. "Found who?"

"The girls. I don't know much, only folklore." He fixed his
glasses, which made his eyes appear bigger. "Most of these," he
gestured to the wall while talking, "were my great-grandmother's.
Close family members claimed she was pretty tight-lipped about this
story. Most of the locals have speculated they got lost in the woods
or maybe even murdered. Their bodies were never recovered. It's a
bizarre happenstance, right?" His explanation held a feeling of loss
as though he knew them. "They were last seen by Skelton Lake." He
pointed at the pictures. "These two girls were the daughters of one

of the miners killed in the explosion that day."

The air became frigid, and I stepped closer to Kailee and Jaci for comfort.

Albert continued, "Some campers have reported seeing a girl or girls in the forest. Females camping by the lake have said they would start crying for no reason. Men seem to be affected differently. One woman reported that her husband started spitting up a dark substance. If I recall correctly, he was rushed to the hospital. Ya' know, they never went back to retrieve their gear from the cabin. Just left."

"Well, I guess it's a good thing we're only staying for a couple of days." I picked up the map he had handed me before. "I'll take this since we'll be hiking by the river tomorrow. Oh, and I'll take this postcard too." I pushed past everyone and headed for the cash register.

Albert slipped behind me. "Hiking by the river, are you? Be careful; it's slippery along the edges this time of year. But if you fall into the water, make sure you don't stay in there too long; you don't want to catch anything you might bring home." His thin smile left me cold.

I paid and left.

The incident at the general store was slightly unnerving. I wanted to tell the girls, but at the same time, I didn't want them to worry. So, I decided to keep it to myself. If I had time to process the information, I would understand what the manager's warning meant.

The moon outlined the peaks of the mountain range from across Skelton Lake. Mathew backed his truck into the campsite so we could unload faster, and Kailee parked next to his truck and left the headlights on so we could see until Trey started the campfire and set up the lanterns. Unpacking gave me time to reflect on Albert's storytelling. I couldn't decide if he used the story to drum up business or if it had a deeper meaning.

When the guys finished securing the tents, the girls and I went inside ours to arrange the cots. I excused myself to retrieve the box of goodies I snuck from home as a surprise for the girls. I had stashed it under my sleeping bag behind the bucket seats of Kailee's Jeep.

A tiny bubble of happiness was the first sign I was beginning to relax. Humming, I shuffled through the items to ensure I grabbed everything. My rhythm was thrown off by the crickets and cicadas interjecting their song and a rushed conversation that seemed a bit harsh coming from Mat and Trey's tent next to the vehicles.

'Were they arguing?'

Figuring it was none of my business, I went back to retrieving our things. Lifting the box out, I balanced it on my hip and slammed the door. At the same time, their heated discussion peaked, and then someone started swearing. Their argument caused my stomach to flip-flop.

Not realizing what I might be walking into, I shuffled apprehensively back to the tent. When I turned the corner by the guys' tent, Mat was on the ground, and Trey backed away. Unthinking, I dropped the box and rushed to help Mathew stand.

"What's going on here?" My shouting alerted the girls.

When Trey met my glare, the harsh lines of rage began to smooth out and were replaced by a shocked expression. "What did you hear?" He said sharply, then took another step back.

"What do you mean? Was I not supposed to hear something?" My voice wavered.

Mat started to dust off the dirt. Glancing at our tent, I saw the girls running. Jaci followed right behind Kay. Then I saw Kailee's eyes widen, observing the hunched posture of her brother and me next to Mat.

Jaci gasped, "Oh my goodness."

Trey started to pace like a trapped animal.

A marred expression crossed Kailee's face as she glowered at Trey, then tersely asked, "Okay, spill. What's going on?" She didn't even acknowledge Mat, which I knew why, and that meant whatever explanation her brother gave wasn't enough to save him from her wrath. "Well, Trey, care to explain? I know we're all tired, but what could you two possibly be fighting about?" Her voice was shaky from holding in her annoyance.

"It's something between Mat and me. Everything is…all right." The last sentence came out through his teeth.

With a hand on her hip, she pointed a purple manicured nail at her brother. "Look, Trey, I came here to be with our friends and make some memories, not regrets. Now, I know you. You don't get physical unless it's a last resort."

He shook his head.

"Tell me!" Kay's demand could've shattered glass.

I went to stand by Jaci and Kay and placed a hand on her arm to calm her down before she woke the other campers nearby because it was well after eleven. Then I remembered Trey's question to me before the girls showed up. I didn't believe he would be straight with me, so I asked Mat instead. "What wasn't I supposed to hear?"

Mat gestured toward me, but Trey kicked a pine cone, and we watched it sail into the forest.

"Ceanna, don't press. It's nothing," Trey said. His face reminded me of when our French teacher made an escargot and told the class that the ones who tried it would get extra credit. He failed the course.

"Hey, guys spat sometimes. We're good." Mat caught on to Trey's demeanor and tried to smooth things over. He strolled toward Trey. "I only had good intentions, Man. You know, right?" Then he held out his hand.

Trey looked worried as he scanned from Mat to me and then back to Mat. I grew worried he wouldn't accept Mathew's apology. Irritation hovered between them as Trey mumbled before shaking his hand. "Yeah, I'm sure it'll be cool." Using their handshake, Trey jerked him closer and added, "But if she gets hurt, you'll be in a world of pain."

Briskly, Kailee's brother moved toward us and then asked for her keys. With a challenging scowl, she produced a key ring from a front pocket. Sulking, he fisted them before heading for the driver's side of the vehicle. Trey yanked open the door, got in, and slammed it shut. When the interior lights went off, music broke the silence. I figured he would be in there for a while.

Mat apologized and then tapped Kailee on the nose. Her lips parted, but he left before gauging her demeanor. Confused, we watched him disappear into the tent. From inside the tent, he dimmed the light. I did a double take as two shadows zipped over the forest floor. Right before the light went out, the darkness absorbed Mat's silhouette.

Retrieving the box from the ground, I ushered the girls into our tent. We were sullen as I unpacked the surprise, passing bags of chocolate and Girl Scout cookies to the girls.

Kay smirked, "Caramel Delights, my favorite. Thanks."

I gave them each a fuzzy blanket.

She hugged it. "This is so soft, and I love the dark blue color. Thanks, Ceanna."

I arranged the portable DVD player, but Kailee suggested we skip the movie and go to sleep. I could tell the argument between her brother and the guy she liked had her on edge. Besides the fight ruining our mood, my happy little bubble popped the millisecond I saw Trey's ire.

All three of us said, "Goodnight," as Jaci turned off the lantern.

Chapter: 4

Kailee nominated herself to cook the next morning, and the smell of coffee sent a promise of food. The aroma quickened my steps to the campsite bathrooms. Jaci complained while trying to tag along. From nearby, a campfire and bacon wafted in the air, adding to the demand for caffeine.

Jaci and I chatted while we brushed our teeth and dressed for the day. Dropping the boots under the sink, I stood to tuck in the blue shirt. Scrutinizing my reflection, I decided to braid my long black locks so they wouldn't get in the way while I took pictures.

Jaci's morning chatter faded into the background as I remembered the cryptic conversation with Mr. Owens. His warning was baffling, not the, "Be careful; it's slippery along the edges." But the last thing, "If you fall into the water, make sure you don't stay in there too long; you don't want to catch anything you might bring home." *'What did he mean?'*

"Hey," Jaci said playfully, punching me, "Where are you?"

Using a rubber band to secure the braid, I tossed it over my shoulder and plopped on the floor to wedge on my boots. Exhaling, I apologized, "Sorry, I was thinking about the scenery and if I brought the right equipment." After lacing my boots, I hoisted myself using the edge of the sink and adjusted the flannel shirt to lay flat.

I met Jaci's eyes in the mirror. "Didn't you find the manager creepy?"

Jaci's reflection remained stoic. "What manager?"

Collecting my toiletries, I said, "The old guy from the store."

"Oh, the place we went to after dinner?"

I nodded.

A confused pinch creased in between her eyebrows. "Just an old guy, I guess. The man probably acts that way for the tourist." She shrugged and then tapped my shoulder while pointing at my boots. The lace on my right foot had untied. I dropped everything to retie it.

"Thanks," I said.

As we headed back, the subject wasn't discussed further. Kailee stood by the campfire, holding up two coffees. Jaci and I gladly accepted the steaming mugs. The smell of eggs drifted as she motioned for us to follow her to the grill.

Trey shoveled some egg fluff into his mouth and then pointed at his sister with the empty fork. "Yeah, I'm shocked. Who knew she could cook? She doesn't even make toast at home." His eyebrows rose while laughing.

Mathew's deep laugh joined in with Trey's. They weren't sitting next to each other but close enough to appear on good terms again. Mat motioned to the forest with his white plastic fork. After taking another mouthful, Trey nodded and mirrored Mat's fork trace. It was internal guy talk, I assumed.

There was a nip to the air from the sun playing peek-a-boo. I watched the guys work out the activities for the day. Their casual banter made me think of Seth. I hid my frown behind the mug as a streak of annoyance squashed the emotion. *'I shouldn't feel this way; it was my decision.'*

I spent the rest of the morning listening to everyone's light chit-chat, the chirping birds, and if I strained, the pacifying static of rushing water. It added a soft *'shhh'* in the background. The tension began to erode the longer I listened. Voices rose in excitement, lassoing the negative emotions and anchoring me to what was important in my life.

Jaci collected the trash, and Kailee passed around a plastic bag. As we finished cleaning, the guys left to retrieve their backpacks. The girls and I went to our tent to get ready for the hike. I grabbed a black windbreaker, the trail map, my camera bag, and sunscreen.

Kailee knelt next to me. "Don't forget to fix the lace. It's under your boot."

I huffed. "Damn laces." Irked, I quickly reworked the tie and double-knotted it for extra measure. Satisfied, I finished packing, zipped the backpack, and followed the girls.

Several hours later, we stopped for a light snack and to catch our breath. I took out a jerky stick to munch on. Clenching the meat stick between my teeth, I unfolded the guide. Kailee asked if I wanted a bottle of water, and letting go of the map corner, I absentmindedly took it.

Using half of the meat stick, I pointed it toward the lane. "If we follow this path, it should lead us to the main river. If we head north, it should take us to Skelton Lake."

"Are you getting enough pictures?" Jaci sat on a rock next to me.

"Yes, but I want to take a few of the river."

Mathew stood abruptly when a soft buzzing started. He patted his pockets and finally retrieved it from the back of his shorts. He tapped the screen, his face scrunching from reading something.

Trey grumbled and jolted from his spot. As he began to pass me, his hand fastened onto my wrist since both hands were full. I caught Jaci's hurt expression as I chirped in surprise. The forced reaction made me drop the map as I tripped from being pulled forward.

"I got it," Jaci shouted.

After we were out of earshot from the group, he stopped, causing me to bump into him. The pause between us was long enough for me to assess his agitation before he let go of my wrist.

Trey's pained expression made me wary. "How are you doing, Ceanna?"

Hiding behind a forced grin, I shrugged. "Okay."

"Okay?"

"Yes, Trey." I drolly answered while rolling my eyes. "I'm trying not to think about my grades." I took a sip of water before continuing. "Maybe I can work extra hours to retake those classes." Out of breath, I dismissed the explanations with a one-shoulder shrug. Annoyance from his demeanor made me realize I was clenching my jaw.

"Ceanna, you know that's not what I'm asking you about."

Fingers slightly shaking, I crumpled up the jerky wrapper to hide my nervousness and tucked it into a front pocket. From a distance, Kailee and Jaci laughed at something I assumed Mat must have said. The slight distraction saved me from having to face his unsureness.

All the mixed emotions for Seth fractured, causing my resolve to ooze from the cracks. A burning ire added fuel to my frustration. "Honestly, Trey, I ended the relationship, what, two weeks ago? Give me some time to lick my wounds, okay?"

"Well, time isn't on your side." The muscle in his lower jaw tensed.

His comment made me bristle, and my vision narrowed. "What?"

The noise level from our group rose, signaling their approach. As they came into view, I was both irritated and relieved. They were clueless about why Trey had dragged me away, just as I was too. Kailee was too engrossed with Mat to notice anything awkward. When she passed her brother, Kay laughed and squeezed his arm playfully. I lingered on the spot where she touched him, detecting his stiff demeanor.

From behind, I heard Mathew ask the girls if they needed help crossing the moss-covered log. Jaci squealed when Mathew threatened to carry her. Kailee hollered above their playful banter for us to join them, but a surprised cry abruptly cut off her comment. Then, she redirected her demands to Mat to put her down. Trey's protective nature kicked in as he watched them. Her gleeful yelp made him frown once he detected she was flirting.

His shoulders drooped before closing the gap between us and then hesitantly held my hand. "I have to tell you something, and you have to be honest with me."

"Hey, you two, let's go. I want to get dinner started before nightfall." Kailee's bossiness kicked in.

I was getting irritated because every time Trey began to crack, someone interrupted us. I coaxed Trey to follow so that we could talk privately.

"Hey, I want a few more minutes with your brother." I tugged Trey with both hands, took two steps, rotated my body, and faceplanted into Mat's chest.

A six-foot man loomed over me, smiling. Mathew then asked Trey, "Did you tell her?"

He dropped my hand, stepped around me, and into Mathew's space by forcefully shoving him away. Mat sidestepped, then continued toward Kailee. Mathew tried to hide his annoyance by rubbing the spot Trey grabbed. The action left me dumbfounded. A question formed in a festering lump, making it hard to swallow.

Ignoring my best friend, I pursued the one who could answer my questions. "Tell me what?" I called out, at the same time, taking several strides to follow on his heels. Approaching the fallen tree, I caught the girls watching us like we were on an episode of Survivor.

Anger pulled on my strings as I spun on Mathew. Not realizing my right boot had become loose, I almost lost my balance but steadied myself. "Mat, what's going on?"

"Well." He scrubbed his face with his thumb and finger. "I only wanted to help."

"Help? With what?"

"I think you should give Seth another chance."

I froze.

Pleased to play Dr. Phil's role in my life, he said, "You and Seth need to talk things out, and I thought, what a better setting than up here. Ya' know? A romantic setting, right?"

The discomfort of seeing my ex ignited a new emotion: wrath. *'How dare he? How dare Mathew interfere?'* I cursed at myself for always being tight-lipped about Seth's major character flaw. My temper tantrum instantly melted into anxiety.

Panicked, I howled, "He's coming here? Here? I thought this was my time." I scared a nearby flock of birds. Their wings madly flapped as they took to the sky. I stormed past Trey, stepping onto the mossy log, then turned on a heel to confront them.

Pointing at Trey, I could have scorched him with my thoughts if he was close enough. "And you knew? This is what you've been trying to tell me?" Feeling betrayed and trapped, I whipped my wrath toward the girls. "Did you two know?" The accusation bounced around the forest.

"Ceanna, Honey, come here." Kailee beckoned for me to regain my cool. "You need to calm down and get off the dead tree before you completely freak out."

All reasoning gone, I heard. *'Get away. Get away. Get away.'* The phrase weakly filtered through my head. Whirling around too fast with my arms open, I resembled a broken toy top. Dizzy from spinning and off balance, I overcorrected, causing my right foot to catch on the loose lace. I fell. My scream was short-lived when I smacked into the freezing water. It swelled around me, forcefully propelling me down the mind-numbing current.

Cries of fear replaced my own as I broke the water's surface, briefly hearing their commands echoing across the river. Jaci and Kailee's demands were muffled when the water sucked my body under. Realizing the backpack weighed me down, I fought to remain above the rushing water. The rapids were getting rough, and then a wave pushed me under. I banged into a rock. Finally losing the backpack, I scrambled to breathe. Sucking in the air, some of the spray caught me by surprise, and I choked.

Once I broke the surface, I screeched, "Help. Help me." Water clogged my airway and both hiking boots turned into cement shoes. Fighting the currents, I saw white foam outlining a waterfall's edge, highlighting my impending doom.

The guys communicated back and forth, competing with the waterfall's roar. Then one of them yelled, "She's heading for the falls." Someone responded, but I couldn't tell who when a wave hit me. A small part of me found it comforting that they were trying to help. But the emotion faded when my muscles slowly knotted. The river sucked the warmth from my limbs, turning them into dead weight. I started to sink.

"Hang on. Ceanna, hang on," Jaci shouted.

I barely caught Kailee's commands to the guys. "Go that way. Meet her in the plunge pool below."

Tree roots brushed against exposed skin like fingers, then wrapped around my ankles. I gasped before something dragged me down. Kicking, a paralyzing sensation moved up both legs. Submerged in the inky darkness, internally, I shrieked, *'Let go,'* my lungs starving for air.

The resistance went slack, and the rapids propelled me toward the waterfall's overhang. Freefalling, I glimpsed two blurry forms moving toward the river's edge, not far from where I landed. When I broke the surface, I heard twin splashes as the confirmation of their breach sprayed across my face.

I assumed this was what it must feel like for a dead fish being flushed down a drain. Now, I was stuck in a maelstrom. Suddenly, a girl's face appeared with hollowed eye sockets and framed ebony flowing strands. When she reached for me, I heard, *'I'm coming.'*

I then lost consciousness.

Chapter: 5

I woke to bickering. Their noise grew to a buzzing irritant. The sound wedged next to the intense throbbing. If my head was hurting this bad, moving was going to be a task. Assuming I could.

Cracking one eye, I noticed figures were pacing and flailing. The light hurt but not as bad as I expected. Hesitantly, I opened the other eye, blinking several times to regain focus. Jaci's face came into view.

"Ceanna!" She exclaimed.

Everyone stopped moving to approach the bed. Their presence gave a whole new meaning to claustrophobia. The girls were interrogating me. Mathew knelt beside the bed, and I believed he was holding my hand. Trey had positioned himself at my feet. Another figure approached my cot. *'Seth.'*

He stood behind Mat and then tapped his shoulder. My hand was slightly cooler than Seth's as he slid his over mine. I tried to swallow, but my tongue acted like sandpaper. For as much water as I choked on, I found it ironic that water was the first thing I would ask for.

Not wanting to ask Seth, I reluctantly turned toward Trey and rasped, "Water."

Everyone fell silent to stare at my friend in the corner. Trey jolted for the ice chest. He flipped it open, and both hands plunged into the ice. His actions were so loud that they hurt.

Trey cracked the bottle cap and then handed it to Kailee's outstretched hand. Jaci sat by my hip, patting the other hand. My hand, under Seth's, was still cold.

Kailee asked Seth and Jaci to help me sit up. Moving hurt, but

Kay handed me the bottle when I finally was upright. I took a sip and choked. My body reacted to leftover reactions to drowning, I assumed. Seth patted my back, and Jaci took the bottle.

After the coughing fit, Kailee placed a hand on my shoulder. "Are you okay?"

I know people mean well when they ask you those questions, but it's normally asked in the worst times of your life. You're in the hospital, sick or broken, *'How are you feeling?'* You found out your dog died, *'Hun, are you okay?' 'Ceanna, you've almost fallen to your death and drowned. Are you all right?'* I knew she meant well but couldn't shake my ill-tempered mood. I was seriously tempted to state something extremely uncouth.

"I feel like a shaken cocktail," I murmured.

Seth slapped between the shoulder blades harder than I thought necessary, but it could have been bruised. "See, I told you she would come to."

"You both were worrying for nothing." It came off condescending.

Kailee cocked a hip and then added, "I believe she should see a doctor. The bump on the back of her head is huge."

I reached slowly to feel a welt the size of an egg, but when I glanced at my hand, there was no blood. My father would have said, *'No blood, no foul. You don't need a doctor right now.'* Thinking of him made me smirk. Unfocused, I wasn't paying attention to the people in the room.

Seth misunderstood my small reaction. "Hey, baby, you surprised to see your man? Wake'n you up like the princess you are."

My eyes pinched, and I answered, "Yeah, what a surprise." I pictured Mathew and Trey as Voodoo dolls, punching them repeatedly with pins. Mat raised his eyebrows and beamed. Trey knew I was livid.

Seth scooted closer. "Can we talk?"

Trey scowled and brushed back his short, auburn hair. Clenching and unclenching his fist in frustration, he huffed something inaudible, smacked the tent flap open, and left.

Puzzled, I squinted at Kailee to see the same bewilderment from her brother's sudden departure. Jaci pivoted between Seth and me, smiling. Kailee motioned for Mat to check on Trey. His shoulders slumped forward, but he slipped out. Whether he would find Trey and talk to him was another matter.

Head throbbing, I answered Seth. "Yeah, we'll talk. But I've had a crappy afternoon." I gingerly touched the knot again. Waving at Kailee, I asked, "Can I have some aspirin or ibuprofen?"

Frowning, she handed back the water bottle. "I think you need to see a doctor. You've got a bad gash on your back and side. They were bleeding pretty bad for a while, but the bruises on your legs are a deep bluish purple. I'm worried about the goose egg. You probably have a concussion." She removed my hand and parted the hair to inspect the spot. "It's not bleeding, but it looks nasty. I'll get the ibuprofen."

Affronted, I made a noise from the back of my throat.

"Listen." She flipped into mom mode as she handed over the pills. "People have died from less." She pointed at me. "Maybe I should call your mom?"

I jerked upright, regretting it. Being waterlogged was similar to motion sickness. A bout of nausea threatened, and I had to cover my mouth. Jaci hopped off the cot, and Seth drew back slowly, gauging if I would spew.

Speaking between laced fingers, I asked, "Can I have a few minutes alone?" I didn't remove my hands even though the wave of nausea passed. Instead, I begged Kay. "Please don't call. You'll freak them out for no reason."

She exhaled hard. "If you start convulsing or talking gibberish, you're going to the hospital." At my side, she added, "Here, let me help you lay down." Giving in, I let her push me back onto my pillow.

Breath held, I removed my fingers and noticed Seth was gone. I was torn right down the middle. Hate burned, but love for him froze me into a block of numbness. It left my heart's defrosted button broken.

Jaci frowned. A ping of shame triggered a few tears. I wanted to tell them why I broke it off with Seth but couldn't bring myself to do it. I was weak and mad for how long I stayed with him. There wasn't a good enough reason. In a way, remaining silent might give me time to prove to myself that I was strong enough to move on.

Jaci called out for Trey. Her silhouette faded to nothing as she walked away. With everyone leaving the tent, it felt less confined.

Alone with Kailee, she waved a hand toward a pile of wet clothes. "Your things are there. The outfit you were in was ruined, so I placed it there." She gestured next to the goodie box. "Call if you need anything, okay?"

"Sorry for ruining our nature walk. You know, by almost drowning." I said miserably.

Kay ignored me. "Mathew and Trey worked together to save you. Trey said you were caught on some roots, or something was swathed around your feet. Mat kept diving beneath you until he freed your boots. Trey held your head above the water, and they both swam you to the edge." Kailee's voice trembled as she relived it.

"I am sorry for overreacting," I whispered, genuinely meaning it.

She gave a small nod and left.

Finally, alone, I closed my eyes and counted. *'One, two, three, four...'*

Instantly, the little hairs on my body rose. Next to my ear, I heard an airy phrase: "I'm coming."

Hitching a breath, eyes wide. I brushed the hair from the left ear and scanned the tent. No one was in here but me.

The pile of soggy clothes was in the same spot. One of the hiking boots was on its side, and the other faced me. The laces were in a huge knot, but something was caught in the middle.

Slowly, I stood. A sharp pain stabbed my stomach. My ribs had to be bruised. Taking a deep breath confirmed it. The pain was agonizing. Wobbly, I made my way to the shoes.

Holding my side, I bent down to pick it up. Settling onto the cot, a spike of anxiety spurred me to move faster. The knot seemed to tighten while I tried to solve the puzzle. With a shallow breath to steady myself, I slowly dragged the lace through the knot. A small leather bag fell to the floor.

It had some weight to it as I jiggled it. Working the worn string that held it together, I paused. *'How old is this? Ewe, what if I'm holding something dead?'* It smelled rotten and musty. I held the bag away from me.

'Open it.' A flutter of air hit the side of my face. Hands moved swiftly to untie the pouch. I tipped the bag to shake the contents into my palm. In a rancid pile of debris, there was a glint of silver. I set the pouch down to remove the trapped object. I studied the silver chain and oval floral picture on the front of the locket.

There was a sting in the back of my eyes, and I started to sob. Clasping the trinket, I rocked to soothe the waves of emotion. *'You're so alone.'* The tears flowed, but my breathing slowed. I rationalized that this all stemmed from my brush with death.

Being overwhelmed by so many emotions drained me. *'I'm the only one who understands.'* A voice echoed inside me. Dropping the locket into the pouch, I instantly felt better. Wiping my cheeks and nose on the sleeve of my pajamas, I couldn't grasp these emotions. I wasn't a sobbing wreck five minutes ago. These feelings were different. I was petrified and full of fury.

Too tired to think, I slipped into the sleeping bag. Placing the pouch under my pillow, I repositioned myself as I spotted something unexplainable. There were wet footprints all over the ground. Two were side by side next to the cot facing away. My sleeping bag had an indentation as if someone was sitting next to me.

My voice shaking, I said, "You need to go." Tentatively, I reached for the spot beside me. The air was the same consistency as dry ice vapor. I withdrew from the space and then heard the cot creak. The footprints next to the bed instantaneously dried.

'Was I alone?'

Chapter: 6

Campfire smoke and hot dogs made their way into the tent knotting my stomach. I took some time to change and comb out the tangles. The night air had lost the day's warmth, causing my skin to react. I unzipped the sleeping bag to use it as a blanket.

Stepping from the tent I chuckled to myself at what lay before me. It revealed a complete picturesque of a camping supply commercial. The group was huddled next to the fire, having dinner. I gathered the open sleeping bag high enough so I wouldn't faceplant and advanced to join them. Flickering orange faces fell silent as they acknowledged my presence. Rising, Kay asked if I was feeling better.

Jaci handed her skewed hot dog to Mathew so she could open one of the blue folding chairs. My nerves frayed when she placed it by Seth. For some reason, he wasn't interacting with the group and seemed deep in thought. Acknowledging Jaci with a nod he clutched the arm and scooted it closer then gave me a wink. The twisting in my gut took on a different meaning. We were a good eight to ten feet from the group. It was obvious, that he wanted to talk, alone.

I watched Jaci move her chair closer to Trey, then snatched her skewer to finish cooking the hot dog while Mat turned a few sausage links above the flames. To the side of me, Kay held out an empty plate for me while I tucked the lower half of the blanket under the seat and sat down.

"Want a drink?"

"Something light, maybe. I'm a little nauseous," I said. Kailee went to the cooler and then came back with a Sprite.

She then nodded at Seth and me before heading back to the

group. Her attention returned to Mathew on the other side of the fire pit. She joined in the group's conversation as though she'd never left. None of them mentioned fishing me out of the river, and I was grateful.

Trey made a joke, and the four of them laughed. It made me glad to see Mat and Trey getting along. A sliver of contentment worked into my aching muscles as I watched them by the crackling fire. After taking a swallow of soda, I bent down to place it on the ground next to the chair.

Switching the plate, I pushed myself back onto the seat so I could use my legs as a table. Long fingers slithered across my left arm. Seth took his other hand and slipped it into mine. The smile was genuine, but his posture seemed guarded. The reflection of the fire danced across both pupils, adding heat to his gaze. My heart wanted to melt from the intensity, but my head told me to be reasonable.

"Ceanna," he spoke low enough for me to hear, "Did you sleep well?"

Lying, I said, "I did." Even though every time I tried to fall asleep, the female I saw in the river would find me. Then, right on cue, a sensation similar to frosty fingertips skittered down the side of my neck.

Seth turned his chair, invading my personal space. "I was wondering if I could stay with you tonight?"

His presence burned away the chill and left me with raw annoyance. Screwing on the fake familiar grin, I answered in the same hushed tone. "No."

Not expecting a negative answer, his grip became tighter. "I'm sure the girls won't mind sleeping in the other tent." He moved his hand from mine and tapped my chin. The other one remained possessively clamped around my arm.

Slightly turning to face him made it seem like we were having an intimate moment. Disappointment rained down on me. If loneliness could be displayed as a pictured emotion, it would be me right now. Our little altercation didn't seem to affect our friends or their conversation. They had no idea Seth was intimidating me.

Challenging, I asked, "And where do you think the girls will sleep?"

He glanced at them and then back to me. "Didn't you hear me before? I said they would sleep in the other tent. I'm sure the guys won't mind."

Fury spurred my reply, "What makes you think you can just show up and shift things to what you want?"

"We both want this." His lips twitched.

I hissed, "How do you know this is what I want?"

Seth's fingers dug in. "I understand. You were overreacting. And I'm willing to forgive you this time." He loosened his grip but only slightly. "Guilt makes us do regretful things at times." Seth patted me sympathetically.

"You forgive me?" I gushed out, "You gave me a black eye."

"I only slapped you. You're making my actions seem monstrous."

"You hit me. My face was bruised. I took two weeks off so I wouldn't have to pretend like everything's okay and lie for you." Clenching my teeth, I bit my tongue. Swallowing the blood, I heard the whisper of laughter.

"You could have worked. That was your decision not to. I didn't force you to stay home." Seth removed himself from the blame by making it my fault. He used that tactic when we fought, but I didn't expect him to do it now. *'He had hit me.'*

A female's voice provoked, *'What will you do about it?'*

I went to move when he latched onto my wrist tight enough to cut off the circulation.

The voice in my head boomed, *'Get away.'* Frightened, I dropped the plate. My free hand seized the top of his wrist. An airless "Let go" trickled out; I knew the voice was not mine but the foreign tongue didn't scare me. What terrified me was the controlled energy that empowered my actions as my nails began to draw blood.

He bent my hand and pulled me toward him. "I'm staying with you tonight." With our backs to the group, we probably appeared to be getting closer which was further from the truth. This lit my anger.

"I said, 'let go.'" Fingers wedged under him, I firmly wrenched his hand back, feeling the tendons protest.

Scowling, he grunted, "Let go."

My vision blurred like someone was using me to focus on Seth. Seeing double our hands, I tried to process what was happening. Switching into defense mode, I released him, and at the same time, something spoke through me. "Don't touch her." Both hands flew to my mouth. I could feel the blood draining from my face when I heard Trey and Mat approach us.

Trey addressed me first. "Is everything all right here?"

With a shudder, I closed my eyes and pressed against them. The coldness dissipated. Everything was clear except for the throbbing pressure at the base of my skull.

Seth pushed off the chair. "Yes, everything is fine." He turned to Mat and playfully punched his shoulder. "You have room for me in there? Ceanna is okay with me staying if it's all right with you all." Pouring his charm over everyone like kerosene made me fear that we'd blow up if one of them objected.

Kailee regarded the situation and I could tell she knew something was off, Redirecting the mood, she playfully looped an arm around Jaci and then helped me from the chair. "The more, the merrier, right?" She added.

"Come on, let's hit the sack. I want to head to the docks early to rent the boat." Mat said before ushering Seth away from us.

"I'll help with the trash." The need to keep moving jolted me into action.

"Trey, can you lock up the food." Kailee pushed him in the opposite direction from the guys.

"Um, Trey, do you need help?" Jaci picked up the bags of chips.

He wrapped the meat and said, "Sure, thanks, Jaci."

Kailee put both hands on her hips. "I'll put out the fire once I find the bucket of sand."

When we finished putting everything away, Jaci, Kailee, and I hit the bathroom before getting settled for bed. Right before entering the tent, Kailee held me back as Jaci went in.

"Ceanna, are you really okay with Seth staying here?"

Rubbing my arm, I shrugged. "Not really, but as long as he stays away from me, I will try to make the best of it."

"Ceanna, I'm sorry. Honestly, Jaci and I didn't know what Mat was doing. I'm sure he meant well."

My emotional dam broke, and all the ugly, negative comments flooded my mouth. I wanted to gag. Realistically, I knew Mat meant well, and it was my fault that none of them knew why we'd broken up. Not wanting to offend her, I didn't respond and stepped into the tent.

Stirring from the whispers in my dreams, I jolted awake to hear screams. Men and women were screaming at each other. Smoke filled the tent. I kicked the sleeping bag off and slipped on my sneakers.

Running out of the enclosed space amplified the exclamations and demands. Shielding my eyes from the popping and crackling, I pushed forward. Heat swamped me, and I gasped. The girls were ordering the guys where to put out the flames.

Their tent was on fire.

Swiftly, I moved to assist. "Jaci, where's the extinguishers?"

"We've used both of them," She bawled.

Trey bumped into me carrying a bucket of water. I spun to get out of his way. He splashed water along the side where the flames were the highest, then threw the empty bucket to Mathew. "Your turn!"

Mat took off toward the lake, running past us. Helpless, I became irked. I turned on a heel, went back inside the tent, collected two sleeping bags, and bolted back out. Getting Kailee's attention, I threw one at her. "Help me smother the flames," I shouted.

We began to smack the tent. I could feel sweat dripping down my face. I channeled my frustration and used it to beat the flames into submission.

Mathew came from behind us and heaved the water bucket directly above his head. He missed. The freezing liquid slammed into me in six different ways. It went up my nose and in my mouth, and I stood there choking. A bottom-out feeling pulled in my core as the strangest thing happened. The wail I released shocked my friends into statues. Heat coiled around my neck and lit my skin. It felt as though I was on fire and melting.

Trey wrapped his arms around my waist and then lifted me into a cradle hold. Shuffling my weight in his arms, he backed away from what was left of their tent. I clung to him until the sensation subsided, forcing a few more coughs to clear my airway. Peering through wet strands of hair, I scrutinized the damage to find that the flames had consumed most of the area except where I once stood.

"Please put me down."

Trey hesitated, holding me tighter against his chest until the whine of faint sirens grew louder. Shaking uncontrollably, I touched the areas where I was burned, discovering a hard lump under the nightshirt. Hoarse, I said, "Trey, you can put me down." Reluctantly, he slid me down his torso.

Turning away, I stuck my hand down the shirt and retrieved the locket. *'I was wearing the locket,'* I thought in shock. The locket I never remembered putting on. There was a faint pat of reassurance as I watched the firelight glitter off it. One thing was for certain: It was now mine.

Chapter 7

Once the flames were out, we all collapsed in the girls' tent. It was big enough to accommodate the six of us with room to spare. A few of us were restless, which made it hard to fall asleep. In the back of our minds, I'm sure we all wanted to know how the fire had started. I couldn't put my finger on it, especially since I had watched Kailee pour sand on the campfire until it was out. I would stand by that in court if they tried to accuse her.

Feeling I would have better luck waking Kailee, I nudged her first. She snorted and cracked one eye. "You poke me again, and I'll use your travel pillow to suffocate you." She rolled onto her side.

I huffed. "You could try."

Quickly, she moved and took her pillow to smack me.

"Well, I see the girls are up." I heard Trey state candidly. He wiggled out of his sleeping bag and started to roll it up. After tying the green roll, he stood, yawned, and then stretched. "Well, I want a shower before breakfast. Who needs a token?"

"Good, 'cause I'm starving." Mat muffled as he flopped around in his smoke-scented sleeping bag. "Hold on." He then followed Trey's routine from folding the bag to stretching.

Kailee used me to aid in propping herself up to see what Mat was doing. I wanted to know, too, but I was under her and couldn't move. She croaked a morning laugh. "What on earth are you doing?"

A zipper answered us, and we both started laughing. Jaci grumbled and stifled a yawn. "Next time we go camping, I'm getting my own tent." She pushed Kailee off me and then stated tersely, "Your morning breath woke me up."

Provoked, I sat to face her. "And you snore."

"I do not."

Everyone moaned and said in unison, "Yes, you do."

Peeved, she yanked back the top of her sleeping bag. Kicking her legs, she smacked into Seth. Without missing a beat, Seth swatted her foot away.

"Hey!" She recoiled to massage her foot.

Trey dropped his things and headed for Seth, but Mat intercepted by clutching his arm. "Man, what are you doing?"

Seth repositioned himself, unfazed by Trey's actions. Mat let go of Trey when he stopped advancing. My ex-boyfriend cocked his head and shot me a smirk.

'Why did Mat defend him?'

Trey collected his things and abruptly left.

Trey's actions spurred Kailee from her spot to follow her brother, hollering for him to come back. We last heard her say, "Wait for me."

Mat rolled his bed, tied it, and then stood to slip on his shoes. "Come on, Seth, we need to clean up."

"What is there to clean up? There's nothing but a charcoal mess."

Mathew paused and arched an eyebrow. "Seth, come on."

"I'm coming." Deliberately, he moved like a sun-drunk cat.

Mat frowned slightly.

I inspected Jaci's foot where Seth's slap had left a mark. After examining it, she shot an abominable expression at Seth. It would have made him spontaneously combust if we were in a supernatural movie. *'If only.'*

Jaci put her boots on and started to lace them. "Ceanna, I have to go to the bathroom." She raised both eyebrows. "You coming?"

Dropping my gaze, I shook my head no.

Unsure, she said, "Okay," then left with Mathew.

"Ceanna, I'm only going to ask you once: did you start the fire?" Seth loomed over me.

Slack-jawed from the accusation caused me to hold my breath. His smug expression meant my silence indicated guilt. He crawled out from under Kailee's extra blanket backward.

Appalled that he would even suggest I could do such a thing, I hiked the top cover higher and busied myself with more assumptions about last night. Trying very hard not to glance in his direction; I didn't want to give him the satisfaction that what he said had bothered me.

Kailee popped in and addressed Seth. "Are you still in here? The guys are waiting for you."

Standing in a t-shirt and underwear, he shot a bemused expression at her. Seth gave me a curt nod. "Yeah, I need to ask the guys something, anyway." Instead of dressing, he scooped up his jeans and shoes. He ducked under Kay's arm and left.

Kailee reached out to me. "What's wrong? Did he upset you? You're as white as a sheet."

"No, I'm perhaps a little weak from yesterday. I'm sure nothing a few cups of coffee couldn't fix."

She grinned with her hand resting on my shoulder. "Well, hurry and get dressed. Trey and I have a surprise for everyone."

"Kailee," I said, squinting at her, "the last time you said that we ended up here." Laying out my clothes, I hesitantly said, "I'm not sure I can take any more of you and Trey's surprises."

"No, I think you and Jaci will love this idea."

I gave her a skeptical glare.

Kailee beamed. "Okay, I'll tell you. Trey and I are going to see if we can salvage this weekend."

"And how are you going to do that," I asked.

"We are going to rent one of the lake cabins. Isn't it great?" Kay snickered.

"Yeah, great," I said sarcastically, adding, "I hoped we'd go home instead."

"You don't mean that," she said with a slight tinge of hurt.

"What about the fire last night? If we stay out here any longer, someone is going to get hurt or worse."

Kailee's brow creased. "Maybe I didn't put out the fire completely." I went to protest, but she stopped me. "I'm just glad

Trey and the guys got out okay."

I couldn't add to her guilt, so I gave in. "Okay, okay, let's see if a cabin is available. But Kailee, can we go home if there isn't one?"

"Yes, I promise. We'll pack up and head home if nothing is available. You'll see, everything will be fine." She left, shouting for everyone to start packing to leave.

I tugged my arms through the outer long-sleeve shirt and wiggled into some black jeans. When I finished dressing, I collected my things. I turned the sleeping bag upside down for a good shake to ensure there weren't any creepy crawlies hitching a ride. My flint stick made a thunk when it hit the ground, followed by several long strands of grass. Confused, I bent down to grasp the flint stick.

"How did that get in there?" I whispered. Dread crept along my skin as I remembered Kailee's last remark. I wasn't so convinced things would be fine.

Jaci popped in with both eyebrows raised in alarm.

Hiding the flint stick behind me, I said, "Jaci, what's wrong?"

"It's strange, but someone drew several X's in mud on the outside of our tent."

Yeah, everything's going to be, *'F. I. N. E.'*

I lost the chance to leave. Trey and Kailee rented a cabin on Skelton Lake. The little log cottage had a kitchen, one bathroom, a sitting room with a fireplace, and two bedrooms. The front faced the river, and a long boating dock was in the back. The guys talked about splitting the rental fees on a fishing boat. While they hashed out details, Jaci, Kailee, and I fixed brunch and chatted about going with them on the boat. Not to go fishing but to sunbathe.

After brunch, the guys took turns unloading the vehicles as we added our personal touches inside the cabin. Trey set up the grill on the back deck, and then the guys decided to head into town.

When they returned, Trey came bursting in to show Kailee his new hat with a smiling bass jumping out of the water and Mammoth Lakes scrawled across the bottom of the picture. Afterward, he told us we had thirty minutes to get dressed and change if we wanted to go out on the lake. Jaci shrieked and took off for our room. Kailee draped her arm across my shoulders for a quick half hug. "See, what could go wrong now?"

I bit my lower lip to keep myself from saying something that would wreck her mood. I thought about the movies when the disposable character said, *'What could go wrong?'* Right then was our moment.

About an hour later, we were in the middle of Skelton Lake. Mat and Seth were baiting their fishing hooks, and Trey was sitting in the middle of us talking to Jaci. Kailee and I were slicked with oil soaking in the sun. Uncomfortable in my old two-piece swimsuit, I kept fidgeting. Kailee told me not to sweat it and relax. I wanted to, but I sensed Seth's possessiveness every time I moved.

I kept the necklace on, even though I didn't want an oval tan mark three inches below my neckline. So, I tucked the locket behind my neck. It was odd that neither Kailee nor Jaci ever said anything about the locket, and for some reason, it hurt that they didn't inquire about my new trinket. I fiddled with the chain before readjusting the towel by my head. The sense of eyes on me was back.

Behind tinted glasses, I watched Seth. A few times, he stared at me from under his hat and after the fifth lingering glance, I decided sunbathing was not good for my nerves. I shucked into a mauve top and scooted closer to Trey who decided to fish and was baiting a fishing hook while he continued his conversation with Jaci.

Jaci sat cross-legged on the other side of Trey, scrunching her nose when Trey put the salmon eggs on the hook. I tilted forward and shot Jaci a wave. The breeze across the lake hit the sweat on the back of my neck, making my teeth chatter.

Trey noticed and reached for his hoodie. "You're shivering. Thought you might need it." His eyes crinkled, and a dimple appeared on the left side, right below his mouth. I shuddered again, but from what, I wasn't sure.

He misunderstood my movement and went to put it back, but I reached out and gently touched his fingers. "Thank you. Sorry, I spaced out for a bit." Then I tried to play off spacing out. "Laying down in the sun, I couldn't tell it was gusty."

He checked the sky, and I followed his gaze. Huge gray, puffy clouds were heading in our direction. "I guess we got out here just in time." Trey called out to Mat, "We might have to head back in about an hour."

A blast of air slammed into the starboard side and blew off Trey's new hat. Kay bolted to an upright position and then rolled into a crouch to keep her balance. Mat dropped his fishing pole and seized the chair. Seth cursed and swiveled in his chair so he could face away from the wind. Jaci latched onto Trey's arm to steady herself, and I followed her example by anchoring myself to him, too.

Another gust hit the boat. "Where did this come from?" Mathew hollered. His fishing pole dropped into the water. "Oh, crap," he swore.

We didn't move as the wind's mood went from friendly to a scorned lover. A few more gusts rocked us so hard that we fell on top of each other. Lying in the middle of the boat, we stayed there for several minutes, waiting for it to die down long enough to start the motor and head back. Waves tipped the boat on its side as if the lake was checking to see who was in it.

As fast as the storm hit, an eeriness followed. Mat had fallen across my legs. It startled me, and I watched his face contort in pain as he tried to right himself. Cradling his left arm, he winced.

Jaci crawled toward him, and I removed myself slowly, trying not to jostle him too much while asking, "Mat, where does it hurt?" I knew I was talking too loudly because the wind had caused a ringing in my ears. "Mat, do you think it's broken?"

His wince turned into a baffled expression. "Damn, it hurts, but I don't think it's broken. It feels like I jammed it when I fell."

Kailee pushed in between Jaci and me. "Do you need a doctor?"

I shook my head. *Why was she adamant about us getting*

medical treatment?' But I saw the misery in her eyes that matched the pain in his. He tried to give her a smolder-type grin to calm her uncertainties.

Trying to mask the pain, Mat said, "I'll be okay, Kailee, thanks."

And that's all it took. I call it the Nightingale syndrome. Mathew was seeing Kailee differently. She knelt and whispered something in his ear. His demeanor changed. I believed Kay told him her secret.

Trey and Seth untangled from each other. Seth scrambled to the steering wheel, and Trey headed toward the anchor to tug the chain free from the bottom of the lake. Seth turned the key, but nothing happened. He did it several more times, but the motor wouldn't spark to life.

I left Jaci and Kay tending to Mat; he was in good hands. Advancing to Trey, I asked, "Can I help?"

He shook his head. "Nope, I almost have it, but it won't matter if we can't start the boat." He shot back at Seth, "Try it again."

"Man, I've tried several times already. It's dead." He turned the key forcefully. Nothing. His irritation flickered across his face. I couldn't tell if it was because the boat wasn't cooperating or I was too close to Trey.

I stepped even closer to Kailee's brother to test him. Seth gritted his teeth. *'Yup, I was too close to Trey,'* but Seth didn't have the right to be angry. I'm not with him anymore; he had no say in how I interacted with others. Besides, Trey was one of my best friends.

Lightning flashed, adding a charge to my swelling foul mood. A pool of heat blossomed under the locket. There was an ache branching down to my fingers, making them cramp. It gained in strength until it was painful to move them. *'Maybe I scrapped my hands when I fell?'*

In the weather's newfound calm, the breeze stirred around me. It carried a high-pitched noise. I heard a pained scream off in the distance. Quickly, I glanced at Trey. He heard it, too, and stopped pulling on the rope.

I needed confirmation. "Did you hear that?"

It was loud and clear in the distance, but this time, it was multiple cries for help. Jaci and Kay gawked at me. Both of them were pale. Seth even stopped trying to start the boat to listen.

Panicked, I moved toward Seth. "We need to get the boat started. Someone needs our help." I frantically scanned the tree line. Cupping my hands around my mouth, I shouted, "We hear you." I began to pace from side to side. "Where are you?" Seth smacked my hands. I jerked from him as the cramping intensified.

"Knock it off. What are you going to do for them from here? If you haven't noticed, we're on a craft with a flooded motor in the middle of this godforsaken lake." He went back to the driver's seat and wretched the key.

Fingers throbbing, the urge to feel his pulse under each digit increased, but instead, I pushed him down into the chair next to me. Placing one hand on the steering wheel and the other on the key, I sobbed, "We're coming," and rotated the key. There was a loud crack of electricity from my fingers to the metal, and the boat roared to life. Disoriented, I let go of the wheel.

Seth shoved me to the side to position himself behind the wheel. Making a sharp turn, he steered us toward the cabin and pushed up on the throttle.

I stiffened. "What do you think you are doing?"

He looked back at Trey, then yelled over the boat slapping at the water, "I could ask you the same thing."

"You're heading the wrong way." I accused.

Black eyes squinted in judgment. "And Mathew's arm needs to be looked at." He glanced at the girls' tending to Mat.

I went to argue but lost my fervor when I heard Mathew's low groans and Kailee trying to console him.

The boat plowed across the waves. I turned in the direction where we heard the screaming. The swell of my aggravation drained into a pool of failure. I couldn't get to them and hoped whoever was out there would be okay. In my head, a familiar voice said, *I'll be with you soon.'*

The clouds dissipated, and the evening sun lit a path across the water to our cabin. Automatically, my hand wrapped around the locket. Watching my friends tend to Mat, I said into the wind. "I know."

Chapter: 8

When we reached the dock, everyone sprang into action. The girls and I gathered what we could and ran straight for the cabin to unlock the door. Seth and Trey helped Mat to his feet. Trey wedged his shoulder under Mat's good one, and they hobbled through the door. Seth followed, carrying Mathew's things.

"You're going to have to pay for the fishing pole, Mat," Seth said while tossing his things on the table.

In a stern rebuke, Kailee said, "Really, Seth?"

'Yes,' I thought. They were all starting to see his true colors. Even Mathew's uncomfortable expression soured at Seth's snide comment.

Trey passed Mat to Jaci and Kailee. The two had guided him to the couch, and without speaking, I left the scene and went into the kitchen to get Mat some water. When I came back, he was propped up in the chair with an extra loveseat cushion behind his back.

Giving him a concerned grimace, I handed him the glass. "Would you like some aspirin or something stronger? Oh geez, I just remembered I have a couple of eight hundred ibuprofens at the bottom of my travel bag." I smacked my forehead.

He took a sip. "The ibuprofens." Then handed the glass to Kailee.

"Hold on. I'll be right back," I said before padding toward the bedroom.

"Let's take a look." I heard Trey say as I shut the door.

Rummaging through my travel bag, I found the pill bottle and tossed it onto the bed. Retrieving the small suitcase, I plopped it next to my travel bag, making it bounce. Feeling the need to cover myself,

I took out a pair of light blue jeans, a white tank top, and a floppy, blue coyote sweatshirt. I didn't want to get the locket caught, so I slipped it under my shirt. For extra measure, I flipped the hood over my head. After putting on a clean pair of socks, I snatched the pill bottle and padded across the carpet to the hall.

In the hallway, there was harsh whispering. It was high and crisp, like a female's voice. Straining to hear, I started to think it was Jaci and Kailee, so I tentatively took a step in their direction. The pitch changed, and a third voice joined in.

Frozen in place, a static zap of air jolted me, forcing an exhale. My breath puffed out in a thin, misty cloud. The muscle in my chest thumped, once twice; I wasn't sure if I wanted to react in panic or see what was around the corner. Curiosity possessed me.

Clutching the bottle so it wouldn't rattle, I took a silent step forward. I noticed a trail of water, but it wasn't coming from the bathroom. My sock was now wet. The door was wide open, and the lights were off, but I didn't hear the water running.

Confused, I followed the small puddles down the hall. The trail led into the kitchen and then the living room, where it stopped, and so did the soft conversation.

"So, what's with all the secrecy?"

My friends gaped.

Jaci shrugged. "No one has said anything. Trey was talking to Mat, and Seth went to the kitchen with Kailee." Believing it might be Kailee whispering to Seth, I tossed Jaci the ibuprofen and turned on a heel. Before I entered the kitchen, I heard Kailee angrily whisper, "Stop it." Pain pierced my stomach, and I placed a hand on the doorjamb for some leverage.

Coming around the corner, I asked, "What's going on in here?"

Seth had Kailee pinned between him and the counter with one arm behind her back. I couldn't process the scene fast enough; I exploded in possessed rage. "Get off her." The need for vengeance pushed me to shove Seth away from her with such force that he lost his footing. The ache was back in my fingers, and the corners of my vision swallowed everything down to a pinpoint. I was going to blackout.

All the windows in the cabin cracked at once as if someone had swung a heavy object. Glass splintered and popped. We heard Jaci scream from the main room and the guy's holler.

Seth righted himself and ran into the other room. Kailee and I followed close behind. Trey tried to hold Jaci, and Mathew's face was ashen.

"What the He–" Seth's booming voice cut off when Jaci pointed and screeched.

Wet footprints were forming all around the room. *'Just like the ones in the tent,'* my brain concluded. Several were by each window and door. I went to calm Jaci down when I noticed both socks were soaked as a puddle formed underneath me.

The locket ignited, making me imagine my skin melting under it. Frantically, I yanked the sweatshirt over my head and threw it onto the floor. The heat traveled across my chest. Unable to move, I warbled, "Help me."

The lights popped, plunging us into darkness right after Jaci exclaimed that she didn't want to stay anymore. Moonlight filtered through the double glass doors, highlighting the fissures in the glass. Mesmerized, I tried to walk toward the doors. A girl with long dark hair stood outside them, pressing her hands on each window. Blood began to drip down the glass from her fingertips. She appeared to be intently saying something to me, but I couldn't hear her.

Kailee spun me around in the commotion and yelled for me to follow them. My friends ran for the front door. Trey helped Mat outside, and Seth held the screen so it wouldn't instantly close on the ones trying to escape.

I turned back to the double doors. She was gone, but her bloody handprints were there. Curious, I stepped forward and rested both hands where hers were, and then I lost consciousness.

Plummeting through empty space, I landed running. Barefoot and bleeding, my shoulder brushed against the bark of a tree, and I winced in pain. I could hear the blood pumping in my ears. Despite the moonless sky, I knew where I was going. The river seemed to be calling for me.

Insistent, muffled urging coaxed me on.

Tears marred my vision, but I could make out three lights forming next to me. The shadows from the lights sent a wave of fear crashing into me. Their outline was so murky that it wasn't easy to keep track of them skittering across the forest floor.

Above the rushing water nearby, I heard their movement, and it broke my stride. I stopped briefly to see who or what was chasing after me. With my heart racing, everything was painted in shades from a moonless night. I couldn't see more than two trees beyond my point.

"Get back here," echoed sharp enough to cut the trees.

The exhale made me choke. It was Seth. I knew I couldn't shout for help. He would then know where I was.

"Run," responded a female with vehemence.

Moving swiftly, I came upon the waterfall. A shadow passed me, and then another shoved me. I tripped, almost falling face-first into the frigid river. A third specter whispered, "Tainted." My foot lifted above the water. I stepped out. Freezing water flowed around each foot placement. I stood on top of the water.

The taller apparition materialized beside me, and my mouth unhinged, but nothing came out. The soft voice came back. "It's time; you must be cleansed; come." When the apparition reappeared, it took my elbow, leading us toward the rushing water.

Pain arched from the middle of my back as I took a second step. Something struck me. There was a chorus hissing all around. The locket burned, and the pain intensified as I forced back the tears.

A question of need skated over my skin. "You want the burning to stop?" I wanted to dive into the river, but the tall manifestation embraced me and said, "Come. Be one. I'll protect us."

"Ceanna, come back to me." A male's pleas bridged through to my subconscious; it wasn't Seth.

An inferno burned within me, and I reveled in it. My hair began to float. Another presence smothered me until I was numb.

Patiently, I watched for the predator, and our roles reversed. Seth was my prey, and his sin needed to be cleansed so we could be freed.

I found him crouched behind a fern. "Seth, what are you waiting for?" The voice from within taunted him. "Are you afraid? Come and get me if you can."

Seth turned red and swore. He leaped forward and ran toward me, us. Arms outstretched, I splayed my fingers and growled, "So, be it."

By the time he reached me, he was hip-deep in the river. The waters swelled around him. He went to take another step and went taut. Seth's eyes widened when it registered that he had been tricked and started sinking. Struggling against the current, six white hands emerged from the water, forcing him into the depths.

Sinking next to him, I realized the river was going to cleanse our sins. This is our fate. But two strong arms caught me.

Trey's tenderness soaked into my brain. "Ceanna, I'll protect you. Trust me."

Then someone lifted me from the water, and right before the scene disappeared, I saw a pair of dark green eyes.

Chapter: 9

My lids fluttered from the coolness of a cloth that was placed on my forehead. Someone sucked in a gasp. A hand squeezed mine.

"Ceanna, Honey, wake up." Kailee's voice was full of disquiet.

Moaning against my better judgment, it bounced within my skull. Nausea crested, but nothing traveled north of the equator. My throat was raw and made me hesitant to speak.

"Come on; don't subject me to Kailee's incessant fretting." Jaci tried to jest.

"Hey." Kailee removed her hand from mine, perhaps getting ready to smack Jaci.

I timidly touched the top of my head. "Was I struck by lightning?" The question came out gritty. Timidly, I moved my jaw back and forth. "What happened?"

"Nothing." A hard voice answered from the side.

"Nothing, my butt. You can play 'Let's Be Real,' but we all saw what happened." Jaci's voice held an edge. She wasn't going to take any crap from whoever was speaking. I hoped it wasn't Trey.

Exhaling, I forced myself to focus on everyone in the room. Mathew was in a sling and sitting in the armchair beside the cracked bedroom window. Odd scenes flashed from memory. The last one was two hand prints dripping blood. I rubbed my temples slowly. "What's going on?"

"You fainted." A flat male voice said.

I followed the sound from the comment and saw Seth standing in the far corner of the room; his arms crossed in front of his chest, his appearance slightly radiating hostility. There was judgment behind his glare, and I'd been found guilty of something. Again. He appeared unharmed, so the dream or nightmare of Seth being swallowed by the river was just that: a nightmare.

Jaci sat on the bed with too much eagerness. Annoyed, I wanted to push her off for rocking my brain but used a hand to stabilize myself instead. Her face took on a serious mien. "We decided things have gotten too weird, and we've started packing to go home. Personally, I don't care to stay here one more night." She paused to glance over her shoulder and then back to me. Leaning in, she spoke just above a whisper, "I don't think I can take one more day of them disputing. They can't seem to agree on anything."

"Plus, I think Mat needs medical help." Kailee smoothed the quilt down to give her hands something to do. "We'll leave tonight if you're capable." Worry creased her brow. "Do you feel okay to travel?"

Honestly, my insides were cooked. But going home was much better than dealing with Mat and Trey's disputes, Seth's aggressive posturing, and the unexplainable phenomena. *'Yes, going home got my vote.'*

"Yeah, I can make it. I would like to take a shower before we go," I said.

"Sure, it will be a while since the guys have to return the boat and equipment." Kailee picked up a bowl and the damp rag. "Let's pack up the kitchen, Jaci." She eyed me. "You sure you're strong enough to stand in the shower? My nerves can't handle you fainting again because if this has to do with the concussion then I won't be able to forgive myself."

A lighthearted laugh flitted from the back of my throat. "The world seems to be tilted on its axis, but I'll manage. Now scoot, all of you." I waved a hand at the open door.

As everyone filed out, I noticed Trey didn't move. Wondering why only spurred other emotions. None of which I needed to deal with at the moment. He hesitated, then gave Seth a glare before following the group out of the room.

Seth lingered. When the group was further down the hallway, he shut the door slowly and softly clicked the lock so as not to alert the others. Split in half, I wanted to yell for them to come back, but the fear of his unpredictability had me holding my breath.

My ex-boyfriend slowly turned. Vexed, he advanced to the bed in two steps. The locket zapped me, and I held up a hand defensively. He paused long enough to realize my hand cautioned him from touching me. He growled and seized it from the wrist. Gritting my teeth from the pain, he bent down until I felt his breath.

Lips next to my ear, he growled, "When did you and Trey hook up?"

Pain forgotten, I sat there in a stupor. *'What? Me and him, for real? Trey, one of my best friends? He was off his hinges. Besides, Kailee would kill me if she thought I had feelings for him.'* In my head, I panicked. *'Wait, what?'*

Sensing my attention elsewhere, Seth practically spat, "When?"

"Are you crazy? Trey and I have been friends for years. Now, let go of me." Bending my arm in the opposite direction, he let go. Breathing hard, I demanded, "Get out."

He stepped back with the audacity to appear hurt. "I understand we've had some problems, Ceanna, but we can work them out. I'm sure of it." He touched his arm where I had the night before. "You make me all crazy when you flirt and get friendly with other guys. Come on, give me another chance."

Frustrated, I tried to kick the covers off me, and then, like a snake, I slithered out from under them. I stood in front of Seth, dumbfounded at his one-hundred-and-eighty-degree reasoning. "Seth, let me clean up, and we'll talk when I'm ready." *'Next year to never,'* I thought.

He backed up. "Okay, sure. We'll talk. So, we're back together, right?"

Titling my head slightly, I said, "No, Seth, we're not back together, but I promise we'll talk soon." I massaged my wrist.

Seth unlocked the door and never looked back when he closed it.

Inching my way to the suitcase, I removed a set of fresh clothes. Placing them on the bed, I discovered a dark brown smudge by the footboard. Leaving my clothes, I ran a finger passed the mark. It was slimy. Rubbing the substance together between my thumb and forefinger, befuddled, I said, "Mud?"

Glancing at the partly opened closet, I couldn't shake the gnawing feeling of something attached to me.

Two childlike voices intertwined in a shared inaudible whisper, *'Hazel is coming.'*

I collected my things and left for the bathroom.

Chapter: 10

Shaking off the incident by using rationalization as my bare feet squeaked down the hallway. A male's low chuckle caused me to lift my head impulsively. Seth was leaning on the door. It seemed I couldn't get off this ride.

Playing dumb, I said, "Is there something wrong with the bathroom?"

Desire smoldered behind his eyes. Passion once dormant stirred when I remembered his attentive touch. But then, I recalled his Hyde-side and steeled myself.

Seth consciously sensed my newfound control. Using his athletic frame, he opened the door leisurely. "After you, my lady," he said while gesturing for me to pass.

Mentally, I chastised myself for being gullible. "Seth, I'm not sure what you want from me, but if it's what I think you're implying, you can forget it."

Starting for the door, he wrapped his arms around me and kissed me softly. I didn't return it. He pressed harder. Both my hands slapped against his chest, and I pushed. His tongue tried to gain access. I locked my jaw.

He ripped his mouth from mine, followed by the absence of his hands. Every muscle in my body tensed, awaiting the impact of his wrath. The chain around my neck hummed. There was a grunt. I cracked an eye. Beaded sweat collected on his forehead.

Something fractured from inside. I knew he tried to force himself on me, but Seth was in pain. I didn't want him to blame me. Awkwardly, I asked, "Seth, what's wrong?"

He pushed me out of his space and clenched his chest. "Stop

playing these pranks, Ceanna, or so help me." The threat made his face look like a tribal tiki mask.

As he took a step toward me, the sink and tub sputtered with gushing, steaming, muddy water. Startled, we jumped to the back wall. Across from us, the wall mirror was big enough to reflect both of us at the same time.

The stench of wet dirt and decay filled the small space. Condensation covered everything in a filmy haze. I watched my double disappear behind the mist. In the foggy mirror, I followed a trail to the spot between Seth and me and did a double-take. A distorted figure of a girl stood there. Pale, dripping wet long, ebony hair, eyes vacant and fixed on nothing, or possibly everything. Forest debris poked out from under her tangled locks. Dark green eyes leaked muddy tracks down her cheeks. Watching the figure in the mirror swamped me with a mixture of horror, sorrow, and awe.

Unexpectedly, tendons and muscles snapped and popped as her jaw made several bone-crunching cracks, disfiguring the lower part. Broken, it fell agape to her neck as muddy water poured from her mouth. The girl produced a blood-curdling screech at Seth. The shock made us turn away from the grotesque figure.

The air around us grew heavy with moisture, and then my skin burst into imaginary flames. The locket burned hot as though it was melting into my body. My hands flew to the spot, and I tried to yank it off. The chain tightened. The girl's figure flickered, followed by a static hissing when she tore her eyes from Seth to direct her hollow glower at me.

Phantom fingers traced letters across the fogged mirror. My eyes widened in horror when I read, "Hazel." Then the girl released an earsplitting shrill. The pitch cracked the mirror as though someone had smacked it with a bat. Glass webbed, stretching the length of it.

Muddy finger marks appeared instantly, raking down Seth's torso. White as a sheet, he seized his chest and swung his arm back. Jerking the door open, he fell into our frantic group, knocking everyone into the hallway.

Startled, the girls shrieked. Jaci managed to push Mat out of the way before Kay and Seth crashed into her. A tangle of bodies hit the floor. The only one missing from the group was Trey.

Mathew shouted, "What the hell?"

Seth untangled himself from Kailee. Sneering, he yelled, "You're dead."

With no time to process what he threatened, I used the balls of my feet to launch myself over the pile of humans. Panic fed my desire to run. I flew at the screen door, tearing right through it. I didn't stop. Seth could run, and I was no match for the length of his stride.

I only hit one stair before my other foot struck gravel. Minuscule rocks embedded into the soft flesh. I whimpered when the pain intensified as my other foot landed to support my weight.

Then, my nightmare blended with reality. Seth was after me, and I was heading for the woods. I was moving so fast; it was a miracle that I caught sight of Trey by the edge of the lake. Our connection seemed to be in slow motion as I ran for my life at full speed. This moment was out of place and I didn't recall it from the outlandish dream from the night before. I pleaded to the universe that Trey understood what was unfolding in front of him, and that this was an actual life-or-death situation.

A male's venomous voice said to come back.

'Right, as if,' I thought.

Another matched Seth's potency, but this voice was directed at my pursuer.

A moonless night had swallowed the forest. My feet were bare and bleeding but pressed on as I breached the forest line. Every beat from my chest moved me faster. Dread, panic, fear: these emotions were nothing compared to what I tried to process. Death was hunting me.

Unrelenting, she offered an angelic promise. "We are here to help you."

The clouds rolled in, threatening to storm. I allowed myself to be led blindly. The need to become cleansed made me want to scratch and claw at my skin. I had to get to the river and rid myself of what tainted me.

From my dream, I only remembered the black, misty outlines as they looped and whirled past me. But this time, a tall one stayed very close to me.

Over my panting, I heard the gurgling of the river beckon in the distance. Pausing to hold my side, I peered behind me briefly to see if Seth was on my tail. I forced my heart to slow to hear what was around me.

Seth snarled, "Get back here!"

I choked on fear, and if I raised my voice for help, he would know where I was. I found my mind wandering to Trey. *'Did he know where I was? Did any of them know?'*

Running past the ferns and several trees, I could feel the mist building in the air. The ground gave way under my movement. Parting the vegetation, I saw the waterfall. Shade inked from the treetops, creating a canopy, and placing negative images all around.

"Tainted." Something pushed the thought as if it was trying to remove it from me.

Lips trembling, I said into the air, "No."

Her voice raised in volume. "I am here, Ceanna; let me help you." I stumbled back. "Vengeance is mine, saith the Lord. This is our chance to move on." The tall spirit morphed into the girl from the bathroom, the one from my nightmare. Her dress was torn, muddy, and dripping. She took two steps to stand in front of me.

Barely audible, I said, "Hazel?"

Green eyes sparkled as she sneered wickedly.

Both my feet were stuck in the mud, I tried to move away from her, but one of the spirits swirled and zigzagged over the locket. Hazel reached for it. Her fingers passed through. "I've missed you both." There was heartache in her confession.

The second phantom enveloped me in darkness.

Hazel said, "Come."

I wasn't controlling myself when my right foot lifted to hover above the water. I stepped out. Freezing water flowed around my foot. My body took a few more steps until I stood on top of the rushing water.

The third presence loomed over me. My mouth was unhinged, but nothing came out. Its form morphed into Hazel. She floated next to me. "It's time; you must be cleansed; come." She faded into the tall silhouette, looping her arm around mine several times. She towed me across the water.

I then realized almost every action up until now had mirrored my nightmare. Maybe this was a warning or worse; a premonition.

Pain bowed from my toes to my skull, making me cry out. Hazel had taken both arms from behind. Hot sulfuric water dripped from the locket. It left welts down my chest and stomach. I screamed.

Hazel asked me the same question from the dream. "You want the burning to stop?" She pressed me from behind and offered a remedy. "If you'll accept me, I will protect you."

"Ceanna! Ceanna, where are you?" Trey! But I was too afraid to alert him. Choosing to remain silent ruptured my resolve. I needed him, no, I wanted him.

I knew what was coming next as the burning sensation consumed every one of my thoughts and dried the tear streaks along my cheeks. My locks of hair lifted from the breeze traveling over the flowing water. The river responded to the spectator's demands like it was alive. Hazel dug into my life force. She overpowered me until I was disoriented. Seeing double, I knew we shared the same body as she used me to scan the woods for Seth.

Crunching forest debris alerted us of his coming. He exploded from the ferns lining the edge of the river. He was a jerk, selfish, and abusive, but I didn't believe he deserved what Hazel had planned. I only wanted him to leave me alone.

She manipulated my voice, "Seth, what are you waiting for?" Hazel taunted him. "Are you afraid? Come and get me if you can."

He ran toward me, his hands outstretched. I extended an arm and splayed my fingers as the locket began to glow purple. We growled in unison, "So, be it."

Legs kicked back, arced splashes of water as he ran for us. Seth was almost hip-deep in the river when he caught on that he wasn't running through shallow water but…sinking.

A vortex current started to suck him in. Stretching for a low branch, he struggled to remain upright. I knew what was coming next. My lips stretched in an upward curve and almost reached my eyes. It hurt, but she laughed through me as several small, death-colored hands latched onto him. His eyes bulged as he frantically tried to remove the hands. Broken nails dug into his skin. Blood ran down his neck, arms, and shoulders. The hands were winning the struggle; he continued to sink.

Hazel wanted the river to cleanse our sins. Ours for not fighting to save ourselves and the ones that made Seth seem evil to her. I didn't want to believe this was our fate, and I fought to free myself from her connection.

Hazel stirred from inside me. "No, no, I miss feeling the river's embrace. I'm keeping you."

I plunged into my psyche and found a black mass sucking in my energy. It was her soul. So many negative emotions were emanating from the spot. Rage, sorrow, and worthlessness tainted her soul and probably the other two who were trapped with her.

An idea bubbled up, and I started to express kindness, joy, and self-worth. I thought of my friends and their loyalty, my parents and their self-sacrifice raising me. I thought of Trey. There was a seed of emotion growing for him. Wrapped up in the here and now, I wasn't moving forward. Trey was more than a friend. I showed her pictures of his kindness, devotion toward others, and the fear I saw in the brief moment we shared. He was fearful for my safety.

"Men are evil beings. Fuel their need, their desires, they then infect us with their tainted sins." Hazel projected her agony.

I saw…a monster. These men did unspeakable things. The robbers had hurt her in many ways, from murdering her family to spoiling her purity. She was so young when they took everything from her, including her life. I wanted to ease Hazel's torment and suffering from her curse. I wanted to ease her past and rock her in an embrace. *'What could I possibly say to make things right?'*

"Ceanna." There was a treble boom to my name.

I heard Seth shout for Trey. The spray from them splashing and thrashing hit me. Trey was trying to help him. The movement stopped, and an exchange of hopelessness and despair rang through the woods.

"It's too late for me, save Ceanna," Seth demanded.

'Save me? He's asking Trey to save me?'

Hazel screeched in disapproval.

Trey splashed toward me but barked at Seth. "I'll come back for you; hold on."

"Just save her."

I wanted to argue with Seth, but Trey's hands cupped under my arms. I fought against the touch, unsure if it was his hands, Seth's, or the ones I saw coming out of the water. I was sinking. My head slipped under the water when Trey lost his grip on me for a second. An arm wrapped around my neck to keep me above the fast-moving current. His fingers became tangled in the chain. The metal links pinched my skin as it snapped. I heard the locket plop into the river.

Hazel's wrath echoed until I couldn't hear her anymore.

Trey spoke earnestly. "Ceanna, trust me, I've got you."

As he lifted me out of the water, I stepped on the bank but my knees buckled from exhaustion. Bending to the side, I saw Seth's face sinking into the currents. From his trembling lips came, "Ceanna."

Phantom hands reached for him as the river laid claim to his life. Seth's panicked expression never left mine as I watched him disappear over the falls.

A single comment breached my soul. *'He is no longer tainted.'*

I couldn't help but wonder, *'Was the response from Hazel or the river?'*

Epilogue

TK nudged my cheek. I'd been home for a week, and he finally forgave me for sending him to the Kozy Kitty Kennel. I flopped to a fetal position as a chill settled on top of me. TK's gray fur stood on end as he hissed before running toward the living room.

It was going to take kitten steps. His mood had become unpredictable ever since I brought him home, but at least I could deal with the outbursts. After filling my parents in on what happened and about my grades, they were heading here to visit. Mom was like Thomas from the bible and needed the confirmation that I was okay.

My alarm went off, and I pressed the snooze button. *'What's nine more minutes, right?'* I hadn't been sleeping. The sleeping pills weren't working either. Every time I closed my eyes, I saw Hazel's.

Of course, after we explained what occurred to the state and forest officials, I wasn't about to disclose what I believed had happened. Trey wasn't talking either, which made me both somber and glad. In a small way, I wanted validation of what he remembered, but on the other hand, knowing for sure was overrated.

A muffled tune belted out, "A Pocket Full of Sunshine." I couldn't help but smile; it meant something different this time. Brushing the feeling aside, I figured it was likely Kailee; she never used her phone.

I flipped back the sheets and saw it peeking out from under the pillow. Swiping the bar, I muttered, "Hello, Kay. What the heck are you doing up at this hour?"

There was a pause.

"Hey, I'm kidding. What's up?"

"I wanted to know how you took your coffee?"

Startled as if he walked into my room, I blurted, "Hi, Trey."

"Is this okay? I didn't wake you, did I?"

"No, I've hit the snooze five times already." I leaned back into the pillows. "Did you say something about coffee?"

He cleared his throat. "Yeah. Do you want donuts or something else?"

"Donuts will work."

"Sprinkles?"

I laughed. "Chocolate sprinkles and a vanilla coffee, please."

"Okay, got it." This time, he hesitated. "I can't wait to see you."

Anticipation fluttered inside me, and I wanted to trap it in a jar.

"Hold on, talk to Kay for a minute."

There was the click of a car door opening and some mumbling between the two of them before the door slammed.

Kay cleared her throat next to the mic. "So, Trey received another phone call from the investigators working on Seth's case. He said they might call you again. Have you remembered anything from that night?"

I did, but nothing I wanted anyone else to know, besides, who would believe me. I puffed out, "No, it's all fuzzy. All I remember was Seth threatening me and then him chasing me into the trees."

'Had it only been eight days since I watched Seth disappear?'

I could tell she was messing with the car vents as her voice mixed with the wind. "They searched for him for two days. I think he's holding up in some cabin nursing his pride." She said candidly, "Who knows where he is?"

There was a pause between us, and then she said, "Oh, here comes Trey. We'll be there soon. Now, get up. I know you're in bed."

Stomach knotted, I asked quietly, "Kailee, I need to tell you something about Seth and me. Will you listen?" My voice trembling. I was going to tell her everything. My soul couldn't take keeping it in any longer.

"Anytime, you know I'm here for you." There was a mix of compassion and reassurance in her statement.

"Thanks, I appreciate it. I'll see you soon." Feeling coy, I added, "Kay, can you tell Trey, I can't wait to see him too."

"Sure thing," Kailee giggled before she hung up.

I dropped the phone next to me. My body shivered from another arctic spell. I snatched the phone once more and clicked on a picture of Seth and me. Kailee's question loomed like a presence in the room. *'Who knows where he is?'* The oval burn mark in the middle of my chest was lukewarm. I laid my other hand on it.

Saltwater rimmed my eyes as I whispered…

"I'm sure Hazel knows."

Clipped Wings
By Kathy-Lynn Cross
An angel made
a choice.
A demon changed
his destiny.
Did exercising
free will
doom their future
or alter
their destiny?

Copyright

Clipped Wings

Clipped Wings

Skipping through the graveyard chasing fireflies made me giddy. I adored this time of day when twilight becomes magical and mysterious. Jumping over a mound of fresh dirt, I feather-landed on top of a brand-new upright tombstone. Stretching my iridescent wings behind me for balance, they caught the moonlight, creating rainbow specks across the ground.

I leaned over until my long silver locks barely touched the dirt. Reading the name upside down, I tried phonetically curling my tongue around each syllable. DROFKCERB NIKLIVED. After a few bell-chimed snickers, I slipped off the stone to pay my respects to, Mr. Devilkin Breckford.

In a crouch, I touched each engraved letter. "Devilkin? How strange. Who would name their child, Little Devil?"

Frost rapidly formed under my feet. Ash and charred vegetation penetrated my nose. I sneezed. Once my eyes opened, I was face-to-face with a cloaked man kneeling next to me. His gaze held the heat of hell. Expression hardened, he said, "My father, I would assume."

"Ahh!"

Caught off guard, I went for the dagger in my belt as both feet failed to keep me steady. "Who are–" Dragging my right wing, I backpedaled and stepped on a few long feathers. The pain was similar to ripping out a handful of hair. I winced and involuntarily blurted, "Ouch." My right ankle buckled. "Oh no!" Taking gravity for granted, I overcorrected by kicking out, which caused my left wing to smack the back of my head. Silver locks fell in front of my face blocking the figure squatting by the graveside as I landed on my butt with a loud "Ugh!"

In a thick accent, the male retorted, "That was entertaining. I've knocked plenty of women on their asses but never an angel's. If I had my cell, this moment would be worth preserving on the internet." His chortling lit a fire under my skin.

Irritation was very un-angel-like, so instead, I used embarrassment as a balm to soothe my wounded pride. Swallowing a few selected sinful cuss words, I inhaled nice and slow to keep them from escaping and then parted my hair to take into account what happened. In the four hundred and ninety-nine years I've patrolled this graveyard, I never had such an encounter. He caught me by surprise.

Blinking twice, I rose cautiously, dusting off the backside of my plain grey robe. "And you would be?"

In an instant, his attitude shifted. Rolling both shoulders in discomfort, the amused chuckle soon died. The man ducked his head in a guarded manner.

No sense in wasting the opportunity. I assessed the residue on his soul's aura, then gasped. Jaw agape, I stared dumbfounded at the presence in front of me. No aura–and no aura meant no soul. My analysis concerned me since all creatures, whether living, existing, or dead, carried a mixture of aura and soul. Even the evil little buggers I kept at bay, or sent back to Hades, had remnants of what they once were running through their aura. *'What are you?'* My lip curved in a disgusted sneer.

The cloaked figure must have sensed the spell. Brows furrowed, he straightened with a solemn air encompassing his space. Stoic, he pointed to the gravestone and then to his chest.

Understanding, I nodded while fixing my hair, then reached behind me for the wing I stepped on to examine the damage. The tip was sore, and I noticed four marred feathers on the ground. *'Well, that was unfortunate.'* I grimaced, bending to retrieve what was mine.

Ignoring Mr. Breckford, I began to shake the dirt from each feather when he abruptly said, "Well." Then clapped his hands together so loud it sent a small flock of Nightingales, roosting on a nearby crypt, into the night. "I believe we've gotten off on the wrong foot." With a hand extended, he jested, "At least one of us has."

This time, I bit my tongue and shook a fist full of feathers. I scoffed, *'He wanted to greet me properly.'* Then I remembered the bigger problem. This was going to be a long night if I couldn't fulfill my duties and then shoo-shoo him into the next plain. But not being able to read Devilkin's past would be problematic. *'How would I know what sins he must repent before I allowed him passage into the Light?'*

Lips puckered as if he'd swallowed slugs. "What makes you think I want to go there?"

'The audacity! He read my mind!'

Marching toward him, I threatened, "Stay out of my head," as four fingers grazed down the dagger's hilt for reassurance it was there. I jerked the robe open to feverishly stuff my broken feathers into an inner pocket. Next, I squared my shoulders and demanded, "What are you? I know, you know, I scanned your aura. What happened to it, to your soul?"

Devilkin's stiff form reminded me of a cemetery statue. But, before I finished the last question, he took a side-step back. Then I thought, it might be the finger in his face. Which, I didn't realize, was about two inches from skewering his nose. On impulse, I extended my wings to appear taller than my petite five-foot-four stature.

Hands raised in surrender, he said, "Down kitty, retract your claws, I was only playing."

I gave him one of my prejudgment smiles, showing hints of teeth. "I'll back down when you start answering questions. Let me refresh your memory. How did you die?"

Face blank, his dirt-caked boots stumbled back two feet. "Die?" He examined the mound of overturned dirt. Astonishment washed over his features before exclaiming, "I'll be damned; he wasn't joking. The bastard killed me." Devilkin regarded his attire, then gawked at me with a bemused expression. Right then, as if someone on a movie set said, "cut," and smacked a clapperboard, he broke character. "And you're an angel, right?" He shifted his stance and then lunged for me.

I yelped before grabbing the dagger. The unsheathed bone blade hummed with Light energy. Devilkin stopped a foot away before the tip almost pierced in between his rib cage. I arched an eyebrow. "You were saying?"

Masked behind a slow blink, Devilkin sighed and took a moment to collect his thoughts. "Okay, okay, this reality just sunk in." Two sunlit orbs scanned the trees and across rows of tombstones. "I'm not supposed to be here."

Removing myself from his space while still holding the dagger, I mocked, "Like I haven't heard that line in the last five hundred years."

Agitated, he clenched and unclenched both fists. "No, really, I'm not supposed to be here. I can't die, you see."

I took a breath to retort, but he squashed my words. "I'm a Kull and, therefore, can't die."

Smugly, I quipped. "Well, I'm a Judge, and I can't either."

Then it dawned on me what he was. In the ranks of demons, Kulls were almost the head of the food chain. But my main concern was, why didn't he have an aura or even a thread of soul?

Stunned, Devilkin Breckford once again scrutinized his surroundings.

Off in the distance, a church bell pealed, and at the same moment, Devilkin and I came to a realization.

In unison, we spoke over each other…

Devilkin declared, "You can't judge me."

My words rushed out, "I can't judge you."

Taken aback by my admission, his eyes brightened. "You can only see the souls you judge, right?"

Wary, I nodded. "Yes, I pass judgment on those who stand before me."

"But you just said you can't with me. Why?"

'Did he not know? Didn't he feel different? How would he react if I told him he had nothing there for me to judge?'

Several answers danced around his one question. Irritated, I repeated, "How did you die? I need to know. The situation might shed some light on your past, and we can piece together what happened to you."

Devilkin inched closer. "If you are the judge of the damned, wouldn't you know how the soul expired?"

Drat, that didn't work. Nervous, I curled in one of my wings and stroked the feathers. Feigning indifference, I answered, "In most cases, yes. But, in yours…" I dropped my hands in frustration. "Mr. Breckford–"

"Devin," he clipped. "I expect we'll be in each other's company for a while, so you can call me Devin. I never cared for my real name anyway." The sharp intensity in his glare diminished, replaced by a friendlier warmth.

"Okay, Devin," I amended. "You don't have an aura to read or even the slightest hint of soul residue. Your past is a blank slate, and I can't judge your life without it." I was wringing my fingers so hard the skin had become purple. Then I gestured before interrupting my explanation, "Wait. I retract what I said. For now, I will not judge you. Not until we can sort out your past. Then, once I've properly judged you, I'll see you on your way." Hardening my gaze, I added, "Even if it's in the Light's direction."

One crystal clear note resounded throughout the graveyard. We both faced the direction as the volume magnified, filling me with a sense of inner peace. "It's time for me to work. I will leave you now." Something tickled as it trailed down my leg. I swatted at the spot but didn't stop walking.

"Wait," he cried out. "You dropped…" the rich tone of his voice faltered. Then, as if he remembered the situation, there was a shout, "What about me?"

Self-righteous satisfaction fueled my pace, and it never wavered.

"We're not done here. I need to go back, and you're the only one that can reverse my fate." When I didn't respond, he shouted, "What's your name?"

The question had an air of defeat to it and stopped me in my tracks. I took a few seconds to contemplate whether it was proper to divulge my past position within the universe or allow him to believe I was an Angel of Judgment. No one ever asked for my name. Most of the time, the souls referred to me as Angel, or when the soul realized they were dead, there were a plethora of descriptive names not worth recalling.

Two wing flaps pushed me into the night sky. Mimicking the pose of a fallen angel, I extended my wing span as moonlight filtered through them, creating a soft haze. "I am Raziel, Infinity's Demon Slayer. I protect what is pure and slay all that is evil."

Devilkin was dead, this I was most sure of, but I found it somewhat amusing that he'd become a bit paler.

Chapter Two

Zig-zagging around each plot, careful not to step on or drag my wings over the flat headstones as I headed for the soul on the other side of the cemetery. The chime we heard was from the ward placed around the circumference of my domain. It also worked as a beacon, lightly coating the repentant sinner in energy so I knew exactly where to find them.

Dry leaves crunched under aggravated footfalls; there was a muffled trip, then a thud. When I heard the demon complain about the death shroud covering him, I came to the conclusion the cloak was to blame. It somewhat pleased me karma was still working, as I remembered landing on my backside.

"Serves you right," I mumbled.

A huff came from the darkness as he tried to match my pace. "If you have something to say, say it. Don't be a coward." Another harsh cuss word echoed through the trees.

"Excuse me, I'm not a coward. I'm an angel. The comment was more for my benefit than yours." I used a bit of levitation magic to do an about-face in midair before landing on the pebbled path before him. "Besides, you've already proven that you can read my thoughts. One would assume you knew what I was thinking before my tongue linked the words together." Lowering my wings so they wouldn't scrape under the branches, I proceeded to my next task.

He was fighting to match my stride without stepping on the hem. There was a heat signature next to me. The sign of a presence. Tucking my left wing underneath the right one, I glanced in the direction as his shadow came into view. No aura, no soul, but human in form and a thread of presence. It was baffling.

I couldn't contain the exasperation.

"Frustrated?"

"Yes," I admitted.

"Am I too complex for you?" He taunted.

Exhaling, "You are an enigma."

A dirty boot kicked a stone out of the way. "So, if you won't change my fate and I can't be judged, I guess that means you have a new sidekick."

"What?"

"This is my new future. I'm stuck here." His canter slowed. "I can't go haunt anyone else, right? So, you'll have to show me the ropes," he scanned over the graves, "Who's your next victim?"

Doing an impression of a clogged sprinkler, I sputtered, "You can't help. You're not a Judge. A demon can't do an angel's job." My wings jutted out, causing him to stagger off the path. "And the souls I judge are not my victims. It's not as though I snuffed out their existence; they have a choice, you know."

He made a back-throat rebuke.

I opened my wings with enough velocity to make the air crack.

He kept about a five-foot radius from me, mainly from my wingspan. Strolling along the grass, he kept his distance while avoiding the above-ground walkway lights. The solar bulbs were dimming, but between the patches of moonlight and illuminating ability, I could see a fair distance along the path.

"Devilkin, all creatures have free will and can decide to repent if they want to. Remember, I defend what is pure. Truth and repentance can cleanse the soul." I wrapped my hands behind me and laced my fingers together. "I cannot change the law; I can only uphold it." Even though it was the truth, declaring it made me seem powerless and dejected. Being a Judge was an honor, but I missed soaring through the clouds or racing against a comet. No, this was wrong of me; I was serving out my penance until deemed worthy to return.

"So, you do not enjoy what you do?"

My head whipped in his direction. "You were in my head again?" Instinctively, my right hand fumbled for my dagger.

"Calm down. No, I wasn't. Anyone with eyes can see it on your face. You are a troubled angel. But why–"

"It's none of your business." Anger fueled my words, and I waited for him to catch on fire.

Distracted, the night breeze lifted my hair, cooling my mood and drawing my attention upward. The wind filtered through the high canopy, causing the leaves to flap. It resembled a cloud of bats searching for their next meal.

Footsteps slowed to a stop. His expression closed off, and in an act of frustration, he rubbed his temples. I found the hush growing between us disheartening.

'If he kept trying to read my thoughts, would I be able to sentence him properly?' It bugged me this demon could penetrate my mind. I also found it irritatingly unfair, being a Judge and all. *'Shouldn't it be the other way around?'* I used to be a demon slayer. That phrase got caught in my web of thought more than I was used to.

"I rarely ever do this, so listen well." He stepped back onto the path in front of me. The puckered expression returned as the demon said, "I'm sorry."

Slightly irritated, I countered, "An apology only works when you explain what you are remorseful about. Sorry on its own is an emotional Band-Aid to make you feel better or justified for doing whatever you got caught for."

"It's a demon thing. Most can't control their talents."

"Talents?"

"Transcribing electrical pulses, from thoughts to words to sentences." He coaxed.

I waited.

"What you keep accusing me of."

Interlocking my arms, I groaned. "Devin, I have a soul waiting on me. Can you stumble on your lame attempt of an apology while we walk there?" Using a heel-to-toe motion, I rocked forward.

"I'm sorry for invading your mind." The words were tight after he choked out the sorry part, but he went on to add, "While we work together, I will try to refrain and respect your privacy."

Amused, I put on my best-stunned visage. "Devilkin, you get a gold star. Was that your first apology?"

"If you tact on it being sincere, then yes, it was." Eyebrows angled in annoyance. "And stop using my real name."

Another chime rang throughout the graveyard. Exasperated, I exclaimed, "Great, now I have two waiting on me." The robe opened slightly. Shocked to see him focused on the open slit. In short jerky moments, I retied the robe but kept talking to recapture his attention where it needed to be. "Look, we will work together on finding out why you are here, but that's all. My duties are mine alone."

"One is a lonely number."

I gave him a sidelong glance. "Cute, but not convincing. As long as you stay out of my head, you can come. But don't interfere, especially when I sentence a soul. Understand?"

He acted as though what I said required some thought as he scratched his chin. "What about…"

"I am the Judge, the jury, and the prosecutor. You are the silent court recorder–keyword, silent. If you can't agree to that, I will drop you into the grave I found you at, head first."

He chuckled. "Most partnerships have a probation period."

"I have a feeling this is going to be a very short one." I jumped onto the base of a stone replica of what the humans assumed passed for an angel. I didn't want to ask for help, so I slid my hand into the outstretched marble to maintain my balance. Perusing the area, I saw a wispy form take shape. Opening both wings to cushion my landing, I turned to my temporary, demonic assistant. "Let's go to work." As soon as those words slipped from my mouth, I knew there was no turning back.

Chapter Three

The image of a human girl, about fifteen, sat cross-legged by a vase of dried sunflowers and baby's breath. She fingered the ratty teal bow on a waterlogged stuffed horse. It was beginning to show signs of weather wear and stuffing rot. As I approached, she kept her focus on the toy she tried to move.

Frustrated, she swung, knocking the horse and the vase of flowers over. Both hands flew to her face. "Why?" She shrieked, "Why–why–why? I don't understand this dead thing."

I knelt next to her. "You won't be here long enough to worry about it."

Tears glistened along the rims of her eyes, but I knew they were only her projecting an emotion and would never fall. Still, her soul would recall the physical action of crying. Watching her compelled me to drape my arm across her shoulders in a side hug.

"Angel, can't I stay?" The spirit whispered, "They need me here. Why did I die so soon? My family and my little sister, Tessy, they're hurting."

If I was allowed to express what I disliked about being a Judge, it would be right now. To be tethered between life and death was the worst part of the trial. Depending on how long their penitence stretched, most watched the living learn to cope, accept, and eventually move on. Leaving the dead to become disconnected bystanders. By then, the pain would shift from helplessness to hopelessness, and more often than not, the soul was ready to leave.

"Nadine, deep down, you know you can't stay. Losing someone is part of the chain. There is a special task set aside for you if you're interested."

Using the back of her hand to rub away the phantom tears displayed her fear and sorrow. "I knew Rapunzel was a flaky horse, but she seemed so accepting when I strapped my saddle on her. She blew her air out and everything. I did what I was taught. Why did she buck me off? Why? I loved her."

Patting down her wavy curls, I cupped my wings around us. "She knew you loved her, but I'll share a secret."

She sniffed, ignoring me, and trying to poke the toy again. "What's the secret?"

"Do you remember what happened before you died?" I had an inkling she wouldn't since I'd tried to judge her for almost six months. "It was hot that day, and you decided to take a lower trail by the river."

"Dad told me not to because it was dangerous. He never explained the reason, only said not to."

It never changes, the defiance of a teenager. Even young angels went through it, believing they knew what was best. A cough came from the shadows, and it made Nadine lean forward. "Is someone there?"

The demon inched out from under the shade, taking on an appearance that stopped my heart. The cloak was gone; his eyes weren't gold but dark as a moonless night. He was pressed and ready to ride...a horse? Dark leather riding boots tromped over to us as he questioned Nadine.

"When did you start to ride?" His silky voice hit every note of sincerity.

Within a moment of a blink, I no longer existed. The teenager twisted out from our space to stand, never breaking visual contact. "We've always had horses. My mom rode with me when I was little. They started me off Western when I was six and tried to switch me to English at age ten. Barrel racing is what I loved most." There was an excited edge in her voice that hadn't been there before.

Bright white teeth appeared through a hardened grin. "Didn't you want to prove to your father the horse would obey you? I mean, look at how many years you practiced with trainers. It was time for him to stop treating you as a child. Right? You knew what was best." He outstretched his hands as the spirit took a hesitant step forward.

Curious and somewhat perplexed about what he was doing, I used her tombstone to help me stand. Extending both wings, I flapped once to get his attention. It didn't work. His focus on Nadine intensified. This worried me.

Quietly walking on my toes, a few steps in their direction, something blocked me, or more like, I banged into a wall. Devin's image faltered, becoming a hazy black, causing silver streaks to swirl over the energy dome. Intense gold spheres blinked at me as if I'd snapped my fingers and broke some type of trance. Turning his focus back on her, the riding clothes reappeared. It was an Allure enchantment.

Fury tore my throat. I was going to stab him twice and bury the foul creature in a bottomless pit. Extracting my blade while simultaneously screaming a counter invocation. The blade pierced his set circle. It shattered, intensifying the sound of glass imploding. Rage aided my velocity, and before one could blink, I pinned the demon against a nearby tree. The dagger's blade rested under his chin by the time the last tinkling of his spell hit the ground.

Righteousness fueled my aura to a blinding white. Devilkin tried to turn away, but the cutting edge dug in as he writhed. Inky, blue liquid ran down his neck and burned my fingers. Demon's blood. The smell made me bristle as I remembered the scythe and sword I wielded to kill his kind. *'Why was I trusting him?'* He was the enemy I fought to protect the innocent.

A thought wormed its way into my head. Devin's presence was heady. "Raziel, wait! I don't know what's going on. Why are you trying to judge me?"

Gritting my jaw, I forced him out of my mind. "You were using Allure on this soul, trying to glamour her. Why?" I wasn't about to remove myself from him until he explained.

Craning his neck made the cut deeper. Peering over my wing, he tried to focus on Nadine. "Who? I was doing what?" He seemed confused.

"Don't take me for a fool." That statement was already too late. I was a fool for even allowing him to roam. Exceptions could always be made; hence, free will. I could judge him based on this incident and be done.

"No," he bellowed and grabbed my arm.

My voice became ethereal. "Devilkin Breckford, why were you using your powers on her?"

"Really, I don't know." His form trembled while licking his lips. "I'm thirsty. I'm so thirsty."

"You are dead!" My exclamation echoed several times before dying out. The rustle from the tree leaves, and Nadine's quiet sobs filled the eerie silence.

A hiss from the demon made me lean in, and I lowered my voice. "You are dead. You don't eat–don't sleep–don't breathe–you are a projection of what you once were. A spirit." I eased up on him but didn't remove my blade to keep his attention. "I told you not to interfere; why did you?"

The demon strained to shake his head. "There's a need. I need her. I don't know why, but I need her." Desperation laced each word.

Realization was a hard slap as I began to connect the dots. He had no aura, no soul, and Nadine's, in a way, enticed him to react from need. The probability of this demon telling the truth disappointed me some. But, *'Would it be right to put him out of his misery?'*

"Please, Raziel, I need her."

Rearing up, I withdrew my blade and then struck him so hard his spirit form crashed into the adjacent crypt two lots over. Comprehending our situation followed a pent-up sigh. Nadine was in full meltdown from seeing her docile angel turn into an avenging otherworldly creature.

Applying a little persuasion, I tugged on her arm to follow. The next task was to retrieve my rabid pet before he found another soul to covet. It was another puzzle piece to his problem–I mean, our problem. Nadine's whimper shifted my priorities. First, I must sentence her, retrieve Devin, and locate the other soul.

Another chime resonated, and my wings drooped. This was going to be a long, long night.

Chapter Four

I was miffed. Six months, trying to coax the girl to remember, and the demon jogs her memory in five minutes. After sentencing Nadine for the guilt she carried about disobeying her father, she repented, and I declared her sin nullified. Producing one of my feathers from the inner pocket and handing it to her. It granted those worthy passage into the Light's ever-after. Once she disappeared into the sliver of holy shimmer, there was a longing to escort her there. *'Oh, to have a glimpse of home.'* But a certain creature needed my immediate attention, and I had to find him.

"Clip my wings," I mumbled in aggravation while scrutinizing the figure staggering in between plots of overturned earth.

Devin kept tripping on the shroud while cussing loud enough to wake the dead. I scanned the grounds to make sure we were alone. My attention averted for mere seconds; there was an "oof" and an "ugh" before panning back in time to see his feet fighting to regain traction on the loose earth. The demon's form upends, arms and legs askew as he tumbled into an open grave.

I facepalmed and muttered, "Saints have mercy on me. Please." Devin was walking around the cemetery half punch-drunk. *'Did I smack the sense out of him?'* Answering my question, I frowned. *'No,'* I reassured myself; the hit was to knock the sense back into him.

Gliding to the open grave, I peeked over the edge. "Hello, down there. Need a hand?" I was met with silence. Cupping my hands around my mouth, I complained, "I know you're down there, little devil. I'm offering to help; do you want it or not?"

An airy cough foretold Devilkin was clearing his lungs. *'You're not breathing,'* I thought sarcastically.

He matched my sarcasm. "No, I'm checking to see if this grave is deep enough for the next poor soul." Another cough followed, but louder. "Yup, seems roomy enough."

"Fine, you want to hang out down there, then consider this spot your time-out. Nadine has been sentenced, and I have two more souls to judge, so I'll be on my way." From a tip-toed stance, I jumped over the opening, making sure I flapped a little loose earth to rain down on him.

"Angel, did you just flash me?" A teasing purr rose from the darkness.

"Rude." I kicked a clump of dirt, but it didn't give as easily. The *ka-thwack* it made on contact confirmed it was a rock. The entity's string of profanity made me giggle. "It's called Karma, demon, roll with it."

The note I heard after Nadine's unstable soul began to ring again. The spirits were restless this evening. Exasperated, I stomped toward the sound. Turning onto the path, there he stood, wearing a fierce expression. The scent of wet earth and Bermuda grass hit me. I sniffed. Maybe a hint of chemicals. *'Weed killer? Would it work on him?'*

Unfazed by his sudden appearance, I sauntered around the cloaked figure. His throat clearing led me to believe the demon was insulted by my reaction. As I finished a sigh, the heat of his presence was back.

Facing forward, I affirmed, "You're not coming."

"Why not?"

In mid-glide, I jolted to a halt and hovered. "Are you serious? 'Why not'? Well, for starters, I can't trust you."

Indignant, he reiterated, "Why not?"

It was as though I was talking to a child and took a different route. Leaning in, I spoke slowly. "Devin, I know why you went for Nadine."

He opened his mouth but clamped my hand over it.

"Look, you have no soul and no aura. Your essence craves it, and you need something for me to judge you; I get it. But we need to find out why you showed up here in the first place and then go from there. The dead have something you crave, but as long as I'm protecting them, you can't steal what isn't yours." I removed my hand.

Tenderly, rubbing the area I smacked, he winced. "I was trying to take her soul?"

It confounded me he didn't recall his actions. "I believe so, yes. So, let me do my job and send these two souls into the Light, and then we'll tackle your problem." The same hand I used to cover his mouth I now placed on his shoulder for reassurance. "Demon, you need to be patient. There is a reason you popped up here."

"Raziel, there is one thing I don't understand."

The bell-pealing laughter from my gut made his eyes widen, making me laugh harder. The gongs reverberated from my chest, causing me to shake a little. Gasping, I wiped a tear. "One thing? Tonight, my dear demon, has never happened to me before. Most of this evening has been a mystery." Curling my wings, I snatched the one I stepped on and started examining the area of missing feathers. "Can an angel feel self-conscious? The mere fact I can't judge you is a huge conundrum."

His back to me, he made a motion toward his neck. "You could kill me. Wouldn't that solve most of our problems?"

The tinge of demon blood tickled my nose. He reopened the neck wound. A prickle from ancient instinct grew into an ache as the dagger began to hum. *'Dumb demon,'* I thought.

"No, a realistic demon. You can't judge me. All I recollect is my father threatening imminent death by sending me to Earth, and then I ended up here."

It ticked me off that he was in my head again, but the weight of his last sentence made my breath hitch. "He tried to kill you?" Appalled, I stammered, "Who is your father, Devin?"

Rotating to face me, his features became more demon-like as two searing slits held my attention. "Mastema is my father. The memories of him finding me are fuzzy, but I've been hiding from him for almost five hundred years."

The name Mastema spun in my head. His father was the ruler of all the demons in the universe. My jaw dropped. If my wings could have molted, there would have been a pile of feathers around my feet.

Chapter Five

Sitting on a stone bench between Gordon and Cecilia, I massaged my temples. They were bickering in broken German and English. And here, I thought this would be a quick sentencing. The married couple shared a checkered past, both dealing with hardships, mistrust, and adultery. I knew he was innocent of the adultery part, but his sin was making Cecilia believe her jealousy held merit. Love was a sweet poison, and I was relieved that this kind of emotional definition didn't afflict my kind. I could love but did so out of kindness; I didn't need to mate.

"Meine Blume, ich nicht schlafen mit Deiner Schwester." Gordon kept repeating over and over. 'My flower, I didn't sleep with your sister,' was etched into my brain. They worked out most of their problems, but her insecurities kept them bound in spiritual limbo. I pleaded once again on his behalf, but she silenced me in German, *"Ruhig, sie Krähe."* 'Quiet, you crow.' Dumbfounded, I froze openmouthed as the phrase impaled my pride. A crow. Now, I wasn't going to give her a feather but instead, shove it somewhere unclean.

Gordon softly expressed, *"Meine Liebe für Dich ist immer wahr."* Telling her, 'My love for you has always been true.' Then she started crying when he began to sing their song. I couldn't take much more of this. Plus, there was a demon waiting for me to knock into another plane or slay. Thoughts leaned toward the latter since his chuckling and mocking echoed from a distance.

Abruptly, I stood, regaining their attention. "Enough." I bent down in front of the woman. "Cecilia, do you see my wings? I'm an angel. You and Gordon died several years ago in a fire, and I can see the fire still burns between the both of you. He has loved you unconditionally through life and will continue to do so in death. *Bitte, vergib ihm*–please, forgive him." I patted her hands and then brushed her phantom tears away. "He has lied, but not about this. Really, look at him. He loves you."

Rotating her weepy face in his direction. Nodding, she whispered her forgiveness, and the exhale both Gordon and I did would have crushed an elephant.

I placed judgment on the couple and reclaimed my last two feathers. Shaking the rest of the dirt from them, I handed one to each soul. The sliver of Light opened, illuminating their once corporeal form. Both waved goodbye, but before I waved back, Gordon smiled tenderly and then blew me a grateful kiss. It was an honest gesture, and I acknowledged by nodding once as the portal closed.

An empty silence fell over the graveyard; the trees were eerily still, and even the crickets were not singing. I was about to shout Devilkin's name to annoy him and break the quiet. But, squashing my playful banter, his heat signature popped up next to me. My smile was a dead giveaway; I was getting used to his presence.

"Are you blushing?"

My hand went out to smack him. "Don't be absurd. You, my little devil, are an annoying pest I can't wait to be rid of." Whipping around, my wing connected with his shoulder. "Oops, sorry."

He reached for my wing and ran his fingers through the flight feathers. Playfully, he accused, "I thought angels couldn't lie."

"Umm, there is a difference between couldn't and shouldn't. And if you recall, I, too, have free will." Snickering a few notes before I placed my hand on his lower back to usher him toward his gravesite. "Have you evoked any of your memories?"

"Yes and no; I'm working on rearranging the questions to match my answers." He moved my arm, leaving a trail of warmth over my skin, before slipping his hand into mine as we interlocked our fingers.

A moment of mutual silence broke when he braked hard, making me rock back.

Startled, I dropped his hand. "What is it?"

"Raziel, when did you become a Judge?"

Being an angel has its perks. I didn't need to breathe but enjoyed the swirls of clean air when it entered my lungs. At that moment, I regretted the action because the gulp of air made me dizzy.

"Why do you want to know? I forget exactly. One day, I was fighting for justice; the next, I was passing judgment. Besides, it was a long time ago." The scenery became a convenient distraction, using it to avert my gaze.

Almost inaudible, his whisper pierced my soul. "When, Raziel? When did you become a Judge?" Once again, his eyes burned intensely, illuminating the area, and I could no longer avoid him.

The chill in the air was perhaps crisper because of the demon next to me, but I found the cold to be telling, more ominous. "I believed in free will, and because of my belief, the Light's court deemed me unable to uphold the position of a Slayer." I blinked back tears before scanning the cemetery while absorbing where I had spent several centuries and how I got here. "There was a Kull. He was out of control, causing havoc, and his kind put out a contract to end him before his folly exposed our world." I couldn't hold the weight of my wings as I lowered myself to the grass. "I was sent to slay one of their own."

Devilkin moseyed away, putting a few feet between us. "Did you?"

"What?"

"Did you slay it?"

Not wanting to relive this sin, I hugged both legs tight enough to rest my chin, then instinctively barricaded myself within a prison of feathers. Sliding each hand to my mouth, I cupped them over to muffle my reply, "I don't want to talk about it."

'Why did he want me to relive this?'

Knuckles rapped on a wing. "Knock-knock." His voice carried a jesting vibe, but it also conveyed an underlining sense of caution.

"Devin. I'm not in the mood. Anyway, I don't see what this has to do with you or your missing aura." I was still talking into my hands.

Again, he said, "Knock-Knock."

Giving in, I answered, "Who's there?" And then sniffed, not

realizing I started crying.

"Devilkin."

"This is dumb."

"You're supposed to say–"

"Devilkin who?"

"Devilkin Breckford, the demon you couldn't kill."

Involuntarily, both wings opened, exposing me face-to-face with the Kull I was supposed to slay five hundred years ago. It was as though someone had poured concrete over my figure. The reason I was bound here stared at me.

"Pardon me for not recalling our first meeting. It's been a while. I never thought I would run into you again once Mastema turned me human. Now, I know why." He rocked back from a kneeling position and began to pace.

"Why," I asked, through chattering teeth.

"Because he removed what I was and placed me in this shell." He gestured to his form. Staring at the ground, he continued, "I went into hiding, but from him," Devin's gaze steeled, "…not from you. I was stuck with the frailties of a human. When death becomes aforethought, it weakens the mind. Actually, I'm quite shocked it took him this long to find me, but it must have been his plan all along, for if I died as a human, it would once again make me your prey."

He was right. They told me if I could fulfill my duty, they would welcome me back home. Before I could think it through, a feather was in front of me. One of my feathers. Patting my robe, he shook his head.

"You dropped it during your temper tantrum. Uh, right after we met."

Lips quivering as I formed the question, "You're the reason they clipped my wings?" I lunged to snatch it but missed.

"Raziel, why didn't you kill me then?"

"They stated you were crazy and would someday expose our existence." Staring at him, I saw the demon for the first time behind those golden orbs. "I watched you save a little girl that wandered into the path of an out-of-control, horse-drawn carriage. I thought, if this demon was sane enough to perform an act of kindness, he should be given a chance to explain his actions, not killed."

"I was young, bored, and rebellious. I remember the day now, everything from the girl's lavender sent to the blinding moonlit wings of the angel sent to slay me."

The feather was all I could see as his face blurred behind it.

"I was out of control, Raziel. That little girl–I pushed into the horses' path, but when I saw you, something happened."

"Something," was all I could muster.

"After I saved the child, I watched you battle within yourself. You backed away, smiled, and then whispered…"

We both said in unison, "For one good deed."

"I will always be a demon, but if you had the restraint to save even the likes of me, then…" His voice trailed.

I was in shock, staring at the feather in his fingers. "Why didn't you use it to leave?"

Devilkin's smile was charming as he handed me the feather. "So, I could return the favor. I'm considered dead right, even though I technically didn't die by your hands." He shrugged. "This may work as a loophole. We won't know unless you try to use it."

I reached out to accept it, and a sliver of Light opened next to him. In a panic, I scanned the grounds. "What about the souls and passing judgment? I can't leave them."

"Yes, you can, Demon Slayer. I'll stay here. I've grown a healthy respect for death. It will be my honor to cull the sinners from the repentant. Send on those who are worthy," he grimaced, "to the Light."

My scythe and sword materialized beside me. *'I was going home.'* In my excitement, I exclaimed to the dead, "I'm going home." Then I hugged Devin. "How can I ever thank you?"

Side-eyeing my weapons, he asked, "Can I have your scythe?"

I beheld it longingly but nodded and then handed it over. "Please take care of the dead, and I promise to drop in from time to time to check on you, my little devil." I teased.

His expression held a whisp of bewilderment. "It's nice to know even a demon can have an angel watching over them.”

I can’t explain what compelled me to lean into him. I wanted to express my free will, my choice. Soft and tender lips grazed across mine. Thoughts of red wine, white roses, and unspent tears, spun in my mind. I realized Devilkin was my want, desire, and cardinal sin. Our kiss lifted me from the ground. Internally, I was flying through the clouds during sunset and burned this moment to memory.

He pulled away briefly to whisper, “Stay with me?”

A thumb brushed under my eye. It was wet. *‘Tears?’* I was crying, and it confused me as to why. Unable to respond, I finished our kiss, leaving a soft sigh as a sign of regret.

Breaking our embrace, something foreign stirred within me. *‘Fear.’* Fear of what he meant to me and the burn to protect what I claimed…mine. *‘Was this the emotion of love humans spoke of?’*

Before Devin could answer, I whispered, “This will be our dance between life and death, yes?”

He chuckled, cupping my face in his hands. “Thank you for saving me.”

The warmth from his fingers was replaced by swirls of chilled air mimicking trails of ghostly fingertips trailing down my cheeks. A figure stood a grave plot away, putting some distance between us.

“Go, you’ve been away from your home long enough because of me. Raziel, I will always search the stars for you.”

I kissed my fingertips and then held out the feather with the other. Leaving him a vow, “I will return.” The words chimed somberly, akin to the Knell’s death toll. This sealed the promise between us. Focusing on Devilkin, my foot slid back toward the opening, and the Light’s warmth enveloped my body to take me home.

MISPLACED

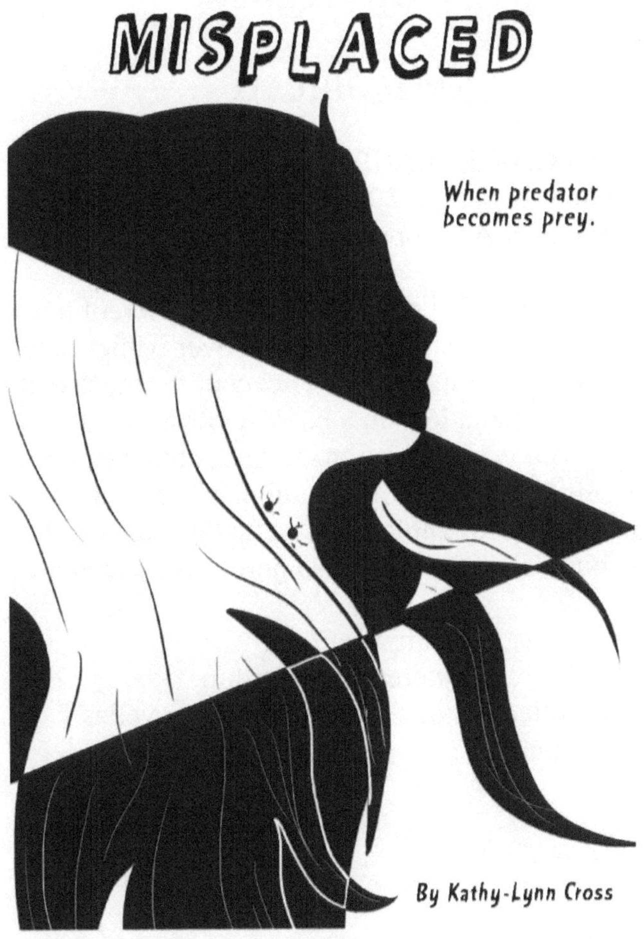

Copyright

Misplaced

Misplaced

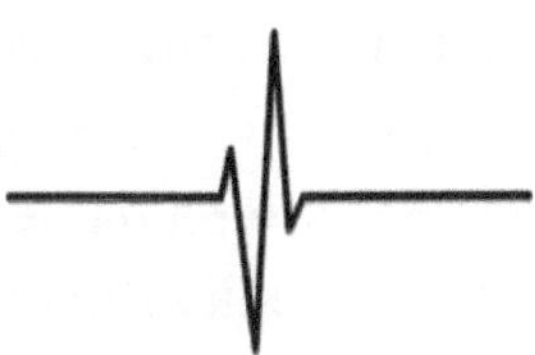

*I*t was surreal. The rough ground was cold, but the world was cloaked in harsh shades of flickering orange, yellows, and reds. Scent-blind from singed hair and skin penetrated the air. Vaguely, I pondered on a few favorite aromas: white roses, a dark Merlot, and fresh emotions from unbridled desire, but none of those memories sparked to replace this repulsive smell.

Debris from the crash had scattered in all directions.

Would they consider the body I was in part of the debris since it went through the windshield?

Something jagged dug into the spine. The arm was numb from the shoulder blade down, and I couldn't move it. I detected a cold, prickly sensation as it traveled from below the navel toward both feet. They throbbed from the pressure, becoming heavier with each strained pump from the main organ. Different forms of pain branched out chaotically, overloading my phantom senses. A breath hitched as I forced the body to exhale. Air rattled from the body's throat. This was difficult as I tried to force the link with it and choked on warm liquid rust. The combined action was the last thing I heard and tasted.

Involuntarily, a few fingers twitched in a sticky substance. The head position faced the sky like a broken traffic camera. Using the body's peripheral vision, I caught glimpses of emergency personnel running frantically, trying to contain the situation. Body language from the police and firefighters appeared over-animated. A policeman came into view and pointed at me. He cupped an open hand against his mouth to get attention. But I heard nothing.

A human male with large, burnt-cinnamon eyes bent down, grabbing the right wrist. Shaking his head, he switched positions before placing two fingers against the jugular to search for a pulse. Bloody fingers shined a penlight into both eyes several times. I wondered if the neck wound was still bleeding.

He grabbed both shoulders to give a slight shake. His lips moved wildly. I believe he kept repeating a name. The outline of a woman knelt beside me. She was a medical magician, as certain supplies materialized out of thin air.

The male checking vitals started to converse with his partner while ripping the shirt to access the wounds. From this position and the body's condition, I could only make out the woman's shoulders and head as her ponytail bobbed in response. Her mouth pressed into a straight line as she scrutinized the injuries and then rubbed the side of her neck. For some unknown reason, I wanted to choke the female until she turned blue.

'What an odd emotional reaction,' I thought.

Distracted, I hadn't noticed the man bending to position himself by the right ear. His presence felt familiar. A voice reverberated with intense pressure. It was as though I was submerged, but the words couldn't break through the liquid barrier.

Again, he tried, but "Ava" came through this time as a fading echo.

Internally, I snickered. Ava was gone. This broken body was mine.

It was an unfortunate mistake that we were in this dilemma. As a Pranic Cypher, I should've known better, but the need to feed trumped my judgment. I was a predator with plenty of time and enjoyed playing with my food by gaining the victim's trust before feeding. For centuries, observing humans, or sleeves, as we called them, improved my acting abilities. The young woman cracked within five minutes. In the vehicle, I was her trapped therapist as she gushed about problems, finances, frustrations, and a string of romantic failures. Ava's inner turmoil simmered, reminding me of raw steaks on an overheated grill.

This naïve female must've been sick the day they taught about 'stranger danger.' She had made a poor choice by deciding to take pity on an old woman by the side of the road, with no walker, on a cloud-covered night and dragging a stiff leg. The sleeve I was occupying had begun to fail. Older humans were not a substance preference of mine, but they eased the hunger in a pinch when traveling between ideal hosts. Inhabiting the frail female did give me the ability to appear harmless, but because of the aura's age and years of damage, it lacked potency. But, I had to admit, they were a convenient disguise to blend in with humans.

Moments before instinct shattered predator composure; I scrutinized the aged sleeve's emotionless face reflected in the passenger window.

Saliva pooled under my tongue. Ava's emotions were boiling as she ranted about lost love, betrayal, and avenging herself. I couldn't refrain from inhaling the young human's scent, mimicking a wine critic, inviting her scent to tease the senses. Within a matter of seconds, two hollow fangs breached the upper gum line, pushing both canines behind to make room. Streetlights caused my reflection to strobe at a hypnotic pace as both irises flashed to royal gold. The color intensified until each pupil narrowed, similar to a feline's when they stare directly into the sun.

I kept my answers behind closed lips, nodding while occasionally adding an agreeable "mmmph," until her aura became so irresistible that I attacked without thinking in a high-velocity moving vehicle.

It wasn't the cleanest aura transfer as I plunged my existence into Ava with the speed for survival. *'Leave no witnesses'* was vital in keeping our species in the mythical realm. After establishing myself in her body, I broke the old woman's neck after the process was complete. I was positive her soul felt no pain. Ava's consciousness, in all likelihood, didn't have enough time to register that she was in a different body. The timing was unfortunate since the human went limp in my arms, and I didn't have enough time to regain control of the car. It clipped the guardrail and sent the vehicle spinning into oncoming traffic.

Honestly, I should cease to exist for such a miscalculated

blunder.

After being ejected, laid out, and broken, I assumed the sleeve had remained in the vehicle. Since Ava wasn't wearing her seatbelt, her body crashed through the windshield. With a weak grin, I remembered buckling the passenger's safety strap. Hopefully, it would be destroyed by the fire. If this body survived, I would probably have to give a statement about the dead passenger. *'How would I portray her as?'* A relative, friend, or stick to the truth that she was someone I'd picked up for dinner.

I was having trouble finishing the sync because of the damage to this sleeve and the rushed transfer. It needed power, and I didn't have enough to sustain the body and my existence. Ava's consciousness was gone, but certain senses and some of the main organs were beginning to glitch. One beat, another light and faint, and the heart stopped. Faint gray swirls etched the outskirts of what I could see. Two electrodes were lifted over me. A grim glance was the only warning. A female silently mouthed, "Clear."

Electricity bridged the gaps in my synapse.

Ava's body remained unresponsive.

"Again. Up the voltage," I read the EMTs mouth.

Water-laden clouds from above the scene released their burden.

Dammit, if only I had waited until we made it to a parking lot somewhere. It would have been easy to convince her to pull into a store or restaurant or tell her I was getting carsick. Regret slithered next to me, cold and unnatural, but it was there.

Rain pelted the humans working on me. A few drops landed in my unmoving eyes. I couldn't blink. All the senses were gone but one. Sight kept me grounded, but it also started to fail. In a tick, the male stood above me with a jacket outstretched to protect my face from the rain. I never detected his movements, so either his reactions had become heightened or my comprehension of time had slowed.

Firelight danced over the name badge before it became blurry. Zak's jaw clenched with professional determination, but a flicker of hope crossed his face. It was then I detected a tender connection. I toyed with the notion that this human knew the woman I now inhabited.

Dark glitter pixeled, snuffing out the dim light. *'So, this is what it's like to die in a sleeve.'* Interesting. Well, I technically wouldn't die, only cease to exist. The only casualty was Ava. Well, and the sleeve I previously used.

Pranic Cyphers were aura extractors, always searching for another tank of gas to sustain us. We are empty souls described as a spirit parasite existing without a body or living essence. For this reason, we are the unknown calamity to the unfortunate. Our existence is never acknowledged except in altered versions of horror stories, twisted fads, or for entertainment as bloodthirsty, immortal vampires. We are never mourned nor would be missed when our auras flickered out. Realizing this intensified the loneliness.

Part of me wondered if I had blundered the chance to play a human. As a rule, we only stayed in one sleeve for a short time. Feed and move on. That was the natural order of things. But this time, I had grown fond of the name Ava. *'I could wear her sleeve for a while, couldn't I?'*

Once the foreboding thought sluggishly made its way into my conscience, regret bit down like a rabid dog and began to shred my new aura. The body was shutting down. I needed to obtain more power to heal. On a panic high, I commanded my abilities to mesh with Ava's body. My fangs wouldn't extend. I was trapped within the sleeve.

Lightning illuminated the female's face long enough for me to register a hint of frustration as she readjusted the paddles.

"Clear."

The body arched from the electrical surge. Pain exploded into strobing spots of color. Then the aura—I desperately tried to latch onto—shattered. Frustrated, I wanted to scream, *"Stop that!"* The mouth wouldn't move. I heard a high-pitched, erratic giggle as the darkness saturated the core of my existence. Blurred images faded to black. With the body's senses gone, I drifted along a motionless void toward a warm glow. But then, an unknown presence rushed in and robbed me from reaching the light.

A small pinpoint of light no bigger than the size of a pinhead floated in front of me. It was frustrating. Every time I tried to concentrate on its position, it would move. I felt misplaced. The darkness was a bit jarring and disappointing. Succumbing to death was draining. Periodically, there was a lukewarm sensation that made certain thoughts sluggish. It reminded me of the time I used an exercise instructor for a few days as a host. She would float in a weightless tank when stressed.

Light zipped across my vision again.

'Should I head toward it?'

There was a sinister sensation emanating from its direction. A female silhouette stepped in front of the light. One word slithered from the shadow. '*Mine.*' A hazy hand reached for me. I backed away and screamed possessively, *"This is mine!"* The shadow morphed into a familiar face. An old woman's figure turned to dust; its anger swirled around me and disappeared.

'Oh, boy!' I needed to find a way out of this darkness before I cozied up with crazy. Human dreams were confusing.

The glow caught my attention again, but this time, it appeared bigger and gliding toward me.

"Maybe I'll wait here and see what happens," reassuring myself.

There was a pinch, a light purr from a motor, pressure, and a high-pitch shrill, followed by an incessant number of beeps. Slow and steady, the rhythm made me transfixed. While concentrating on the beat, the white spot positioned itself a few feet away.

"Ava. Ava, can you hear me?"

'Ava? Who's Ava?'

A familiar snicker echoed in the space I was trapped in, but I couldn't see anyone.

Beep…beep…beep.

I forced myself to remember the name. It sounded important—

an image of an elderly woman opening the car door. Fingers curled around a steering wheel. Anger and treachery slithered from the gloom. A desire to kill. Flashing emergency lights. Snippets of time smudged like fingers swishing through paint. The last moment dissolved as I stared into a pair of sad brown eyes.

These memories were from two perspectives. A side effect that could happen when auras are mixed during a transfer. It could be problematic if I harbored part of the person's life essence.

"Ava, honey, please open your eyes." A woman's soft pleas hit like an electrical jolt. The beeps were louder and out of rhythm. This voice wasn't the one connected to the laughter. "It's been three weeks. Please open your eyes. It's Aunt Mimi."

'Three weeks! Where was I?'

Distracted, I hadn't noticed that the glowing spot wasn't a spot anymore. Once I had acknowledged its presence, the distorted sphere exploded. The force punched through my essence. Shards of color shot into me.

I felt feverish. It was a struggle, but finally, I cracked my eyelids enough to see a blurry figure to the left of me. Blinking a few times, a pudgy woman with pink-rimmed eyes and short curly, gray hair came into focus. Small, aged, freckled hands clutched a stack of pictures to her chest. A tiny hiccup and sob trailed as she glanced in my direction.

Bloodshot eyes widened as though the woman had seen a ghost.

I tried to speak, but the mouth had a tube sticking out of it. Instead, I blinked in acknowledgment.

"Oh, Ava." Pictures scattered into the air as she lunged forward. "Precious girl, you gave us a big scare. Here." She pressed the remote on the side of the bed.

A loud hiss of static filled the pause, and a voice said, "Hello. Can I help you?"

"Yes, yes. My niece is awake." She spoke through tears. "Can you notify her doctor?"

The senses were on overdrive, so I took a moment to adjust. *'Gave us a scare? Us? Who's us?'*

When I adjusted the body's weight, a stiffness developed between the back and shoulders. The pain morphed into several knots, which triggered a dull throbbing. I remembered this irritation: a headache. Squinting, I saw hints of a cast resting across the abdomen. On the right, a heavy presence enclosed the hand. When I tried to lift it, thick fingers squeezed several of them. Cautiously, I blinked a few more times. There was the male I recalled from Ava's memories.

Zak's eyes mirrored the woman's, except for two dark half-circles displaying his exhaustion. His smile was weak, with a hint of distance behind his eyes. He cleared his throat, patted the hand, and leaned in before whispering, "I don't know what you've done, but we'll work it out between us soon enough." He lifted his head and made eye contact. "We'll make things right again. Second chances shouldn't be ignored."

None of this made sense. Bewildered, I rocked from side to side. I wasn't Ava.

'No. Wait. The body I transferred to survived? They thought I was Ava.'

Zak leaned in as if to kiss me, but he brushed his face against mine at the last second. A heated breath lingered at the curvature base of the neck, causing a pulse jump. I winced from the reaction.

His hot words slid over the skin. "Take this time to heal. I'll see you soon." Straightening his stance, he retrieved a jacket from the back of the chair and slipped it on. Responding to Ava's aunt, he released a weighted breath. "Mimi, my shift starts in an hour. I'll be back afterward to check on you both. Maybe bring you dinner?"

"Thank you, Zakary. That would be nice. I've appreciated your support during this time." She pursed her lips. "I'm sure your fiancé misses you. Please tell Veronica we said, 'Hello.'" Her last sentence was rigid and stiff—strictly out of human formality. I wondered why the body protested against dwelling on the matter, but I obeyed its silent plea not to press on the matter.

He fidgeted with an uneasy smile. "Sure thing. Ava knows I'll always be there for her. It's part of the job requirements from once being the guy next door."

Sidetracked by the squeaky wheels from the hallway, a doctor and two nurses entered. A muscle jumped along Zakary's jaw as he stared at the man. *Either the medication was messing with me, or my brain was scrambled.* The two had an uncanny similarity, but the doctor was marginally shorter and wore wire-rimmed glasses.

The nurses were on autopilot as they briskly avoided the men and headed toward their target, me. One of them was a petite blonde with a pixie-style haircut. As she approached the machines, I received a reassuring smirk from her, which appeared genuine. Inwardly, I sighed. *Ava must've known her, too.* I'd have to piece together who this human was later. It hurt too much to retrieve bits of her memory or what was left for me.

With complete disinterest, I barely glanced at the second woman as she typed on a portable computer. Right now, the testosterone was distracting. Zak's brow pinched as he coolly addressed the man with a quick nod. "Dr. Steinman."

Rigid, the doctor held out his hand. "Brother, there's no need for formality."

Zak didn't return the gesture and backed two steps to the side while reaching for the door handle. "Considering the history in this room. I think formality is required."

Mimi cajoled, "Oh, Kristopher, will you two ever stop fighting over Ava."

I choked on the tube. *'Who exactly was this Ava?'*

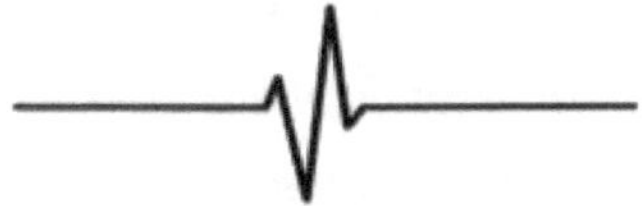

It took a few months for the physical aspect of the body to recover. I was still weak from only using the body's life essence and not hopping from host to host. I desperately needed a recharge. It wasn't as bad as the night I found this sleeve, but it was getting close.

Since Dr. Steinman and Ava had some history, which also involved his brother, I played the amnesia card whenever he tried to discuss their past. Considering the severity of the accident and the extent of the injuries, the loss of memory seemed feasible considering what 'attentively' Ava had been through. At least it would also buy me time to acclimate to the sleeve's life.

'I get to play human,' I thought mischievously, hiding a smile as I sucked on a rectangle box of orange juice Aunt Mimi had given me earlier.

Because of my memory issues, Ava's aunt had pretty much taken over things. She insisted I should stay with her since it would be another two weeks until the cast could be removed for me to start physical therapy. Whenever Ava's aunt visited, I secretly extracted information about her niece.

Her birthday and last name, Peyton, were a freebie from the wrist tag. She was twenty-six. Height and weight weren't indicated. I'd have to get a glimpse at the chart. She lived alone in a one-bedroom apartment. Wasn't sure where. Her parents were deceased, which was information I wouldn't have to spend too much time remembering—a positive point for death. I'm not sure how or when they died, but I would find out the factors for portraying Ava. She was a law student about six months shy of taking the bar exam. She must've been left-handed since her aunt kept handing me things and apologizing when I hesitated to grab things with my right. Since Pranic Cyphers were ambidextrous, I would make this mental adjustment to use the left more often to keep the act going.

Next on the agenda was to learn more about this awkward, emotionally charged drama triangle I was now a part of. Mimi hinted that Zak and Ava might've been involved once, but I couldn't tell if it was before, during, or after Veronica. Zakary hadn't been back. Again, I'm presuming it's because his brother was my doctor or possibly his fiancé barred him from visiting. Whenever Dr. Steinman came to discuss my health status, he remained professional with a sterile, stiff distance, especially when he examined the wounds, dressings, and chart updates. Never did he hint at anything personal. Ava's part seemed more like she was swimming in the middle of Kristopher and Zak. Veronica appeared to be fishing in the same river and happened to catch the younger brother. She had him chomping on the same bait for almost two years. It made me wonder how Ava remained the tethered desire between the two males for so long and if there was something I would have to instigate to find answers.

There was an annoying tickle against my right ear. Over time, it felt more natural to act like the body was mine and I was Ava. *'Yes, I am Ava now, and Ava is me.'* An annoyance tickled against my right ear, eventually turning painful. I became crossed as I didn't know whether to swat it away or rub the area.

The orange juice was a deterrent, so I sucked harder to finish it.

I could've sworn an inhuman whisper of laughter invaded my space. It made me uneasy as I pondered the possibilities of playing human and becoming more like them before realizing it wasn't a good idea. The pros and cons were getting muddled and a bit concerning. It was too emotionally complex and uncomfortable to remain in this skin. The physical side wasn't so bad, except humans took forever to heal. And a lot of their medication and healing methods did more harm to their auras than my kind did from power feeding.

One high priority on my things-to-do list was extracting an aura. I needed my kind of food soon before another misstep clouded my judgment and misplaced me again. But on the other hand, being Ava for a spell has driven away the loneliness. I disliked that part of being a cypher. *'No,'* I redirected those tainted thoughts and reiterated my main concern. *'Maybe remaining in this particular human wasn't a good idea, and I should extract myself into a new host.'*

During my stay, I found out the nurse with the short haircut was named Samantha. She went by Sammy. Ava had given her the nickname when they were young. But her demeanor and general questions made it seem as though the two were not as close anymore. During our brief encounters, I shoved Jell-O into my mouth instead of answering specific questions.

An image of me swapping auras with Sammy teased the predator within. But I forced the impulse away and finished the juice box with a final suck of bubbled air. She snickered as I placed the concave box next to the untouched food. Sammy removed the breakfast tray.

A second later, Mimi click-clacked through the door. "Good morning, Samantha. I finished the paperwork for your release, dear. Do you have everything?"

Nervous, I scanned the room, unsure of what was mine, but gave her a dismissive nod. "Yes, I believe I do. Thank you for filling out most of the paperwork. I only had to sign my name."

An orderly came in with a wheelchair. The man was emotionally charged, and his scent made me bolt upright. It was a struggle to keep my fangs from extending. His stature reminded me of a basketball player. I watched him set the brake, retract the footplates, and then start to free me from my blanket cocoon.

Saliva began to pool in my mouth. This was bad.

Mimi lifted two bags. "I'll take these with me and pull the car around. See you in a tick."

Leaving me alone with this male was not going to bode well. Since the crash, the desire to feed would disappear and reappear like fog. Early in the morning, it would stir or settle over me in the middle of the night. But today, of all days, it was all I could think about. Ava's aura was sustaining me, so I didn't need to at first since she was young. The damage was draining it faster before it could heal. But, his scent. *'Damn me to Hell.'* His scent caused my fangs to extend a little more. I bit the inside of my cheek hard enough to draw blood.

Deep brown-black eyes dove right into my existence. "Good morning, Ava."

I nodded in reply.

He grinned mischievously, which made me nervous. *'Was he waiting for a response? Did he know her too?'* Pretending to be Ava was getting harder by the day.

A male dressed in a gray uniform popped in the doorway. "Jackson, let me know when the room is free to clean."

'Thank the cosmos for dropping this man's name.'

"We're wheeling out of here shortly." He helped me into the

wheelchair and locked the footplates. His long fingers were gentle as he lifted the cast to make room for the overnight bag and placed it on my lap.

Sipping on my blood helped to redirect the hunger. The sharp points began to retract. Pretending to be shy, I mumbled, "Thank you, Jackson."

A wide, pleased grin spread across his face. "No problem, Ava."

As the orderly pushed me down the corridor, a few medical staff waved goodbye. Within minutes, Jackson positioned us in front of the elevator doors and pressed the down button. Across the reflective surface, our images were somewhat distorted. Intuition raised the hairs on the back of my neck and arms. The air around me dropped in temperature. The chill sent me into defense mode. *'Was another Pranic Cypher nearby?'* I chewed on my lower lip; it couldn't be the man behind me. I detected his life force well before he entered the room.

'Could I be having trouble distinguishing which human was a sleeve?' I'd never been in a body this long. It might be a drawback to remaining stationary. If I couldn't detect another cypher, things would get problematic.

The elevator chimed. When the doors opened, a figure wearing a white coat pushed Jackson politely aside and stepped behind my chair.

"Jackson, I've got her."

I held my breath.

"Sure thing, Dr. Steinman. Take care, Ava."

Robotically, I said, "Thank you."

Kristopher's aura was a blend of beach-baked sand and raw honey. I pressed the bag against me with the cast. This was a dreadful happenstance. I had to focus on something other than feeding. If I lost control, I couldn't conceal my actions in an elevator. It would be the end for us both.

The doctor said nothing as he pushed me into the metal box and turned us around to face the entrance. When the doors closed, Kristopher pressed the number one button.

On the descent, my stomach uncontrollably flip-flopped. I placed a shaky hand on my forehead.

He bent down. I noted his eyes were the same color as his brother's. "Are you lightheaded, nauseous, or both?" Kristopher took my hand and replaced it with his to check my temperature. Next, he turned my wrist to place two fingers on bluish-green lines.

We were too close. Perspiration was forming along my hairline. "Yes." The word came out with a lisp. Both fangs were almost fully extended. "Fun fact about me: elevators make me feel claustrophobic."

He chuckled. "Really?"

"Yes. They make me think of coffins."

"What a bleak comparison."

I needed a diversion. "What did you want to talk about, Kristopher?"

"Give my brother some space."

That did it. I completely forgot about my fangs as I blurted, "You want me to what?"

"Veronica's good for Zakary. Both of them are in the same profession. They have more in common."

Hearing the woman's name triggered a hostile sense of ending. An avalanche of rage and unfaithfulness plowed into me. The pressure of it made it hard to breathe. Without thinking, I countered, "So, you're condoning what he's done." I slapped a hand over my mouth. *'What was I saying?'* My eyes widened. I wasn't planning on answering.

The comment didn't faze him. "No. I don't condone what he's done to you. But, we're not exactly innocent either." He reproached.

'Oh, crap! Did he say we're—as in us?'

Positioning himself behind the chair, I stared at our warped images. An outline of a woman stood behind him. My mouth fell open as our reflective doubles, plus one, disappeared when the doors slid open.

In a harsh tone, Kristopher clipped, "Why do I trip over my tongue whenever I'm around you? It's unfathomable how you affect me." We headed for the entrance, where a lighted exit sign hung above the doorjamb. Honestly, it should've been marked freedom.

'How should I respond?' His words had no meaning since he was talking about Ava and not me. Remaining tight-lipped would be for the best.

When we reached the sliding glass doors, I ran my tongue across the upper row of teeth. They were normal again. I puffed out with relief and continued running my tongue across the even row of bone.

Misunderstanding my actions, he exhaled hard and asked, "Ava, do you still love him?"

I snorted and began to choke.

Sidestepping into my line of sight, he dropped to one knee and clasped my good hand. A few onlookers took out their cell phones, probably taking pictures or videos, believing this was going to be a confession or proposal of sorts.

I grimaced.

"Ava, you're intelligent, beautiful," he moved several violet-black locks from my face and placed them behind my ear, "bewitching." A hint of passion settled behind his admission.

Sticking to my plan, I kept mute and unmoving until I had to blink.

Within a few minutes, this well-composed doctor had morphed into a flustered, lovesick human. His aura shifted to a sickly crimson-blue, and for a brief instant, a knife bite of empathy twisted in my stomach.

My face flushed, contorting to pity, while my chest burned from lack of air as he waited for a response. Guilt wasn't something I normally experienced. It compelled me to do the unthinkable, I responded honestly. "Kristopher, things are not always as they seem." On impulse, I withdrew my hand from under his.

A white Cadillac crept into view and parked in front of the doors. Aunt Mimi waved from the driver's side. Kristopher nodded, then gradually stood. He steered the wheelchair to the car in silence. After helping me onto the seat, his touch shifted to a doctor-patient professionalism. It was very awkward.

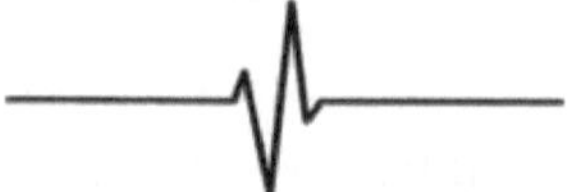

Since I was staying with Mimi throughout my recovery, she insisted I collect a few necessities from Ava's, which was now my apartment. I didn't argue against the idea. It would give me the chance to quickly scan and make mental notes about the life she led. Mimi helped with the packing. A stack of law books and notebooks was scattered across the desk. I asked if I could bring them with me, and she retrieved a duffel bag from the closet with a frown.

"I know you've been working hard, and the accident was a setback with your studies, but realistically, maybe you should take a break. You could always take the bar at the end of the year." While packing the books, she unearthed a photograph of Zak and Ava.

On impulse, I frowned and picked up the picture frame. For a moment, I pondered on how Ava would answer her aunt, making my way back to the desk. I retrieved the laptop, mouse, and power cord and replied, "I'll consider your suggestion. Either way, I will have to study twice as hard for lost time."

"I had a feeling you would continue your studies." Zipping the duffel bag, she clicked her tongue and held out her hand. "Do you want to bring the picture with you?"

Studying the portrait for a moment, I shrugged. "Why not." As I was handing it to her, the glass cracked under my thumb, and blood filled the crevices, forming a bloody spiderweb over Ava's face.

"Oh dear, are you all right? I'll get you a Band-Aid." She disappeared into the bathroom.

I placed the picture on top of the duffel bag and examined the cut. The wound was deep, slightly angled, and resembled a puncture from a cypher fang. Scanning the room, I felt nothing. *'Was it even possible?'*

The landline started ringing. Mimi came out of the bathroom to answer it, but I stopped her. "No, wait." I wanted to hear the message Ava had left. Plus, I had no clue who was calling or what I would say to them.

On the third ring, the answering machine clicked on.

"Hey, you've reached Ava Peyton. I'm away from any communication technology at the moment." There was a brief nervous laugh. "I'm either A) studying, B) studying, C) trapped under something heavy, or D) that's none of your business. If you must, leave a brief message and the best phone number at which to reach you. I'll return your call as soon as possible unless it's C."

There was a long beep. For a few seconds, it seemed the person was considering answer D, but then a male voice sighed. "Ava, it's me. I heard you were released from the hospital and staying with Mimi. I'm sure you're wondering why I never came back to check on you." His pause was measured. "I think we need to discuss our future." Another pause. "Plus, Veronica divulged some information about the accident, which concerns me. I'll call you at your aunt's. I'll see you—" Zak's message abruptly cut off.

Mimi appeared agitated while waving around the Band-Aid. After taking it, she shrugged. "It's your mess now, and you'll have to deal with it."

Ava's aunt had no idea how truthfully messed up her statement was.

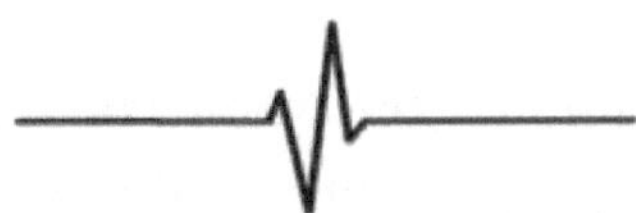

At Mimi's condo, I was unpacking when a light knuckle tap caught my attention. She was fidgeting with her purse. "I haven't gone grocery shopping in a while. Is there anything special you want?"

I ducked to hide the smile. I had done a little reconnaissance through the refrigerator and cupboards. "I would love some Cherry Garcia Ice Cream. A jar of maraschino cherries. Oh, and Cherry Coke."

She frowned. "Is that a serious cherry or sugar addiction?"

Backpedaling, I played it off as if I was joking. "Okay, okay, diet Cherry Coke."

Jiggling her keys, Mimi backed into the hallway. "By the way, Veronica stopped by earlier."

Curious, I cocked my head. "Why?"

"She dropped off a get-well bouquet from her and Zakary."

I frowned.

"It was a nice gesture." Sounding disappointed, she turned on a heel. "She might stop by later to check on you."

Throughout the condo, a doorbell chimed.

"I'll go see who it is."

Once she was gone, I went back to unpacking. After placing a book onto a stack, I rounded the bed to listen from the doorway. Not far from the threshold, a blast of chilled air smacked against my body. I heard the front door open, followed by several greetings. From down the hallway, three voices intertwined until Mimi replied, "I wasn't expecting you both so soon."

There was a male response I couldn't make out, and then Ava's aunt mumbled, "She's in the guest room."

A fight or flight surge shot through my body. Oppression and emptiness rolled into the space. At the far end of the house, there was nowhere to escape unless I locked myself in the bathroom. While considering the option, a figure rounded the corner. I assumed it was Veronica.

Readjusting the sling for the weight of the cast to be centered, I positioned myself in a guarded stance. Pulling on the body's aura to charge my powers was difficult. It was similar to sucking frozen malt through a straw. Fangs barely poked through the gum line as I searched for a life force.

Strong, erratic pulses indicated that a human within the condo was nervous.

Scuffled footsteps over carpet approached and stopped short from the doorway. I relaxed to some extent and stuffed my free hand in the front pocket. "What are you doing here, Veronica?"

She regarded me with uncertainty. "We need to talk."

"What about?"

"Since the night of the crash, Zak's been behaving differently."

Flustered, she acted as though I was supposed to explain his behavior. We remained silent until Veronica's voice became meek. "Um, I'm having trouble recalling certain events."

A light electrical charge made my arm hairs stand on end. "Trouble? Trouble about what?" The body's reaction toward this woman made me concerned.

"Tell me the truth. Did you hit someone?"

Feigning ignorance and waving a dismissive hand, I answered sharply, "No. I don't think so. The incident happened so fast. All I remember is hitting the guardrail and spinning. Honestly, I don't even remember going through the windshield."

Events clicked like a slideshow. Each one raised a new worry. *'Did Ava survive the crash? Hadn't I broken the sleeve's neck? Was Ava's aura still in the sleeve? And, if so, how could I finish what I'd started? I had to find her before she talked.'*

Veronica's face twisted in pain as if recalling what she had witnessed hurt. "There was an elderly woman with extensive neck, torso, and hand wounds." She grimly added, "I heard the police have started an investigation."

Confused, I blurted, "Did she die?"

"It was touch and go for a while."

I felt the blood drained from my face. "Was?"

"Yes. Zak kept checking to see if she was breathing. After a while, he started to perform CPR. Once the patient appeared stable, I tagged her for Flight for Life. Then we were informed about you."

Images from that night zipped past like a horror movie.

Veronica placed a hand on her hip. "We found out this morning the patient died during transport."

"But, did she?" An inaudible reply penetrated my thoughts.

A figure slipped from behind Veronica. Two flashes of royal gold caused me to go numb. A small hand grabbed Veronica's ponytail, wrenched it hard to the back, and then a quick jerk to the right. I heard a bone-crunching snap. Her body went limp and collapsed with an audible thud.

Past the small woman, I saw Zakary lying on the living room

floor motionless. Blood trickled from two puncture wounds on Mimi's neck. Her eyes had become predatory. With a mouthful of fangs, she gestured toward the female on the floor. "I couldn't have done it without you," Ava spoke with satisfaction. "It's a shame I had to claim my aunt's life, but you know, those pesky old humans are the best disguises." A malevolent grin spread across her face. "Now, I want my body back."

The realization had me stupefied. *'Had I created a Pranic Cypher?'* Now, I was its prey. Hands lifted like claws as the short, gray-haired sleeve lunged for me. We scrambled on the ground until she pinned me onto my stomach and grabbed the cast to the point I believed she was going to break the shoulder. I screamed as she plunged her fangs into her body.

Her aura flooded in, overtaking mine.

Ava's voice cooed, "Oh, what sweet irony."

The wave of panic and pain was replaced by…by…*light.*

'It's so warm.' My last final thought was, *'So, this is what death is like.'*

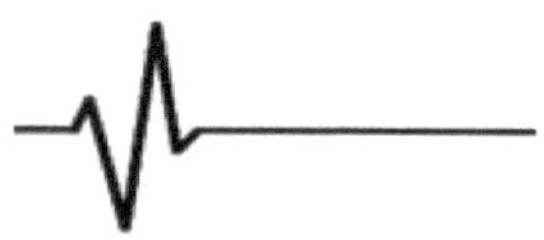

LONELY HEARTS
BY AMBER HASSLER
When the
voices from
your past
haunt your
present...

Lonely Hearts
By Amber Hassler

Gusts of air ruffled the dying leaves from an aging oak tree that sat on top of a hill, alone, until it became a scraggly piece of thick wood.

Mila Webber watched the brown leaflets float to the ground, helpless to their fate. She pulled her black pea coat tighter against the crisp wind. Despite the fall chill, she welcomed it.

Another year and another season had passed. It was her last year in high school, and she had no plans for after graduation. *Depressing*.

The crunch of light footsteps on the brittle ground broke through Mila's solitude, warning of someone approaching from behind. An aroma of coconut swirled in the air giving away the presence of her best friend, Cindy.

"What are you doing out here?" Cindy stepped into view. Her strawberry blonde hair whipped around her face, blocking her features.

"I needed some air," Mila replied while pulling her jacket closer around her thin frame.

"Well, come on, Mrs. Bleevie has started roll call. You don't want her calling home and telling your mom you ditched this field trip." Cindy didn't wait for an answer; she rotated on her heels, leaving an indent in the soft ground and headed back inside.

Mila glanced at the fragile tree one last time. Its branches seemed to reach for her as they shifted from the air's intensity. Her long, vibrant auburn locks, in turn, searched for a connection with its limbs, wanting to accept the invitation to sit among its protruding roots.

With a sigh, she reluctantly spun around and followed her

friend's trail. In her mind, the leaves appeared to scream in protest under her feet as she stepped on the ones she couldn't avoid while fighting against the wind.

Nearing the base of the hill an elongated, two-story, brick building loomed ahead of her. Within the walls, it provided a false hope of change. A change that was to come from what she would learn today. *It was just a waste of time. She was certain it was a setup; it had the parental stench of poor planning. So, why did she agree to come on this field trip? And how in the heck were they able to convince Mrs. Bleevie to make a class trip out of it; that was the real question.* A scoff followed Mila's thoughts.

Mila entered the lobby right as Mrs. Bleevie called her name.

"Here." She spoke without missing a beat and then crossed her arms over her chest while leaning against the wall.

Mrs. Bleevie didn't seem to notice she was absent beforehand as she continued rifling off the last few names from her clipboard.

Mila shifted both feet and glanced at her enthusiastic classmates, moving from one to another, and listening to them gush about the haunting decor. She didn't stop until she caught Cindy eyeing her with one of her criticizing looks. She brushed it off and paid attention to the once thriving entryway.

Even though it had been classified a museum, there wasn't an entry fee. As long as no one took advantage by vandalizing the grounds, then it was free for the public to enjoy. It also meant, no tour guides or floor employees to give direction when needed; except for a lone security guard that moseyed along the property's perimeter. For there being no crew to upkeep the place it looked intact. Apart from a few spots where the plaster had flaked off the wall, and chunks of rocks littering the floor that had fallen from the ceiling, everything else appeared as it did when people once walked the halls.

With the current state of the building, a special bond formed between her and it, because it revealed what she felt inside.

"All right class, quiet down," Mrs. Bleevie's voice filled the room. "No wandering off. Stay close. We were only given an hour to explore. No shenanigans. Listen to your assigned chaperone."

The decibels in the hollow space immediately increased followed by the scuffling of feet as students and parents tried to figure out where to go.

An ear piercing whistle caused everyone to go silent and look at Mrs. Bleevie who removed her thumb and forefinger from her mouth.

"Welcome to Stayville Asylum. Some historians believe the majority of unconventional testing were done here. All their efforts were to understand the brain and how it functioned under certain circumstances. Each room is equipped with a glass case that holds the tools used and a plaque that gives you the reasons behind the experiments performed. Take notes, because I will expect a three-page paper on your findings, due first thing in the morning. Now, explore."

When Mrs. Bleevie spoke the last word, the hair on Mila's skin rose, sending chills down her spine. It could have been the way Mrs. Bleevie said 'explore' that made it sound dark and daring, but it gave her an uneasy twinge in her stomach as if she was doomed.

The small groups of students and parents dispersed in different directions to begin their tour into the depths of history.

Cindy dodged through the masses and emerged on the other side, showing her irritation that they didn't make it easy for her to cut across. "Do these boys ever take a shower? *Ugh.* And what the heck is up with this lack of organization? You'd think Mrs. Bleevie would have already made a list of who goes where before we got here. It's complete chaos," she sneered.

Mila ignored her comments and didn't hold back her own irritation. "An asylum. Really? What made my parents think this would be a great idea?"

Cindy furrowed her brows together, confused. "Umm, what do you mean by parents?"

"This is why I had to come to school today?" Mila spoke over her friend, continuing her rant.

All she wanted to do was take the day off, lay in bed and catch up on rest. So, it still made little sense as to why her parents were persistent on her attending class today. She may have found out the where, but it was the why that plagued her.

Cindy dropped her line of sight to the ground and used a rock to divert her attention by pushing it back and forth with a leather boot. "Maybe, it's because you have been distant with her lately."

"I'm a teenager, what do they expect? A cheery cheerleader?"

"It's more than being a teenager, Mila. You have gone through how many therapists in the last year? And all it's done is turn you into a recluse."

"I can't help that they did absolutely nothing for me. But forcing me on this field trip? What did they think it would accomplish? To show me where I might end up?" Mila dramatically rolled her eyes with a head shake.

Cindy continued to rotate the rock under her foot, avoiding eye contact. "Maybe."

Mila growled in a low voice, "Unbelievable."

Mila pushed herself off the wall with her shoulder and left Cindy behind to figure out why she was mad. She headed after her group, steering clear of the fallen debris that scattered over the tile.

It was disappointing that this place wasn't sacred enough for anyone to keep up the grounds. It had potential; she thought. *And what in the heck made her parents think forcing her on a field trip to the asylum would help express her darkest feelings!*

Anger rose in her chest; the betrayal a little too surreal. She marched around the corner, following the faint voices of her group. While trying to catch up, Mila peeked into each room as she passed. The first three rooms had been used for sleeping quarters, its scenery holding no importance, so she continued in a fuming silence.

The fourth room held the same appeal as the others except for an old metal bed frame laid on its side, and a cracked mirror occupied one corner. Mila resumed her stroll down the hall. She had just passed the doorframe when a faint sound stopped her. It had come from the last room.

With eyebrows raised, she rigidly backed up and peered into the room. Mila surveyed the area, searching for the source. Apart from the things she noted before, it was empty.

She waited a few moments, her breathing coming out in thin, short bursts.

It was quiet.

Rotating on her heels, she focused on her classmates, their faint voices echoed from the end of the hall.

"Mila…"

She froze.

Her name whispered with every letter drawn out caused chills to ricochet up and down her spine before using her limbs as an outlet. The blood pumped loud in her ears.

In seconds, a battle raged within her mind. *Should she turn around, or keep walking and then get the heck out of that place?* Not knowing who or what was behind her, added to the fear, making every muscle burn and her joints ache.

Could it be a straggler, someone playing a trick on her, or taking their time as she was? Unless, it was Cindy, but, *why would she whisper?*

A burst of laughter from down the hall made her realize the group had proceeded further into the depths of insanity.

"Mila…"

This time, the hair around her ear moved in the breeze of her name. Her breathing hitched in her throat, heart pounding harder against her chest.

Drawing in a breath, Mila slowly, and cautiously, pivoted to face the unknown.

Her eyes grew wide while she released her breath.

No one was there.

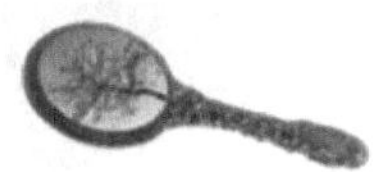

Mila stepped into the dingy room and eyed every corner. She noticed a closet with the door half hanging off of its hinges. Inhaling a large breath, she squared her shoulders, then stormed to the vacant space.

Peeking in, she saw it was empty.

Stumped, Mila scanned her surroundings again until she was face-to-face with the broken mirror. Her uncombed, multi-layer appearance stared back at her.

She frowned.

It frowned back.

Mirrors never did her justice, which is why the only one in the entire house was in her parents' bathroom. It only reminded her of how bleak and unwanted she felt, and how it had ways to destroy one's life. *Did she really need to have that constant reminder?*

Mila ran her fingers through her frizzy strands, attempting to bring order to her tresses. With a sigh, she gave up, and before leaving watched a single tear slip down her pimply cheek.

In that moment, her throat ached, and a layer of unforgivable sadness began to suffocate her.

Quickly averting her eyes from the image, she forced her emotions to calm down before they overreacted and resulted in a barrage of tears.

As she took a step toward the door, an airy voice reached her ears. "Why don't you just give up then?"

"What?" Mila choked out. She eyed the room with more persistence, adamant to find the face that went with the voice. But again, she was the only one in the room.

"It's simple, really."

Mila faced the mirror, realizing it was the source, and hesitantly walked toward it. Once again, she was one-on-one with her image.

"I could give you some tips."

Mila gasped. Her reflection was speaking to her.

This could not be happening. She must have knocked her head at some point. There was no way it was a ghost; she didn't believe in the supernatural. Mila freaked.

The reflection put a hand on her hip. "No, you did not knock your head. Yes, it's happening. And you're right; I am not a ghost."

Mila's eyes grew wide at the reflection answering her thoughts. "Then, who are you?"

"Isn't it obvious? I'm you." The reflection smirked.

"I don't understand."

She sighed. "You are talking to yourself, Mila."

Mila raised her eyebrows.

"Think of me as your evil conscience. I'm the one who makes you hate yourself. Oh, and don't bother looking for Jiminy the Cricket, he was quite tasty."

Mila swallowed hard. A thousand questions ran through her mind, but she didn't know which one to ask first.

"I've been biding my time, waiting for the right moment to explain a sensitive situation to you. Deep down you know your parents and Cindy are only pretending like they give a damn."

"Why would they do that?"

"To make you think you're going crazy, so they can lock you up and never deal with you, ever, again."

Mila's throat tightened while a trickle of tears flowed down her pale flesh.

"It would be smarter to end it before they do. Because you know if they caged you, you will find a way, it's inevitable."

"What if I talk to them?"

The reflection belted out a throaty laugh. "Don't kid yourself, Mila. A damaged soul is a damaged soul. There is no fixing that."

A steady stream of liquid, now released from Mila's bottom lids.

Disgusted, the broken image rolled its eyes. "Stop crying. You clinging to your worthlessness is your fault, so there is no need for the pity party."

"But… but…"

"Mila!" Cindy's voice rang from down the hall.

Mila quickly wiped at her eyes and watched her reflection performing the same action.

"There you are." Cindy's face filled the doorway. "Everyone is already at the meeting location. It's time to head back."

"An hour has passed already?"

"Yeah. Were you in here the whole time?"

"I suppose I was." Mila breathed, surprised.

"Well, come on," Cindy motioned with her hand. "It's time to go."

Cindy was out the door before Mila could protest.

Mila turned back to the mirror, shocked to see her disconnected form wink while the corner of her mouth twitched.

Turning to follow Cindy, a voice echoed in her head, *You know I'm right.*

The noise in the lobby overpowered the small space. Mila hugged the wall until she found a section that wasn't being occupied and then crossed her arms over her midsection. She listened to the different animated conversations on what they found.

Look at them, so, happy. Maybe, someone should tell them, life is one big disappointment.

Mila scoffed. She thought of what she experienced. Besides, trying to comprehend what had happened, there was nothing her alternate self-said that wasn't true.

Of course, I'm right. We are of like minds. And, it would be so simple, Mila. Who would even miss you?

"You know I'm here for you if you ever need to talk."

Mila jumped and then snapped her head to the right to see Cindy supporting the wall with her.

"What makes you think I need to talk?" Mila hissed, ready to strangle her prey if it continued to interrupt her thoughts.

Sensing the hostile atmosphere, Cindy pushed off the wall and faced her friend. "I'm not blind, Mila. You've been acting standoffish ever since we arrived." She sighed. "An asylum probably wasn't the best choice—"

"You think?"

"But we thought it would help."

Mila straightened, her eyebrows furrowing together. "We? So, you had a hand in this too? What was this, an intervention?"

Heads close by turned, startled by Mila's tone. They watched the exchange between the two friends, probably wondering if they would see a fight.

"Mila, please calm down." Cindy let out a breath. "Why do you act as if we are committing a crime by showing how much we care for you?"

She's lying Mila.

"If this is caring, then I want no part of it."

"You're being ridiculous, Mila."

"Am I?"

Cindy sighed and then lowered her voice. "Why won't you talk to me?"

"Because there is nothing to talk about Cindy. I'm fine. I'm standoffish because this place is depressing, just like this conversation."

Nice save, the voice within her praised.

"You don't have to be so mean about it, Mila." Cindy pouted.

"All right class. Let's get back on the buses," Mrs. Bleevie announced, saving Mila from having to apologize for her behavior. *She shouldn't have to relent when it was them who needed to grovel.*

Automatically, the students migrated to the door. Cindy followed, but Mila lingered behind, waiting for an opportunity to leave without bumping shoulders with people. Her friend glanced back, but Mila gave no indication that she had forgiven her.

The bus ride back was overpowered by noise from students teasing over who got scared in one of the rooms with some disturbing tools the doctors used on their patients. Mila rolled her eyes, deciding to not listen to the details, then rested her head against the back of the seat. She thought about the choice words she was going to share with her parents. *Forcing her on this trip and telling her she would not get the car promised if she didn't go. It was beneath them to blackmail her.* Mila seethed.

As the night sky descended upon them, the jokes and excitement slowly died down.

"Are we good?" Cindy's whispered voice broke through her red fog.

The bus pulled in front of the school and came to a stop. Everyone stood up at once, eager to get home.

Mila faced her friend; green eyes stared back. They had been through a lot since freshman year and were close. It was hard to stay mad at her… sometimes.

"Not right now, Cindy. You tricked me. And that is not what friends do." Mila sidestepped around Cindy and joined the crowd.

"But–" Cindy's words faded as Mila shuffled her way off the bus.

The moment Mila's foot hit the pavement the night air stung her cheeks. She brought her coat closer around her while scanning the parking lot. She didn't see her parents' car. *Oh, how nice of them to not even pick her up.* She growled under her breath.

There's your proof that they don't care, Mila.

"I'm sure there is an explanation," Mila uttered out loud.

Why do you keep making excuses for them?

"I don't know."

By the time Mila got home, her extremities were numb from the cold. A blazing fire crackled and popped as she entered the foyer. The warmth began to bring her limbs back to life but not without an uncomfortable tingly sensation.

She stripped off her jacket and was greeted by the *clip-clop* of nails on the tile as the family's chocolate Labrador, Rex, hurried toward her wagging his tail in excitement at the sight of her.

Mila kneeled next to Rex and rubbed behind his ears. "Hey,

buddy." She placed a kiss on top of his wet nose, and he returned the gesture by giving her a lick across the cheek.

"Mila? Is that you?" Kora, her mother, called from the living room.

"Yeah, Mom."

"Come in here and keep your aging mother company." One glass clinking another echoed from the room.

She's at it again, I see.

Mila strolled to the archway and stopped. Two open bottles of wine sat on the coffee table in front of her mother. Kora had her legs curled under her, and a wine glass gripped between two hands.

There's your explanation.

"Not today, Mother. I haven't quite forgiven you for forcing me on that field trip today."

"Oh, honey. You're being silly. I was only trying to help." Her mother took a sip from her glass.

"Right. I'm sure that's *all* it was. I'm going to bed." Mila turned.

"Mila, hold on!" Her mother raised her voice as she got up from the couch, attempting to go after her. "I have tried to be sympathetic to whatever you are feeling inside. But enough is enough. I want my daughter back. Is that so much to ask?"

Mila whipped around to see her mother standing in the doorway.

Not much of an effort.

"I've always been here, Mother. I never left. If you had just paid attention, you would have seen that." Tears pricked Mila's eyes. She forced down the bubble of sobs in her throat. Her mother's expression left a guilty twinge resting in her stomach.

Reciting what she wanted to say would only cause further pain, and she didn't want that on her conscience, so she spun on her heels and ascended the stairs.

"Mila? Does your behavior have anything to do with Lila?" Kora called after her.

She froze in mid-step.

An overwhelming weight on her lungs began to suffocate her. Hearing that name brought on a slew of forgotten memories. Not ready to relive them, she shoved them back into the darkness and then pivoted to face her mother, rage filling all corners of her being.

"How dare you speak of her! You have no right to." Her insides began to boil.

Kora let out a breath. "Mila, it wasn't your fault."

"You're absolutely right, Mother. It was yours," Mila spewed, then charged up the stairs to her bedroom, slamming the door in her wake.

Lila. She hadn't thought of her name in a year. Then the repressed memories returned, and with force. *Her sister had taken her own life, and their lack of connection at the time had kept her from seeing the signs to stop her.* Thinking of her identical twin brought on emotions she had trapped inside since Lila's death; it was agonizing.

She's not the only one to blame, you know.

"What are you talking about?" Mila challenged.

It was your fault, too.

"How so?" Anger laced Mila's words; she spun back and forth looking for the voice. It didn't respond. "How so?" She growled, demanding an answer.

The silence continued to be the only reply to her question.

"Maybe I *should* commit myself. If I'm talking to myself and expecting an answer, then I must have already lost my mind." Mila disposed of her day clothes with force, tossing them toward the open hamper, but they missed and landed on the floor.

Or, you could just end things and not have to worry about where you belong.

She disregarded the heap, the voice, and then donned her nightwear. Mila skipped her nightly ritual and then crawled in between the sheets.

It didn't take her long to succumb to sleep, and Mila found herself plunged into a red fog, swirling with the mist. Light up ahead forced her hand to cover her eyes from the brightness. When it dimmed, Mila found herself back at the asylum, face-to-face with her reflection in the broken mirror.

A maniacal laugh rumbled in the room. Her image distorted and then morphed into her evil self from earlier.

"Hello again, Mila. You ready to give up yet?" The reflection pushed a hand through her hair, throwing her long tresses away from her shoulder.

"I'm not sure." Mila hesitated.

The image smirked. "You have every reason to. And it won't take much effort on your part."

"What about my parents?"

"What about them?" The reflection let out a breath. "Has it not been blatantly clear that they don't care for you? That they won't miss you when you're gone."

Tears pooled on her bottom lids. She couldn't even have her own thoughts without her evil side having an opinion.

The reflection let out another menacing chuckle. "You were always weaker than me. Never had the guts to live… sister."

Mila froze. *It can't be.* "Lila?" Her mouth dropped open. "How is this even possible? You're… you're dead."

"No thanks to you," Lila spat.

A series of events took over her mind, one after another, knocking her back.

They shifted until it became one continuous reel. It was unclear, but the images twisted and moved in a fluid motion. Even though the picture was hazy, Mila knew what scene was playing out in front of her. It was the day Lila died.

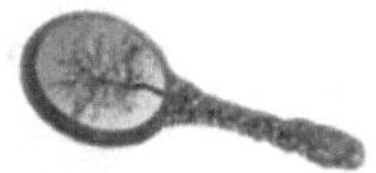

Mila threw her tote bag on top of her unmade bed, a smile touching each cheek. Henry Raven, a percussionist in the band, asked her out to a movie. She was on cloud nine. Her heart fluttered in excitement at the thought of showing up to school the next day to see him again.

Water trickling in the bathroom froze her smile. *Was Lila home, already?* She closed the space and tapped on the door with her knuckles. "Lila? You in there?"

There was no answer.

Mila turned the knob and then placed one foot in the room before she realized something was wrong. Her socks soaked in the water puddled on the floor. She glanced down, confused. Eyeing her surroundings, she quickly assessed the situation.

A scream released from her lungs when her eyes lay upon her sister, Lila. Her twin was submerged in the tub; red mixed with the water spilling over the side. The mirror hanging over the sink had been shattered into pieces. Glass shards littered the tile.

Mila pressed her palms hard over her eyes, refusing to watch the scene, again.

"Why are you showing this to me? I already know what happened," she hollered out.

Not everything. You seem to have forgotten the most important part.

The picture replayed, but this time it rewound to before Mila walked in the door. It stopped and played at normal speed. She watched a fuzzy image of herself bash Lila's head into the mirror, the glass splintering, and then picking up a sliver of the mirror, and slitting Lila's wrists before placing her in the tub.

Mila shook her head at the sight. "No! It's not possible! There is no way I would have done that to you! I loved you, Lila."

Well, that's how I remembered it.

"No!" Mila screamed. "No. No. No. No!"

"Mila!"

Another voice called out to her as if on an intercom. Her entire body started convulsing.

"Mila! Stop! Wake up!"

Mila's eyes fluttered open. What she thought was her bedroom, at first, melted into white walls around her. With a blurry vision, she tried to focus when she spotted her mother and a man wearing a white coat, standing by the door. Both were whispering intently.

"What is happening with my daughter?" Kora dabbed at her eyes with a tissue.

"It appears she is experiencing a psychotic breakdown."

"How? How did this happen?" Kora choked on the tears flowing from her eyes.

"What were the events leading up to this moment?" The man inquired as he opened a file in his hands.

"I forced her on a field trip. Thought it would be good for her to get out of the house and the funk she has been in for this past year. When she got back, we had a fight. She marched up to her room and went to bed. A little while later I heard her screaming. I rushed in to find her thrashing in bed, and she was holding a piece of mirror to her wrists.

"I couldn't get her to wake up, so I called an ambulance. At the hospital, they found nothing physically wrong with her. The staff decided it was best to place her on suicide watch for a few days. When her condition didn't improve, they committed her."

"That's what I'm seeing in her file." He mentioned, and then flipped through several pages before stopping on a tab that was labelled red. "It also states you were to remove any reflective surfaces that could cause her harm." He snapped the file shut. "So, where did Mila get the mirror?"

Kora's breath hitched in her throat. "I'm afraid I don't know where she got it. I had placed those items in storage. It's possible she retrieved it at some point. She and Lila used to have matching hand mirrors."

"Lila…" He flipped open the file again. "Your other daughter?"

"Yes. Mila had come home to find Lila had taken her own life one year ago, today. I knew she was feeling guilty for not seeing the signs, just based on her behavior. That's why I put her in therapy, but it didn't seem to help." Kora shook her head.

The doctor closed the file again and placed it underneath his armpit, and then the two glanced in Mila's direction.

Mila sat hunched in the corner, the padding providing comfort for the throbbing ache in her head. Her mom knelt beside her, then ran a hand through her untamed locks.

"Mrs. Webber, we will take care of her here at Blayville. I want to ensure you we have a very successful program to help teens with psychological issues."

A heave escaped her mother's throat. "Psychological issues?" She whispered.

"It hasn't escaped my attention as I was glancing through her file of who Mila's father is, Mrs. Webber. Trenton Webber has been a resident here for the last year."

Kora closed her eyes, but the tears still escaped.

"He's been diagnosed with Schizoaffective disorder." The doctor stated.

Mila briefly tuned out their talk and focused on the fact that she couldn't wrap her mind around killing her sister. *Why would she have done such a thing?*

You were jealous.

"Never," Mila growled defensively.

Kora and the doctor returned their line of sight toward her.

Her mother leaned in closer. "Mila?"

In a whisper, Mila uttered, "I killed my sister."

Tears streamed down her face. Lila's laugh vibrated in her ears. She put a hand over each ear and rocked back and forth. "Stop, please. I'm sorry!" Mila clawed at her face, her nails tearing into the flesh.

"Mila, honey." Her mother tried to grab her flailing arms, attempting to hold them down, but she only rocked harder and clawed faster.

"Nurse! Get me a jacket!" The doctor hollered out the open door.

Two burly men in white scrubs rushed in.

Kora maneuvered to the side and watched, helpless.

One man focused on holding her legs down but struggled from Mila kicking them out in all directions. The other man shoved her thrashing arms, with force, into the straitjacket. After a few attempts, they finally succeeded and pulled the straps tight. She continued to fight against the restraints.

"Why?" Mila screamed.

"It appears Mila is hearing voices and hallucinating. Based on your family history so far, I'm led to believe your other daughter might have had a similar form of Schizophrenia, and succumbed to her own inner voices." The doctor concluded.

"Please help her." Kora released her tears. "She is all I have."

"We will do what we can. This disease is a powerful illness and is not curable. But there are treatments out there to keep it stable."

"I loved you!" Mila continued to fight against the restraints.

It wasn't enough.

A sharp pain in her arm caused a yelp to escape. Her world became fuzzy, and her mom and the doctor turned into a ripple from a disrupted puddle.

A single tear slipped down her cheek as darkness took over.

About the Author

Hello! I'm Amber Hassler, known as the Twister of Mystery. With the customary cliché, I write, but I love to! (It really does coarse through my veins). Nothing is better than creating a whole world or a set of characters in your head and sharing it for all to read. I have also added ghostwriting, book consulting, and professional editor to my resume. In 2014, I started my own company, Twister of Mystery Productions, to provide those services to others. I write for First Comics News under Twisted News and run the Horror Writers Association Las Vegas Chapter in my free time.

I have published a novella in Enchanted: A Paranormal New Adult Novella Collection, titled K + L, and another short story in Lurking in the Mind anthology, titled Lonely Hearts. Which has won multiple awards:

Finalist in the Fiction: Anthologies category of the 2017 International Book Awards

Winner in the Fiction: Anthologies category of the 2017 Best Book Awards

Official Selection for Short Story Fiction in the 2018 New Apple Book Awards for Excellence in Independent Publishing

Solo Medalist Winner for Short Story Collection in the 2018 New Apple Summer E-book Awards

My latest is titled Porcelain, a novelette with the flair of the tooth fairy legend. Besides my continued accolades, when I'm not writing, I work full-time, and am a mother of two. Every once in a while, I might plug into my Nintendo Switch and play.

Coming Soon from Amber Hassler.

For more information about Author Amber Hassler
visit her wedsite today by clicking on the QR code.

Don't forget to leave an offering under your pillow.

An ancient obsession must be satisfied
or tomorrow may never come...
even for you.

About the Author

Hello and scythe-u-tations, I'm Kathy-Lynn Cross, also known as the Reaper Girl. I'm the author of the Unseen Series. My first paranormal novel, So Shall I Reap, Book One The Unseen Series was first published in 2015 and republished under my logo, Inscytheful Publishing in 2017. It has won the 2016 International Book Awards Finalist in Fiction: Young Adult and the 2019 Official Selection eBook in Fantasy. I've had several short stories and novellas in a few anthologies. My first publication was in 2015. A short story titled Within a Grain of Sand. Featured in the anthology Twists in Time by Clean Teen Publishing. One of my favorite short stories is When Emily was Here. It debuted in the Award-winning anthology, Lurking in the Mind. Published by CHBB Publishing in 2017.

I wasn't always a writer. In 2008, when my niece was hospitalized, I decided to do something special and wrote a short tale for her to read. After consuming it in a single day, my niece and some of the nurses, in the pediatrics wing, asked, "What's next?" I was at a turning point in my life, and this opened up a new chapter. I knew then I wanted to write but also to strive to be something different by becoming a Storyweaver.

I love rose red and obsessively use it in everything, including my bottle-blond hair accented with red highlights. As a pastime, I love to bake and dabble in cake decorating—that is when my fingers are not busy writing mayhem. My favorite pastime is spent on rainy days, when I can sit in my comfy sweats, wrapped up in my favorite blanket, with a cup of vanilla coffee and a story from my TBR list. But, when I need to step away from my writing, I'll spend time with my husband of twenty-nine years, and our three cats.

Links and Author Info

Head on over to my website for new works, and upcoming events, or visit the KLCross Story Merch and More storefront.

klcross7.wixsite.com/authorkathylynncross

My Linktree is under @ReaperGirl07

https://linktr.ee/ReaperGirl07

Coming Soon.

Sweet Scythes!

Five years later, I've finally dusted off my keyboard and will be releasing
Betrayed by Light's Shadow: Book Three The Unseen Series in late 2025. Exactly when? TBD.
Check my website for updates on Tevin and Alexcia's journey into the Unseen.

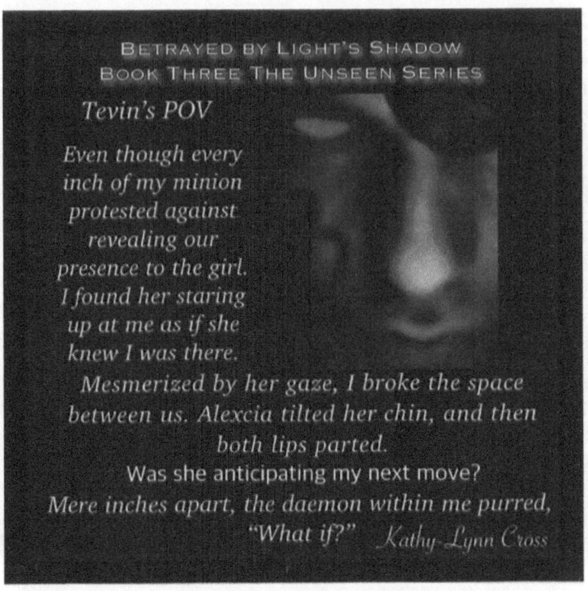

Want to find more?

Available for eBook and Print.

A Spirit's Last Gift: A Winter Novella

Reluctant, I wiggled each toe, before extending both arms out of the crisscross placement over my chest while relaxing each finger. As I shifted, my brain invented the whisper of silk moving against polyester and Lycia. The fabrication, of fictional dress material, gave me some reassurance; this was very real. Following this new routine, I forced my lashes to flutter open. Going through the physical motions made me feel displaced; especially after I woke to ivory silk seven inches above my face.

When the moon rose at 9:02 p.m., so did I.

Who knew, that time had a sense of humor?

Acknowledgments!

This collection of stories would have never seen the light of day if
it wasn't for Amber Hassler.
Author, editor, ghostwriter, and friend.
Some stories were fun to revisit, and others were a reminder of our
growth and education in the book world for the last ten years.

My deepest thanks and gratefulness for your guidance with my
Storyweaving.

You are not alone

Many of these stories touch on sensitive subject matters like physical or emotional abuse, drug or alcohol, and mental illness. These subjects I would like to say, "You are NOT alone." On this page, there is information below for victims of abuse. Victims are not coming forward because of blame and shame. If you or someone you know has succumbed to physical or emotional abuse, please reach out, because you matter - they matter. I have listed a few websites and hotlines for professionals that you can reach out to.

Remember, coal, when it is mined is deemed as unrefined. But over time as pressure and conditions are applied something beautiful is created from deep inside. It's our own form of diamond. Cut yours to the image of your inner beauty and potential.

Domestic Abuse websites and hotlines.
The National Domestic Violence website: Identify Abuse | The National Domestic Violence Hotline (thehotline.org)
They keep everything confidential. Hotline: 1 - 800 - 799 - 7233 (safe)

Also, for the deaf and hard of hearing.
Phone: 1 - 855 - 812 - 1001 (VP)

Or you can text "START" to 88788

National Coalition Against Domestic Violence - Official Site. (NCADV)
Website: http://www.ncadv.org/